IN
PLAIN
SIGHT

IN PLAIN SIGHT
By Laurie Holbrook
Copyright © 2020 Laurie Holbrook

In Plain Sight is a work of fiction. Names, characters, places, and incidents are the product of the author's imagination or are used fictitiously. Any resemblance to actual events, locales, businesses, or persons, living or dead, is coincidental.

Published by Frisson Publishing
Print ISBN - 978-1-7335609-2-4
Ebook ISBN - 978-1-7335609-3-1

Cover Design by Book Design Stars, www.bookdesignstars.com
Interior Design by Kimberly Peticolas, www.kimpeticolas.com

Library of Congress Control Number: 2020905214

10 9 8 7 6 5 4 3 2 1

IN PLAIN SIGHT

LAURIE HOLBROOK

ALSO BY LAURIE HOLBROOK

Still Out There

To my girls. I love you always.

And to all the women, girls, mothers, daughters, sisters, and friends. May you be forever free.

Fear is the path to the dark side.
Fear leads to anger.
Anger leads to hate.
Hate leads to suffering.
— *YODA*

ONE

IT STARTS WITH A CALL AND USUALLY INVOLVES a desperate parent. They're terrified, but optimistic. There's a good chance the parent received Frankie Dowdy's phone number from a policeman or detective. Over the course of two years working in Colorado, Mabel and Frankie had developed quite the list of connections.

Mabel Peters looked down at the only picture they were given. It was from this past Christmas and Emily, the younger of the two, was smiling, but the smile didn't match her eyes. The older one, Melissa, was looking down at the doll her younger sister held in her hands.

Tucking the picture in her back pocket, Mabel set out across the flat, dry field on her stomach. She thought being petite would help her easily maneuver through any obstacle, but army crawling across an empty plane where the naked eye could see over ten miles proved harder than she'd originally thought.

The Great Plains aren't heavily populated, but people live scattered throughout the land. Mostly struggling farmers. Frankie had decided to leave their car a half mile up the road at an abandoned house. They were sure to be seen—it wasn't unusual for people to drive by. From there they hiked in, keeping to the ditches whenever possible. A line of trees ran along the east end of the house where, they suspected, the kids were being kept.

From two hundred yards out, she looked at her watch and smiled. She'd made it faster than anticipated. She poked her head up for signs of Frankie near the tree line. Too far to make anything out, she pulled her binoculars from her pant pocket and looked past the old house, in need of repairs and a good painting, stopping at two men with guns guarding the front yard.

From a distance, the men looked like twins. Not real twins, but like Arnold Schwarzenegger and Danny DeVito, only a Mexican version.

Past the twins and through a small field, no more than ten meters into the line of trees, she caught a slight movement. If she hadn't been looking specifically for it, she would not have seen the branch move telling her Frankie was in place. She hunkered down, biding her time to make her move—when an itch distracted her from Frankie and the twins.

Focus, she scolded herself in Frankie's voice.

The pain sent signals to her brain convincing her she had to scratch it or it wouldn't go away. She tried to focus, but the sensation became stronger. It reminded her of the last hiking trip she and Lucas had taken. They'd decided to go off trail, through a dense forest where they got licked by nature. Not poison ivy—the other pesky green plant, stinging nettle.

Stinging nettle may itch like hell, but you can eat it. It's like a superfood loaded with protein, iron, vitamins, and minerals. The key was not touching the plant, so they'd used their jackets, careful not to make the same mistake twice. They cooked it that night and ate it like spinach. After dinner, Lucas surprised her. He took her hand and got down on one knee.

She knew this day would come. It both scared and excited her.

For seven years Lucas had been a big part of her life, all while she was living a lie. If you'd watched the news, you'd know. Her given name was Melodi Stucker. Melodi was eleven when she died and Mabel Peters was born. Flash forward sixteen years later and she struggled to keep her life a secret. She loved Lucas, but she'd lied to him every day. When the truth about her life finally came out, he was there, just like he'd always been.

She focused back to the men, still arguing, then over to Frankie who had started moving toward the house. *Crap!* She'd missed his signal. If she'd had the time, she'd have beat herself up about it. Frankie told her time and time again how much he liked working with her and what a good partner she made.

No time to feel bad for letting him down, because she wouldn't. Not today.

In a full-on sprint, much like Frankie, she closed the space in just over twenty-five seconds. She didn't need to time it, because she had many times before. She could run a hundred-meter sprint in 10.7 seconds.

If the men hadn't been arguing like an old married couple, they would have seen her coming. With ten yards to go, Danny looked her way, fumbled with his gun and dropped it. She expected him to charge her, but instead he ran to the house with his tail between his legs.

For safety? For help? Either way he'd meet Frankie.

Arnold yelled something incoherent and bent down to pick up Danny's gun, but a swift kick by Mabel sent it flying out of his hands. Now as she stood next to him, he appeared three times her size. She thought of Frankie, a six-foot-five, two-hundred-thirty-pound beast, whom she'd taken down numerous times. She'd find out today if Frankie let her win.

Shots came from inside the house and before she could make

a move, the giant kicked her feet out from under her and she landed on her back knocking the air out of her. Arnold jumped on her, wrapping his big hands around her throat, pinning her down with all his weight. Mabel had found herself in this position many times. For some reason she could not explain, bad men enjoyed choking her. She assumed to watch the life dissipate from her eyes. What they never expected—she was a fighter. Always had been. And she'd been taught by the best.

Just like she'd done many times before, she jammed both her thumbs in his eye sockets causing him to rear back and stumble. She rolled over and jumped to her feet, taking a big rock with her as she did. He looked at her with revulsion. Probably wondering how someone so little could kick his ass. He made to get up but, being a giant and all, he wasn't fast about it. It gave her just enough time to smash the rock into his ugly face. She hit him once and then again and again.

He threw her off like a ragdoll and stood before her, seething and with blood spraying out of his mouth. She hadn't noticed the gun within arms reach and he ended up with it in his hands. He approached slowly, gun pointed between her eyes. His bloody eyes bore deep and his lips drew back exposing his blood-stained teeth. A god-awful sight. He used his free hand to wipe the blood from his eyes. Seizing the opportunity, she grabbed his gun, simultaneously kicking him in the balls. She smiled at him with the gun in her hands.

He flinched to go after her.

"No, you don't," she said. "Get down on your knees."

He took a step forward and she fired at his foot, missing it by a hair and sending dirt flying up. He yelled at her in Spanish. Maybe he hadn't understood her. Frankie'd warned her she'd have to learn other languages.

"Down!" she yelled, because saying it louder would make him understand.

He stood there without moving, his eyes fixated on the gun in her hands.

How do you say down?

"Get down." She motioned with her gun.

He looked down at the ground.

She fired another shot. "Now!"

He did.

While the giant was looking at the ground, she stepped around him, gun pointed at his head. From behind, she whacked him one more time on the side of the head. Finally, out like a light, he fell to the ground—*timber*. He landed next to an old rusted iron wheel. It reminded her of something you'd find in the old west. She tied him to it, glad she had evaded dragging his big ass around. As she tied him up, Danny came running back out of the house and she wondered what a scared little man was doing with criminals. He clearly did not have the courage to fight.

He was screaming in Spanish . . . cursing she supposed. He must have figured he had a better chance with her than the beast inside.

"*Cállate*," she demanded. One of a handful of words she did learn from Frankie. *Shut up.* She found herself using it often.

He saw the gun in her hands and bolted to the right, heading to the open field. Where did he plan to go? She fired her gun, missing on purpose, but he didn't stop. She couldn't shoot a man running away, so she went after him, gaining quickly as he tripped and stumbled through the dry grasses.

In a superman dive, she jumped on him. A dust of dirt puffed up around them as they landed on the ground. He attempted to get up but she pulled him down, rolled him over, and punched him in the face. Besides trying to flee, he didn't fight back. With a tight grip she pulled him to his feet twisting his arm behind his back and escorted him back to the house.

Once she'd tied him up opposite the giant, she headed to the house. Her instincts told her Frankie was fine. He'd had the upper hand; he always did. One hand touched the doorknob and the other held a gun pointed at whatever might come through the door. She slowly cracked the door open, ready to shoot. Relief came over her as she was met with big brown eyes belonging to Frankie. He had two frightened girls under his wings, one older than the other by a few years.

She fired a shot, a foot over the older girl's head, hitting a charging man in the neck. Blood sprayed out like a leak in a garden hose. Frankie had caught the instant her eyes moved from the girls and had pulled them to safety.

It had taken some time to get used to shooting to kill, but after seeing what awful things bad people did to kids, it became easier.

The two girls were wrapped in each other's arms. Both terrified and shaking.

"It's okay. You're safe now," she said. Their heads crept up simultaneously and a lump formed in her throat. They were so young. She reached out and they both moved forward, into her arms. Her heart melted like butter on hot bread.

In her pocket, she felt her phone buzzing, but ignored it. She led them to a frayed brown couch in the middle of the living room. "You must be Melissa," she said to the older of the two. The girl's pale skin was painted with bruises, both old and new.

Her big brown eyes widened and she nodded.

"My partner and I are here to help." Mabel offered a smile. "And you must be Emily," she said to the younger girl who had freckles sprinkled across her nose and cheeks. She had no visible contusions, but was in deep need of a bath.

"Are you a cop?" Melissa asked.

"No, I'm not."

"I don't want to be here anymore," Emily cried.

Mabel knelt next to her. "I know. None of these men can hurt you anymore." She looked at Melissa. "You'll both be home soon."

"No!" Emily shouted, tears pouring down her dirty face, leaving streaks.

Melissa wrapped her arms around her little sister. It reminded Mabel of a past time when Pete had had a bad dream. It was just after they'd lost their dad in a car accident. She was ten and he was seven at the time.

She'd seen a similar scenario once before where a teenage boy refused to go home. Turned out the neighbor had been molesting the boy since they'd moved in. They'd lived there for ten years.

"Can you tell me why?" asked Mabel.

Melissa shook her head. "Don't be scared," she said to Emily. "We'll live with Aunt Charlie. She'll take us in." Melissa rubbed her sister's back, like a mother, nurturing, protecting her to the best of her own childlike abilities.

Emily sniffled.

"Okay. We'll call Aunt Charlie then." Mabel didn't understand, but she trusted the girls. She could only imagine what they'd gone through with the men she and Frankie had just taken down. If the girls were afraid of going home, then something just as bad had to be waiting for them. "I won't take you anywhere you don't want to go," she promised.

"The man you shot, he works for my dad," Melissa confessed.

It all started making sense. He'd only hired them to make it look like he cared. He'd wanted their work done secretly, no police involved. They'd agreed, knowing full well it's not how they worked.

"Are you hungry?"

They nodded.

"Stay here and I'll find you a snack."

Mabel bit down on her bottom lip. If they didn't turn the girls over to their father, in a few hours, he would know something was up.

Bill White stepped out of a white Cherokee Sport and Mabel smiled. He leaned into his old, beat up jeep, snatched his hat from the dash and planted it on his head, right where it belonged. She opened the door to greet him. "You look good, old man," she said, immediately noticing his clean-shaven face and wondering what had prompted him to lose the mustache and goatee he'd sported for as long as she'd known him.

"Young lady." He nodded, tipping his black fur felt cowboy hat. No lift, no spin, no hug—strictly business for the last two years, and it stung now just as much as it did the first time he didn't do it.

Swallowing her self-pity, she said, "You ever going to get rid of that old thing?" She pointed to his jeep.

"Nope."

"I'm surprised it's still running."

"Possessions last if you take care of them."

Possessions or friendships?

Bill White had retired as head detective a couple years back, a few months earlier than planned, and opened his own private investigative firm working with the police on cases. He'd helped conceal Mabel's identity when she was eleven. When the cover-up was exposed a couple years ago, he was forced to retire early. It took some time, but Bill had earned his credit back because of the work Frankie and Mabel had done.

"I treated myself to that gem the day my youngest graduated from high school." He smiled. "Where are the girls?" he asked, changing the subject.

"Asleep. They can't go home." Mabel said, thinking of what Melissa had told her after they'd eaten. She glanced at her watch. "We're out in five. I already called it in: PD and CPS. Oh, and their aunt is on her way."

"Where's . . . George?" he asked.

She and Frankie really had to discuss name changes *before* they went in. Frankie always threw her off with whatever random name he decided upon.

"Checking the perimeter. He texted when he saw you coming. All the assholes are tied up."

"I hear the girl's father is the biggest asshole of all."

She nodded.

He peered into the room where the girls slept. She missed the old Bill, loud and animated—you could hear him coming a mile away.

"How are you?" she asked.

His features softened. "I'm here, ain't I?" he said in his thick Texan drawl.

One of her biggest pet peeves was people answering a question with a question. "You are. Thank you," she said fighting the urge to hug him.

"No thanks necessary." He looked at the girls.

"Whatever happens, they don't go back into the custody of their father."

"Come hell or high water, I'll see to it they don't."

"Gabby, times up," Frankie yelled through the back door.

"Gabby?" Bill questioned.

"That's me." *I guess.*

Bill shook his head, squinted, eyeing her and said, "You look like a Gabby."

She touched his beardless face, now scruffy. He held her hand to his face and smiled.

Frankie entered the kitchen where they stood. "We don't have much time." He paused. "It's not like the first time I've brought it up to you, but we need an answer and now's as good a time as any. You plan on making it official?" Frankie referred to the countless requests for Bill to add the two of them to his private investigation team.

"I reckon you two are going to be the death of me," Bill threw back. He removed his hat, set it on the table, and let out a breath through clenched jaws. Mabel opened her mouth to speak and Frankie shook his head. Bill grumbled to himself, pacing back and forth in the small space. "This is horseshit. I only do these calls from the goodness of my heart."

"Well, okay. There's your answer. You'll never get another call from me." *Bill is his own numero uno. Everyone else comes second,* Frankie had told her once.

"This is my last one," Bill confirmed.

Mabel sucked in her breath and her hand went to her stomach. He might as well have sucker punched her. His refusal to help shouldn't have surprised her. Frankie, of course, had a backup plan, but she'd secretly hoped to keep working with Bill.

They all turned their heads simultaneously to the sound of sirens. Frankie peered out the window to see a big cloud of dust coming down the road.

"Put your weapons on the table first," Bill demanded.

"Right," Mabel said.

She set down the gun with which she'd shot the man in the living room, along with the one Frankie had used. "I used this one and Frankie this one." She pointed.

"Now the rest," he said. "And don't tell me you don't have more hidden."

"This is horseshit," she said, using his own word. "No one knows we were here." She would not give him her other two guns from either of her sides, or the one from her ankle. Especially not her four throwing knives she kept in her boots or the double-edged spear point KA-BAR Commando knife Lucas had given her.

His eyes narrowed, staring at her for a few seconds, he shook his head and said, "Wake up the girls."

The girls were sitting up, visibly shaking. "Girls, this is Bill, he's a private detective. The police are on their way and so is your aunt. I have to go."

Emily started to cry. "No, you can't leave us," she said.

Mabel got down on her knees, so she met Emily eye to eye. "We didn't call him. Your aunt is coming for you along with someone from child protective services. They will do everything they can to keep you safe."

"Time to go," Frankie urged.

Mabel looked back at him and held up her pointer—*One more minute*—Knowing full well he was right to rush her. She didn't have a minute. She gave them each a hug. "I trust Bill and you can, too. He's a good man. I've known him most of my life."

Melissa shook her head, not believing.

"I can't be here when the police arrive. Neither of us." She pointed at Frankie. "It's a long story . . . If anyone asks, Bill saved you. You never saw us." She paused for a few seconds, and added, "I'm proud of you both." Then hurried out the back with Frankie.

TWO

YOU KNOW HOW SOME ADULTS TELL KIDS, "you have no idea how easy you have it?" Well, adults have clearly forgotten how hard it is to be a kid. It sucks. They always say, "Be happy you have a roof over your head and food on the table and clothes on your back." Of course Isabel Dumel was happy, but having things didn't make up for everything else.

For instance—Isabel couldn't come and go without permission. She couldn't eat whatever she wanted, whenever she wanted. And Aunt Susan told *her* not to lie, when her aunt lied all the time, just like her dad.

Dad.

Every morning, without fail, he came to visit. He had impeccable timing, too, which was comical because before they took him away, he was never on time. Yet, the moment her mind slipped from dreamland to consciousness, there he was in her thoughts. Bigger than her mind and heart. She thought she still loved him, but mostly she hated him. She missed him at times, but never wanted to see him again.

His final words, "I'll write you every day," cut deep into every part of her.

Bella licked her face.

"Hey girl," Isabel said smiling, scratching Bella behind the ear. "Need to go outside?" Bella jumped off her bed and stood by the door. "I'll take that as a yes." She slid out of bed wearing a white t-shirt and black shorts. They weren't meant to be pajamas, but she liked to wear them to bed.

She entered the hall to see if Susan was up yet, but the door was closed, so she tried to be as quiet as possible so as not to wake her. Bella had other thoughts though and bounded to the front door in excitement, wagging her tail so hard it struck the wall in loud thuds. Isabel caught up to her to find Bella's nose pushed up against the edge of the door, like an arrow, preventing Isabel from opening it.

"You have to move girl," Isabel whispered loudly. "I can't open the door with you in the way."

Bella didn't budge. If anything, she pressed her nose harder into the door frame.

Isabel squeezed herself between the black Labradane and the door and Bella finally stepped back enough for her to open the door. Then she repeated the whole ordeal with the screen and out Bella ran to do her business in the back yard. The process should have taken a second, but Bella's stubbornness made it last a couple of minutes.

Hungry, Isabel poured Peanut Butter Captain Crunch into a bowl, added milk and dug in. After eating every last bite, she rinsed her bowl and put it, along with her spoon, into the dishwasher. She'd learned long ago to fill Bella's bowl with kibble and water before letting her back in the house or it would end up all over the floor.

The clock on the microwave read 6:23 a.m. *Crap!* She had

less than thirty minutes before Mabel got there. Bella was waiting by the door looking in. Thank goodness, because most of the time she loved sunbathing out back. After opening the door to let her in, Isabel ran upstairs to get ready. When done, she tapped on Susan's door, hoping to find her awake.

"Come in," her aunt called out.

"I'm leaving," is all she said looking at the TV. A woman handed a small, brown puppy to another lady, telling her what a good boy he was, and anyone interested in adopting him should call in.

"Okay. Come give me a hug." Isabel did and her aunt held on a little too long, but the warmth of her arms felt good. "Be careful and tell Mabel I said, 'Hi.'"

"I will." After saying her goodbyes, she opened the front door and found Mabel with her finger out, about to ring the doorbell.

"On time, as expected," Isabel smiled.

"Yeah . . . well . . . if you grew up with my grandpa, you, too, would be on time. Being late was a sin in my house."

Isabel laughed, thinking what it would have been like. Too strict for her taste.

"Ready to take on Trio Falls?"

"What? It's a seven-and-a-half-mile hike, *one way*—remember? You said, 'Best accomplished with a night spent camping.'"

"Relax, Isabel. I know what I said. I was kidding."

"Can we do it in July, maybe for the Fourth?"

"We might be able to do that. First, we focus on today and conquering Black Lake. I need to be back by five to get cleaned up for a dinner date."

"Ohh! You and Lucas have a hot night planned?" she teased.

"That's for me to know and for you . . . not to," she said.

"Now, let's go before our day disappears."

Isabel raised her backpack which she'd stuffed full of snacks, "Ready." From experience, she knew she'd be hungry before they made it out of the car and another three or four times throughout their hike, depending on how long it was. Mabel brought the water and first aid kit. "Better to be safe than sorry," her mom would have said.

They'd taken countless hiking trips together and Isabel couldn't wait for the day when she could keep up with Mabel. She often felt insignificant compared to her, who she swore acted like the energizer bunny. She just kept going and going and going. Mabel told her she'd get there, she just had to keep at it. Easy for her to say, she had someone to do these things with all her life. Isabel didn't start hiking until Mabel came along.

The drive took forever. No wonder Mabel wanted to leave so early. When they reached Glacier Gorge Trailhead, Isabel jumped out and Bella followed close behind. She ran to the small structure with a unisex restroom sign displayed. It was locked. She danced in place swearing if they didn't come out soon, she would pee her pants. Bella squatted and emptied her bladder, then sniffed around where other dogs had marked.

At last the door opened and a man, about Mabel's age, walked out. He briefly made eye contact with Isabel and smiled, before heading out to the trail.

Please don't stink, please don't stink.

It did. She peed as quickly as possible, holding her breath in the process, and ran out panting, taking in as much clean air as she could get into her lungs.

They hit the first waterfall before either of them spoke. Isabel thought of the first time she'd met Mabel, as her teacher. Mabel sort of took her under her wing. She was a good teacher, but a better friend. Some days, Mabel felt like her older sister.

Mabel glanced over to Isabel and her face softened. "What do you think?"

"It's beautiful," she marveled.

"That's Alberta Falls, named after the wife of Abner Sprague. He was one of the first settlers here," she spread her arms, "and in Estes Park."

"Cool." The water rushed down a small gorge. Isabel was tempted to remove her shoes and step into the creek at the bottom. Maybe in June or July, but not April when the water would be freezing cold. She wore the good hiking shoes Mabel had bought for her. They were waterproof and built to hike rough terrain.

Bella ran in circles around them. Seeing her happy made Isabel happy. She stooped over to give her a hug and Bella licked her face and ran off. They continued hiking past Mills Lake, Jewel Lake, and Glacier George Campground.

"What happened here?" Isabel asked. There were dead trees all over.

"Uhm," Mabel paused, "I think it was six or maybe seven years ago. High winds came through. Up to 90 mph." Isabel's jaw dropped. "It's called a microburst and it left this in its wake."

"The wind did this?"

Mabel nodded.

"Ninety miles per hour doesn't seem strong enough to knock trees over."

Mabel laughed. "It is. Ask your science teacher about it."

Isabel winced. "I hate science."

"You can learn anything you put your mind to."

Isabel rolled her eyes.

It seemed like they'd been walking forever when they reached another waterfall. Ribbon Falls, which meant Black

Lake was a short distance farther on. As they neared the lake, Bella barked and ran past Isabel, bumping into her leg as she did. All that, just to mark her spot for the thousandth time. Then glanced back to make sure they were still there, like she always did, decided they were okay and took off again. Repeat.

"Mabel?"

"Hmm?"

"Why don't you hate me?" It was a fair question and one she'd wanted to ask for some time.

"What would make you ask that?" Mabel asked defensively.

"After what my dad did to you?"

Mabel didn't respond.

"I didn't mean to bring it up . . ."

"It's fine," Mabel said, her eyes straight ahead as she continued to walk toward the water.

"It's just . . . we never talk about it," Isabel explained.

Mabel stopped, put her foot on a rock, her hand on her hip, and looked up as if catching her breath. Then she said, "I lost my dad when I was ten. A car accident; no one's fault. Well, maybe I could blame mother nature because of the snowstorm," she paused and took a deep breath. "The same crash killed two others. Your uncle was one of them." She glanced at Isabel for a reaction. Isabel had never met her uncle, but knew he'd died young.

"My dad told me Uncle Will was killed by an idiot who didn't know how to drive."

"It wasn't anyone's fault. Accidents happen and sometimes there isn't a good reason," she said, her voice clipped.

Isabel shouldn't have said anything. She hadn't meant to upset Mabel. "I'm sorry."

"Your dad blamed my dad for the crash . . ." she paused, looking down, then added, "then he took revenge on my family." She stared at Isabel, no anger in her face, just sadness. "Losing someone . . . is tough. Losing your entire family is unimaginable. I'd already lost my father. I didn't have to lose my mom and brother, too. Your dad did that. Your *dad*," she said. "*Not you.*"

Isabel felt shame for her father's actions. "But, how can you stand to be around me?"

Mabel put both her hands on Isabel's shoulders, looking her in the eyes. "You are *not* your father!" She looked away. "Don't blame yourself for your father's sins and don't take on the guilt that belongs to him and only him. I grew up thinking I was bad, like maybe I didn't deserve a family. It took me a long time to work through it." Her eyes glistened as she spoke. "I had people who helped me get through it and so do you. You have me." She smiled, a real smile, her eyes shiny. "You always will. From the moment I met you, I felt a need to protect you and I'm not going anywhere."

Isabel knew it was a sin to take another person's life. How did her dad not know? Or he did, but didn't care. She was part of her mom and her dad. She had her mom's eyes and hair, and her dad's nose. What if she turned out to be a killer like her dad?

"Sometimes I think about visiting my dad," she blurted out. Her heart sped up. Nervous, she picked up a rock and tossed it into the water. Mabel didn't respond, and Isabel was too afraid to look at her. "I know I shouldn't, but he . . . he's my dad."

It was true. As much as Isabel hated her dad for what he'd done, there were times she wanted to see him. But not for the reasons Mabel might think.

The skies were clear, and beauty mushroomed before them. Her dad would never get to see this, ever. In a way, she felt bad for him.

"Can I ask you what changed your mind?" Mabel asked,

reaching into Isabel's bag and pulling out two granola bars, handing one to Isabel along with some water.

Isabel poured some of her water onto Bella's eager tongue, before she ran off again to play. "I'll be thirteen in a couple of weeks and my wish is to see him. That's what I'm asking for." She couldn't tell her the real reason.

"You ready to head down the mountain?" Mabel asked, making it easy on her and putting an end to the awkward conversation.

"Bella . . . Bella," Isabel hollered. "Let's go girl." The dog came running up to Isabel, making circles around her, then settling by Isabel's side. They worked their way down the mountain and back to the car, much quicker than the hike up.

She needed to see his face and then she'd know if he still loved her.

THREE

SUSAN HAD A LOT OF RULES FOR HER, LIKE: clean up after yourself, do your chores, do your homework, no phone at the table or when someone is talking to you, clean up after Bella, and a few others Isabel couldn't think of at the moment. But today Susan had given her permission to go to the mall with Abby, no adults. It had been something she and Abby had talked about since, like, forever.

Isabel's chest fluttered as Susan pulled up to the mall. It felt as though she'd moved up in the world a notch. No one around to watch every move she made. No one to insist she try on clothes she didn't like. No one to tell her to hurry.

Oh, look how cute this shirt is! It will look so good on you. Here, try it on. Then in the next breath, *Hurry up. What's taking so long.*

No, no, and no. How many times did she have to say, "No," before Susan caught on that she didn't like the same things her aunt did?

Susan dropped her off at the main entrance, but before Isabel could make a run for it, Susan said, "Wait."

With the door open and one foot out, Isabel froze. *So close.*

She thought maybe Susan remembered the news last week about a girl who had gone missing and suddenly worried the same would happen to Isabel.

"I'll pick you up right here in three hours. On the dot."

That's it? She rolled her eyes. "I know."

"What are you two planning on doing for three hours, anyway?"

"Stuff."

"Stuff?" she parroted. "Like what kind of stuff?" She laughed.

"What everyone else does at the mall. Shop, eat, look around, people watch. Probably mostly people watch."

She studied Isabel's face. "Do you need money?"

"No. I have some saved up." Isabel patted her pocket.

"How much did you bring?"

"Fifty, just in case I find something I want."

"Okay. Make sure you don't lose it and if you do buy something don't set it down."

Her aunt had already told her all this before. "Can I go now?" she asked, annoyed.

"Yes, go." Isabel ran to the front door and heard Susan holler, "Be safe and be careful who you talk to."

Embarrassing! She couldn't look back. Why was her aunt treating her like a kid? Neither she nor Abby planned on doing any shopping, but if she would have said so, her aunt would not have let her go. So she lied because she had to.

Abby squealed when Isabel walked through the front doors. "She's here. You can go now." Abby told her mom, practically pushing her out.

Isabel hugged Abby with way too much enthusiasm. Abby laughed and hugged her back. They were going to have so much fun.

Abby's mom turned back, "Be good . . . and safe. Don't talk to—"

"Mom, I know." She turned towards Isabel and pulled her down the corridor, away from her mom. "I thought you were never going to get here. My mom insisted on coming in. She's so embarrassing."

Isabel smiled, wishing her mom would have brought her, instead of Susan. She could totally see their moms being friends.

First, they went into Forever 21 because it looked like a fun store and Susan never let her shop there. The place was huge. With her fifty dollars she could have bought two outfits, but they weren't there to buy clothes. Instead, they tried on clothes they would never be allowed to wear, just for fun. Shirts cut too low, skirts too short, and high heels they could barely walk in. They laughed so hard, everyone turned to see what was going on.

They did this for thirty or so minutes and then decided to go to the Apple store and play with the displays. Isabel had the same iPhone 7 her aunt had given her when she'd moved in with her. She was hoping she'd get an iPhone X for her birthday.

After the Apple store, they walked the mall and bothered people for fun. Abby dared Isabel to ask the security guard for his autograph, stating she saw him in Mall Cop and loved it. She did. Then she dared Abby to run up the down escalator. She did, after falling a couple times. She'll have bruises and scrapes to laugh at later. Then they took a break at the food court and found it overflowing with hungry shoppers.

They shared a Sprite and a chicken basket. Total bill, $11.08 including the dollar tip Abby insisted on giving the man even though he didn't do anything but hand them their food. After the fourth request for a refill, he told them it would be their last. If they wanted more, they could pay for another drink. *Who did he think he was, the soda police?*

Abby dared Isabel to buy a ride from the Animal Riders kiosk. "Hi, how much for the rabbit?" she croaked, feeling her face flush when the cute boy behind the kiosk looked up. He had to be at least eighteen, too old for her, but someday, five years difference wouldn't be a big deal. He had dark curly hair that just touched the top of his shoulders, dark brown eyes, long eyelashes, and kissable lips. The thought made her flush again.

He smiled. "Depends how long you would like to ride him for."

"Uhm, what's the least amount of time?"

"Ten minutes." He still had a smile spread across his face. He glanced at Abby, "You want two or one."

"Uhm, just one."

"Okay, that'll be six dollars."

She passed him a ten and his fingers brushed hers, sending a shock through her hand, up her arm and straight down to her belly.

Wow, what was that? She swallowed, trying to compose herself, as he gave her four dollars back.

"Have fun," he said, with a wink. She wanted to say something interesting or funny, but her mind wouldn't cooperate. Instead, she wondered what it would be like to be his girlfriend, to hold his hand, to kiss him. He obviously liked her.

Abby bumped her with her shoulder, pulling her out of her head and into the moment. He'd been waiting for her to respond, say something, but she couldn't. "Thank you," she said hastily, forcing herself to focus on Abby, the reason she agreed to this stupid idea. "I did it," she declared. "Now I dare *you* to ride Bugs Bunny here over to Orange Julius and ask the clerk for a carrot." She grinned, ear to ear, proud of her suggestion. "But first, you have to say, 'What's up, Doc,' then ask for a carrot."

"No fair!" Abby shouted. "I dared you to get it so *you* could ride it."

"You should have been more specific," she replied, laughing. "I did exactly what you told me to. Now it's your turn."

"Fine," Abby scowled, turning bright red when she mounted the rabbit's back. Isabel burst out laughing, watching Abby as she pulled up to Orange Julius, looking back to Isabel with a smirk, then turned to the boy behind the counter.

She took a couple steps closer to Abby to hear better.

"Oh man, you're a mean friend." She turned to see a boy, one she'd seen a couple of times throughout the mall. He was smiling. Was he following her? "But I like how you think," he added. He was by himself, sitting at one of the tables, with a drink in his hands.

She was being paranoid. Everyone comes to the food court.

"She lives for this stuff. She's just mad she didn't think of it first," she replied, looking back at Abby, who had a drink of her own in her hand.

"Look what he gave me, for free," she teased.

"Let me guess, it's made with carrots."

"You guessed right! How cool is that. And it's good." She handed it to Isabel and looked at the boy listening to their conversation.

"Hi," she said, looking back at Isabel. "Who's your friend, Isabel?"

She took a sip and wrinkled her nose. "Not good." She stuck her tongue out making a face. Abby stared at her, eyes wide. "Oh, I don't know hi—"

"I'm Sam," he said.

"Hi Sam. I'm Abby."

He waited for Isabel to introduce herself.

"Isabel. I'm Isabel."

This guy made her uncomfortable. He was cute and all, not animal kiosk cute, but the way he looked at her made her feel exposed. She glanced over to the kiosk guy, who was busy with another customer. It was a lady he appeared to be flirting with as well. She must have made a face, because Sam said, "Don't waste your time with Derek. He thinks he's a ladies man."

"And how about you? What's your story?" she accused.

"I'm nobody really. I came to buy my mom a gift for her birthday. It's next week."

"Isabel's birthday is next week!" Abby practically shouted.

"Well, happy early birthday." His eyes looked directly into her own, like he saw right through her.

Uncomfortable, she looked down, noticing the rabbit Abby still had. "Time to return your rabbit friend," she said.

"Oh, right." Abby wheeled away toward the kiosk.

"Listen, I know we just met, but can I buy you a drink?"

"No, I'm fine," she heard herself say, even though she was really thirsty.

"C'mon. For your birthday." He stood up. "I'm on my way. Tell me what you want or I'll buy you the carrot one."

She smiled. "Strawberry. I like anything with strawberries."

"Strawberries it is." And he disappeared in the crowd of people walking by.

Abby pushed her arm. "Look at you. He is so into you." She sipped her god-awful drink.

This guy she'd been talking to for the last ten minutes had young Justin Beiber hair and a little scruff on his upper lip and jawline. He still had the baby face, aside of the scruff, that some boys held on to.

She stared at him from where they stood, with Abby's back to the food court, when her friend turned to see what Isabel was looking at.

"Don't look!" she barked. "Geez, way to make it obvious."

"Oh, like you're so subtle. Why don't you take a picture," Abby suggested.

"Good idea," she replied.

"He likes you. Talk to him," Abby urged her on.

She glanced at him as he made his way back, drink in hand, and he smiled at her. She hadn't liked him ten minutes ago. Then she was into the kiosk guy. She hadn't seen either one of them before today, and she was feeling things she'd never felt before. It reminded her of the Mind Eraser at Elitch Gardens. Scared at first, butterflies in her stomach, her chest heavy and her skin light, like all the tiny hairs were standing on end. She could feel it now.

He stopped before her. "Hi," is all he said and her heart leapt out of her chest. He offered the drink and she took it. He watched her suck half of it down. "Why don't you two join me?" He turned to look at Abby.

Neither she nor Abby replied, and Isabel stopped breathing all together. "Sure," she squeaked.

He sat down gracefully, like a dancer would, smooth and light, like a feather. The frog in her throat kept her from talking. "I have no idea what I'm going to get my mom. I've been here for two hours and I'm no closer to deciding. Do . . . do you think you two could help me find something?"

"Oh." All she could manage was one measly letter—*O*.

"Sure," Abby replied. Isabel felt the overwhelming urge to hug her friend. *This, people, is what friends are for*, she thought, *to help when you're mute and guide you along until you find your voice.*

"Great!" he exclaimed.

Still hopelessly mute, a smile made it across her face. She lifted her bottom and to her surprise she made it to a standing position only to find herself face-to-face with the guy who slowly melted her heart. His body soap wafted around her and she thought she'd fall back down.

He smiled again and held her gaze with his green eyes. "Shall we," he said, and walked in the opposite direction from where she stood.

Abby pulled on her arm and shoved her face into Isabel's. "Oh my god!" she whispered. "He's cute and so into you."

He's into me, the thought made her smile. She took a deep breath and told herself to be brave. If she continued to act like a freak, she might scare him off.

He must have sensed he made her uncomfortable, because he started paying more attention to Abby, without forgetting Isabel. After a while, she found her voice again. She liked that he didn't say stupid things and then laugh at himself like all the other boys she knew, and he didn't tease her or have other friends tagging along acting like toddlers.

Best of all, he liked *her*. They made plans to see each other again the following week.

FOUR

MAXINE GALLO FOUND HERSELF WITH A RARE afternoon off and the only thing she wanted to do was spend it with Isabel. It had only been six months since she'd learned she had a niece. For so long she thought she didn't have a family. Knowing Isabel made her want to be a better person.

Her niece, her blood—polluted, as it might be. Either way, it felt good knowing she wasn't alone in the world after all.

Growing up, she thought she deserved every bad thing that came her way. In and out of foster homes, she'd stopped caring. It was the only way she could survive.

She hurried down the walk, her heels clicking with each step. She pressed the doorbell, and a chime played within the house. The door opened and the smell of sugar cookies drifted up her nose. Every time. It was like Susan did nothing else but bake cookies all day and night.

"Aunt Max! What are you doing here?" Isabel asked, surprised to see her.

"I'm here for you, of course," Max replied.

"How did you know I didn't have school today?"

"I lucked out. I got the afternoon off and called Susan to ask if I could pick you up a little early from school."

"Yay!" Isabel squealed. "She didn't even say anything."

"I asked her not to," Max smiled. "Surprise! I'm taking you on a girls date."

Susan appeared next to Isabel, "Max. Come in." She looked to Isabel, "Next time, invite your guest inside." Isabel rolled her eyes and moved aside for Max to enter.

Max hadn't come to chat with Susan. She looked at her watch, despite knowing she could afford to spend five minutes, she said, "Oh, we need to run to make our appointment. Thank you so much for letting me take her."

"Appointment? Do I need anything?"

Max reached out and touched her shoulder to get her moving. "Nope. Just you."

"Have her back by six, we have dinner plans."

"Will do."

Isabel turned back to Susan. "Thanks for letting me go." Susan hugged her like she would be gone days.

They walked to the car and Max couldn't help but feel a little cheated. *Don't be negative,* she told herself. *Enjoy the time you do have.*

Isabel looked at Max, "Wait, where are we going?"

"You'll see."

"I hate surprises," she complained. "Please tell me."

"Really? You hate surprises? You seemed pretty happy to see me a couple minutes ago. You changed your mind that quickly?" Max teased.

"No. But please tell me!" she cried.

Max opened the driver side door and Isabel stood on the opposite side of her car, staring her down. "Fine," she laughed. "Get in and I'll tell you." She'd never tire of the excitement in

Isabel's eyes, something Max had never experienced. Before starting the engine, Max turned to Isabel, "Remember my friend, Melanie?" She shook her head no and furrowed her eyebrows. "The one who owns Melz Spa."

Her eyes grew, "We're going to the spa?" she asked, excited.

Max laughed and nodded. Isabel had met Melanie a few months ago and had asked her a thousand questions about the ins and outs of owning her own spa. Max had promised to take her one day and today she'd be fulfilling her promise.

"You're the best!" she squealed, leaning over to hug her.

Max beamed, probably more than Isabel. The words made her heart soar, something that hadn't happened in a long time. She imagined just the two of them, living on some beach, burying their toes in the sand and hunting for seashells. Max had never been to the ocean and she highly doubted Isabel had either. Some day.

"This feels weird," Isabel said as Janice exfoliated her body in preparation for the body wrap.

"It can. Try to relax and clear your mind," Janice responded.

She peered over to Max's table. "Is that the seaweed?" asked Isabel, referring to the clay being applied to Max's body.

"It sure is and it feels so good."

"I'll be the judge of that," Isabel threw back. "When do we get our nails done?"

"After this. Just relax and enjoy the experience."

"I am. Ooh, it feels warm." Isabel remained quiet through the rest of the application right up until they wrapped her up like a burrito. She turned and looked at Max. "You're in a cocoon!" she laughed. "How do I look? Aw! I wish we could take a picture."

"You look comfy, and we can ask one of these wonderful ladies to do it."

"How long do we stay this way?"

"Not long, twenty minutes or so."

When time was up, Janice took a picture of the two of them. Once they were unwrapped, they were told to take a shower. Max hadn't thought of that part and she wondered if she should shower in front of Isabel. Deciding against it because she didn't want to have to answer all the questions Isabel would have for her, she said, "You go first. I'll wait here until you're done."

They finished showering, put on their robes and headed over to get their nails done before ending with facials. Max soaked up every bit of sunshine spilling from Isabel's pores. She could do this every day.

FIVE

TODAY, ISABEL DUMEL OFFICIALLY BECAME A teenager. No longer a teeny bopper, preteen, kid, kiddo, or squirt. And no longer a small fry—a name her mom once called her.

"What are you thinking?" Susan asked, as she placed a chocolate chip pancake on Isabel's plate, and then added another.

She hated the question. Same with, *How was school?* or *What did you do today?* It was always the same questions with the same answers. It annoyed her, but today was her birthday and she didn't want to fight with her aunt. So, she decided on the truth.

"About my mom."

Susan, about to add another, stopped with the chocolaty goodness trickling over the edge of the spatula.

Bet she regretted her question now, thought Isabel. No question should ever be asked unless you're prepared for the worst possible answer. No one ever really wanted to know the truth.

Susan dropped the pancake on her own plate and responded with an, "Oh."

Oh?

Isabel hadn't mentioned her mom for well over a year. Especially on her birthday or Mother's Day or the day she died. Those were the days she least wanted to talk about her.

Now the *Oh* response made her angry. *You really have nothing to say?* Isabel thought. She downed a third of her pancakes, waiting. Waiting for something, anything.

Nothing. She said nothing.

Finally, Isabel said, "Do you even think about her?" It came out rude, but she didn't care.

Susan looked up from her barely touched pancake stack. "Of course, I do," she said, defensively. "I think about her all the time." Although Susan didn't shed any tears, her eyes became glassy and she blinked a lot as if refusing to let her emotions take over. She looked at Isabel, pain spewed all over her face.

"I miss her," Isabel whispered at last, fighting her own battle of emotions, the burn in her nose and lump in her throat making it hard to swallow.

"Me, too," Susan said.

Isabel's brush with sadness turned into anger again, a feeling she'd friended for the last couple of years.

Worn out from thinking about it, she finished off her last bite and put her plate in the sink. In her room, her eyes were drawn to the picture of her grandpa's smiling face. Life had been better with him in it, but then he'd died a week after she'd taken the picture.

When the police took her dad away, she'd hated her grandpa for a whole minute for not stopping her dad from ruining her life and for getting sick and not allowing her to live with him.

He died in an old-age home. The one he put himself in. He'd said, "I'm dying, and I don't want to miss out on all the fun old people have, nurses waiting on me hand and foot. Heck, maybe I'll find me a wife." He laughed. She didn't.

She studied the picture, wondering if he'd known he would die soon. His eyes sparkled from the light. Or was it his spirit talking to her, passing hints of what was to come.

After her dad went to prison, her grandpa said, "My heart is broken in two." For the longest time she blamed her dad for her grandpa's death. He killed him, like everyone else. But the truth was, he'd died from old age and from all the drinking he'd done when he was younger.

She'd had two birthdays since she lost her mom and this would be the first since her grandpa had died. Before doing anything else on her birthday, she had to make a stop.

It was a short, ten-minute drive to the cemetery. Susan parked and Isabel jumped out of the car, making a beeline to her mom's grave clear on the other side of the cemetery. Opposite the Dumel's lot. This time of year, the grass had yet to turn green. The cemetery always seemed deserted. Not from lack of living people visiting. A detached vibe, like the souls of the dead were dried up and gone. She imagined skeletons remaining in rotting coffins, bones disintegrating to dust. All they needed was a strong wind to blow it all away, leaving a smooth flat surface behind.

"Hi, Mom," she said. "I turned thirteen today." She looked up at the sky, then back down to the mound of dirt. "I guess you know that." Lost for words, she added, "Happy birthday to me. I love you, Mom." Susan handed her a bouquet of flowers and she set them gently down next to where her heart would be. She sat there for a few minutes, enjoying being as near as she could to her mom.

She left her aunt there and walked across the cemetery to find her grandpa. Her grandma and uncle were buried next to him, but she'd never met either one, so she only talked to her grandpa. "Hi, Grandpa." She smiled. "I'm thirteen today. Aunt Susan is throwing me a party tonight. I wish she wouldn't, but she said thirteen is a big number, so we had to celebrate. Thank goodness Abby will be there. You haven't met her, but I told you about her last time. Oh, and I met a boy." She blushed thinking of him. "His name is Sam and I really like him. I think you would, too. He's super funny and maybe a couple years older than me, but he's not stupid like all the other boys in my school." She paused, out of breath. It had always been easy talking to him. She spotted Susan making her way over.

Isabel wrapped her finger in the dolphin necklace he'd given her. Before he'd died, she had visited him every Wednesday and Sunday at the retirement center. That particular day he had given her a small box. His face lit up as he watched her remove the shiny chain and small charm. She remembered the day like yesterday. It had been a big day, turning into a crazy day, and ending as one of her worst.

She freed her finger and touched the pendant on her neck. She had squealed in pleasure, wrapping her arms tight around his neck. Then two women interrupted them. One she'd never seen, and Gail, her grandpa's nurse.

"You're not too late, he's right there." Gail said and her grandpa frowned. He'd never liked Gail, or surprises.

"Wilbur?" said the lady no one recognized. She wore a silky white shirt with jeans, her own fancy necklace dangling down between her breasts, and black, single-strap heels. She looked classy, smart, and rich.

Her grandpa turned to Isabel like she had all the answers. She didn't, so she shrugged. He looked back at the classy lady with blonde hair and dark roots, her hair pulled back in a loose bun.

Her grandpa blinked, dumbfounded. "That's me," he replied at last.

"Who are you?" Isabel asked, since no one else spoke up.

"You must be Isabel," the lady said. "Aren't you getting big." She hadn't gone through her growth spurt yet.

"I'm sorry, how rude of me . . ." the classy lady appeared flustered, "I never knew who you were until I read the paper and saw your picture, well not *your* picture. It was Jimmy. He looks just like you, when you were young." Her eyes had lit up. "That's my mom, Julia," she said placing a picture in his hand.

Isabel's throat made a noise without her permission. The picture looked old and worn, and her grandpa had a bushy mustache. She'd always thought if her dad ever grew one, he'd look just like her grandpa.

"Grandpa, that's you?" she said. His hand trembled and the picture quaked.

"I'm Maxine Gallo," the classy lady finally said. "According to my mom, you two dated." Her grandpa's face turned whiter than it already was. "My mom passed away when I was very young, but she left this picture for me. I never knew my father—"

"And you think Wilbur's your father?" Susan accused.

Isabel couldn't believe her ears. She looked at her grandpa for answers, but he didn't give any. He just sat in silence, his face blank.

"Well, yes," she replied.

Susan gasped.

"My mom . . ." Maxine Gallo tried to explain, "here, on the back of the picture," She flipped it over, "you see, she wrote here that this man is my father." She looked at each of them, waiting for acceptance, understanding, a warm welcome?— none came. "I was so confused when I learned this. She never gave me a name, all I had to go by was a face." Maxine looked desperate, turning to Isabel's grandpa, "I'm sorry you're finding out this way. I swear I didn't know. I didn't even get this picture until I was eighteen. My mom had been dead for fourteen years. It was sealed with the rest of my inheritance, and I had no idea where or how to find you with no name. To be honest, I was hurt and mad and didn't want to find you back then."

Susan put her hand on her shoulder. "Listen, Maxine—"

"Please, call me Max."

"Max, I can see you and Wilbur have a lot to talk about, but today he's visiting his granddaughter and they only have thirty minutes left, so if you don't mind, why don't we grab some coffee and give them some time together."

"Oh . . . of course. I'm so sorry. Isabel, it's nice to meet you. I hope to see you again."

Isabel's mind spun with so many questions and thoughts. What had just happened?

For the life of her she couldn't grasp how this lady, Max, was her grandpa's daughter and how he never knew her.

She *knew* back then how babies were made and it usually involved sex. She also knew all about intrauterine insemination, in vitro fertilization, and the turkey baster method. If you're wondering how a kid knew all the ways to get pregnant, it certainly wasn't sex education class in school. She hadn't gone through that dreadful class yet. Her knowledge had come to her by a women's magazine she had read while at the hospital with her grandpa a few months back. There was an article about ways to get pregnant that didn't involve sex. Oh, and she left out surrogacy because you don't get pregnant yourself. The article had caught her attention because without a mom to tell her all these things she figured no one else was going to jump at the chance to educate her. Her grandpa certainly wouldn't, and she figured she probably knew more than him anyway.

Her grandpa, silent, deep in his own thoughts, gave no explanation to her and she wanted to know why he'd never told her.

"Grandpa—"

"Can we talk about something else?"

"But I didn't know I had an aunt this whole time and—"

"Isabel!" She jumped at the rise in his voice. Her grandpa seldom raised his voice at her. "Please, I don't have much time with you, and I don't remember. You know my mind isn't the same. I don't know her or her mom. Now tell me, what are your plans for the rest of the day?"

The new information ate at her and she wanted to know, but her grandpa was a sealed pod and hounding him would only make him mad. She gave up and told him about her week, but she could tell he wasn't listening. His mind, what was left of it, had drifted to another place and time. When Susan returned, Isabel was more than ready to go. A feeling she would regret later.

Her grandpa gained a daughter that day, Isabel gained an aunt, her dad gained a sister, and Isabel lost her grandpa.

"Aunt Max is nice," she said to his grave, thinking he'd be happy to know this about his daughter. "She visits Daddy." She looked to Susan who was out of earshot, giving her the space she always asked for. "He still hasn't written to me." She regretted telling him. He didn't need to be bothered with knowing this. "Did you ever go see him? You never told me and I was afraid to ask. I haven't. Sometimes I want to, but . . . but I'm still so mad at him." She changed the subject. "Aunt Susan is nice to me. We argue sometimes, but no more than you and I did. I think mom would be proud of her. She never talks about Mom. I say I don't want to talk about her, but I do. I miss her. I want to see her . . . and you."

She gestured to Susan who brought over the bouquet for her

grandpa and Isabel set it on his heart. "Love you, Grandpa." A tear rolled down her cheek and she swatted it away. No longer feeling like going to the mall as planned, she said, "I want to see my friends today. I know we had planned on a small celebration tonight, but I want Abby to sleep over."

"I'll talk to her mom," is all Susan said.

She wanted to see Sam and would have to find a way to make it happen without her aunt knowing.

Isabel found her aunt in the kitchen. "Do you think Aunt Max will come to my party with Mabel here?" Isabel asked, knowing full well she wouldn't. Max and Mabel never visited at the same time.

"I don't think so," Susan replied.

"You know what I want most for my birthday?" she asked, obsessing about it half the day and finally coming to a decision.

"What's that?" Susan said, taking her cake out of the oven and placing it on a cooling rack.

"I want to see my dad."

She looked up, confused, her brow furrowed. "I . . . we'll talk about it later. Or tomorrow."

"My birthday is today and I want to see him."

"It's not that easy. They have visiting hours—"

"I know. I looked it up already. Even though he's *my* dad, I need your permission." She handed Susan the form. She didn't take it, so Isabel dropped it on the counter next to her cake.

Susan held on to the counter and shifted her weight to her other leg. Dropping the oven mitts on the counter, she said, "Well, if you want an answer right this moment, it's no."

Isabel frowned, not believing her ears. "Why not? He's *my* dad!" she yelled.

Susan clenched her jaw, as if to keep her unkind thoughts from gushing out. "Can we just get through today—"

"I never get anything I want!" Isabel said, holding nothing back. She could feel her body tense all over and just wanted to get away.

"What are you talking about? All this . . ." Susan spread her arms around, "is for you. This cake is for you, those presents are for you." She pointed at the table where several presents covered the table in rainbow colors, "Everything I do is for you!" she shouted.

Everything told Isabel to scream and cry, but she couldn't. "Liar! If that were true you would take me to see my dad!" She stomped away and slammed the door to her room. She hadn't asked for all those presents, and she most certainly hadn't asked for a cake. She hated cake. How did Susan not know that by now?

Her head pounded, ready to burst, and her heart felt like she'd just run a hundred-yard sprint. Falling face first onto her bed, Isabel gripped her pillow, and let go, screaming with all her might. Feeling no better, she turned her head to breathe and her eyes landed on a purple box with a pink ribbon—a present. Forgetting all her worries, excitement ran through her. Who would put a present in her room? The presents from Susan sat on the coffee table in the living room. She rolled off her bed and stood before her desk, staring at the box. She shook it up and down deciding it had to be clothes.

The card read, *Isabel, Happy 13ᵗʰ Birthday! I hope you like the gift,* a happy face winking back at her followed by, *Love Aunt Max.* She smiled and gave the ribbon a tug and watched it fall to the floor. She stuck her finger under the wrapping, ripping it all to pieces. The box was sealed shut, prolonging her suspense. Her only pair of scissors were at school and she didn't want to get Susan's from the kitchen. A quick scan of her desk and she settled on a pen to poke at the tape. It worked.

Purple tissue paper lay neatly on top, keeping her from whatever hid underneath. Her eyes lit up as she pulled out the most beautiful dress she'd ever seen. Shrieking, she held it up against her body, checking herself out in front of the long mirror taking up the corner of her room. Quickly pulling her shirt off over her head, she tossed it on her bed, followed by her pants. The midnight blue dress slipped on easily over her head and fit nicely on her upper half exposing her bare shoulders, coming in at her hips and flaring out. She spun, watching the bottom half twirl and come to a stop. Frowning, she removed her socks and searched her closet for a pair of shoes suitable to wear knowing full well she didn't have any. This would be her first grown up dress. Come to think of it, she hadn't worn a dress since she was in fifth grade.

The dress wasn't meant to be worn today; she guessed Max bought it for her to wear when she visited her dad. Max had always told her to hold family close because you never knew when you wouldn't have one. She offered to take her, but told her she'd still need Susan's approval. Isabel had flirted with the idea, despite the anger and hate she still felt towards him. Deep inside, she wondered if he had changed, if he was sorry for all he'd done.

She needed shoes. Wondering what size Susan wore, she snuck out of her room and into Susan's. Her closet was half the size of Isabel's room, and bigger than the room she had living with her parents. "Please let them fit." She slid the shiny red shoe on her right foot and straightened her right leg. Doing so brought her left foot off the ground. "What the . . .? How on earth did anyone walk in these? No freaking way," she said, shaking her head. Susan had all colors of the rainbow but none that were flat aside of her running shoes.

Susan caught her on her way out, "You found your gift! You

look so beautiful!" she shrieked.

"Well I can't wear it without shoes."

Her eyes dropped to Isabel's bare feet. "You're right. I guess you can open up one more present before everyone gets here."

In the living room, Susan handed her a present from the stack. Isabel held it—*shoes*—and smiled.

"Here, let me help," Susan said, not afraid to kneel on the floor in her own dress. Isabel took a deep breath and let it out loudly as she watched Susan open the gift careful not to rip the paper. "What?" she asked.

"Nothing."

Susan removed two velvety light-gray flats. "Here," she said, motioning for Isabel to lift her foot and place it into the shoe. "It fits perfect." She beamed, slipping the right shoe on her right foot. "Oh my god, Isabel, you look so beautiful! When Max sent me the picture of your dress saying she was at the store ready to buy it for you, I knew you would need a nice pair of shoes to go with it." She steepled her hands over her mouth and nose, something Isabel did whenever she checked for bad breath, sometimes finding it. Susan's eyes became watery. "Oh, I almost forgot." She took a smaller box from the table and handed it to Isabel.

"You want me to open another one?"

She nodded.

Isabel did, revealing a necklace with a heart locket. She'd never had one of her own, but her mother wore one all the time. She'd asked her grandpa for it and he'd said her mom must have lost it.

"Open it," Susan said, pure joy spreading across her face.

On the left heart, her mom smiled, and on the right, Isabel smiled back. Closed, the two of them forever smiled at one another. Two hearts together, forever. Her bottom lip quivered.

"Thank you," she said, wrapping her arms around Susan's neck.

"Would you like me to wash your dress so you can wear it tonight?"

Isabel nodded, pulling it over her head and handing it to Susan. "Show me how," she said, not sure why, she'd never had any interest in washing clothes before. This dress was special. She wanted to wear it for her birthday, but knew she would also wear it when she visited her dad in prison.

Easy enough. Drop the dress in, turn the dial to small load, gentle cycle, cold water, add half a cap of Woolite and push the button. Water began to pour into the machine. "There, that's all it takes," Susan said.

She wanted to be able to talk to Susan about her dad. He'd done bad things, but he was all she had. Her mood turned sour and she went back to her room to hide out the rest of the afternoon until guests arrived. Two hours later the doorbell rang. It could only be one person, Abby, who always arrived before anyone else. Isabel ran to the door and hugged her friend. "I'm so glad you came early. C'mon." She pulled her by the arm.

"Bad day?"

She rolled her eyes, "How did you know?"

"It's your birthday, you're supposed to happy."

"Tell that to my aunt," Isabel said.

"Isabel, who's at the door?" Susan asked, coming from the kitchen. "Oh hi, Abby."

"Hi, Ms. Landry," Abby replied, polite like usual. Unlike Isabel, she spoke when spoken to, respected her elders, and followed all the rules.

Isabel yanked Abby's arm to keep her from talking any longer to Susan. "Geez, what's your problem?" Abby asked when they were in her room.

"Lock the door," she told Abby.

"I thought you weren't supposed to lock the door."

"My room, my space. I'm a teenager now, I need my privacy." Abby rolled her eyes. "We're fighting, okay. She won't let me see my dad."

"I'm sorry. You want to talk about it?"

"Nope. I want to open the present you're holding." She looked Abby up and down. "Hand it over," she said, holding her hand out.

"You're such a brat. If you're going to be in a bad mood the rest of the night, I don't think I want to give it to you. And besides, you haven't even blown out your candles."

"I'm not five. Now give me my present or I won't share my surprise with you."

"What surprise?"

"The one I saved especially for today."

"What is it?" Abby asked.

"It wouldn't be a surprise if I told you, now would it?"

"I guess not. But you could tell me, and I'll act surprised." She smiled knowing Isabel was not about to budge.

"Good try, but no."

"Fine. You win." She held her arms out, extending a blue box.

Isabel took the offering and shook it, then weighed it in her hands. "It's pajamas," she guessed.

"Just open it," Abby squealed, and Isabel laughed at her big, cheesy grin. Her excitement became contagious and Isabel screeched plopping herself on the ground. Abby watched intently.

Demolishing the paper, she yanked the box open and there sat a single pair of Lululemon leggings and a Victoria's Secret hoodie. "OH MY GAWD!!" she yelled, throwing her arms around her best friend's neck and squeezing. "You are the best!

I can't believe it." She jumped to her feet and was about to rip off her clothes but thought better of it.

"I'm glad you like it. I tried them on, and let me tell you, they feel amazing." Isabel and Abby wore the same size, except Isabel stood almost an inch taller. As if reading her mind, Abby added, "The leggings were a little long on me, which means they'll fit you just right. "Put 'em on!" she demanded.

"I will. But first, our surprise."

Isabel got on her hands and knees and reached into the deepest corner of her closet. She pulled out a little brown chest with a lock on it. She wasn't sure who gave it to her; she'd had it as long as she could remember. She hid the key under her mattress.

Abby's eyes grew with excitement when Isabel exposed a small velvet pouch. "Can I open it?" Abby asked.

"Music first," Isabel replied.

"Good thinking," Within ten seconds Ariana Grande's *Dangerous Woman* blared through the speaker.

"I love this song!" Isabel bellowed. "Don't need permission," she sang, dancing around until Abby joined her twirling and swaying to the music. Halfway through, Isabel handed Abby the pouch singing, "Something about you, makes me feel like a dangerous woman," she bellowed.

Abby smiled, tipped the bag over her palm and out fell a half-smoked joint. "Where did you get this!" Abby shouted.

"Shut up, nerd. You want my aunt to hear you?" Isabel whispered. Here's the thing about Abby, she didn't know how to talk normal. Everything came out too loud and with too much gusto.

"Explain yourself," she ordered, lowering her tone.

Isabel ignored her as she looked for the lighter her aunt had given her to light her candles. *Found it!* She lit her cotton candy candle first, for masking any unwanted scents, then put her hand out, palm up. "Give it," she demanded.

Abby dropped it in her palm and swung her arms behind her back like she did when she refused to hold Rosie the tarantula at the Butterfly Pavilion. Isabel liked the feeling of doing something she shouldn't. Her chest fluttered as she placed the joint between her lips and put the flame to the tip. Like she'd been taught, she sucked in her breath, like a straw, and held it, ending up in a coughing fit. Abby's eyes went wide. "You have to get used to it," Isabel explained.

She offered the joint, like a prize, to Abby who shook her head fast.

"Fine," Isabel said taking another hit, feeling so much better than she did earlier today.

"When did you start smoking that stuff?"

"Sam gave it to me for my birthday. He said I'd have more fun than without it. Don't tell him I told you though, he'd kill me." She attempted another offering to Abby. "C'mon, it's my birthday and you know we'll end up trying it eventually."

"I'm older than you and I didn't make us do anything stupid for my birthday."

"That's because you're a nerd. Now, c'mon. I swear if you never want to touch it again, then I won't either. Just try it, once." She tilted her head and batted her eyes. "Please."

"Just once," Abby conceeded, and Isabel jumped and clapped.

She placed the butt end to Abby's lips, holding it for her. "Now suck it in and hold it there," she instructed, holding her own breath, imitating Abby. "That's enough, pothead," Isabel laughed. "You're a natural. You sure you haven't been holding out on me?"

"No, I haven't. I guess all the swimming classes my mom makes me take, you know, holding my breath and all, helped."

They both started laughing. "That's the dumbest thing you've ever said, nerd." Isabel liked to call her nerd because Abby had never once received anything below a 95 percent on anything. They continued laughing, taking one more hit each, then Isabel smashed the burnt end into the sole of her shoe, like she'd seen Sam do, except on her shoe it left a black mark. "Shoot."

Abby picked up a pair of black shorts from the floor where Isabel had thrown them a couple of days prior. "Here, rub it off with this," she said, throwing them at Isabel.

Isabel frowned, but did it anyway. She put the joint back into the pouch once it cooled and stored it safely back into her locked box. "For safe keeping," she said. "Better open the window just in case." The small breeze felt good. She'd smoked a couple of times prior with Sam, but hadn't told anyone. She knew she could trust Abby but didn't want to get Sam in trouble. She liked him—a lot.

They sat on the floor talking about anything and everything, keeping the conversation light. No longer in a bad mood, Isabel felt relaxed. They'd just taken a giant step, growing up in a matter of fifteen minutes. And here they were, acting like they'd done it a thousand times, knowing full well they would do it again. Susan would kill her if she knew, but Isabel figured there were worse things they could have been doing. They'd broken the rules—no longer innocent and it felt good, tightening the bond between them.

They were deep in conversation when someone knocked on her bedroom door causing them to jump and burst out in laughter. Isabel's heart raced when Susan called out to her. She had no plans of opening the door, it stood between her being grounded for life or her getting away with a secret. "What?" Isabel yelled out.

"Open the door."

"Why?"

She didn't respond for a few moments, then said, "We agreed you wouldn't lock your door."

"You agreed, I just didn't argue," Isabel spat back.

"Isabel! Open the door right now!"

"She's going to ground you," Abby whispered.

"She can try." Her sheer will to be treated like a grownup who had a say in what happened in her life was much stronger than any guilty feelings she pushed down.

They waited a minute for Susan to break the door down and when she didn't, Abby said, "We better get out there."

"Find something in my closet to wear just in case." Isabel stripped and slipped on her new leggings and hoodie. The weather didn't call for a hoodie, but she didn't care.

"Oh my god!" Abby squealed. "You look so cute!"

Isabel grinned, all teeth, because she knew how good she looked. She spun around like a model and said, "Thank you."

"I hate you," Abby cried, then hugged Isabel because they were best friends for life.

"No you don't, you love me," she replied.

"I do *love* you," Abby said. "When will everyone else be here?"

"Not for another hour. No one shows up early, except—"

"Me!" Abby shouted, holding one hand over her heart. They laughed and Abby snorted.

"Nerd alert," Isabel sang, and they giggled.

"What's so funny," Susan asked as the girls walked into the kitchen.

Isabel looked back at Abby and smiled, causing Abby to start giggling again. "Nothing, Abby just said something dumb."

"Mabel is on her way. She should be here any minute."

Regret hit Isabel smack in the face. Susan, she could fool, but Mabel—the freaking psychic who always seemed to know what Isabel was thinking—not so much.

Ten minutes later, Mabel greeted her, "Hey, birthday girl!" And stared right through her soul. She held out her arms, "I have a hug with your name on it."

Isabel smiled and gave her the fastest hug she'd ever given.

"Whoa there. I showered." She laughed smelling herself to be certain. "You too old for hugs now?"

"Yep," she spat out, glancing at Abby, the only other person who knew how much deep shit she was in. Abby turned away the moment they locked eyes. *Thanks a lot, bestie,* she thought.

"Okay. You too old for presents, too?" she asked

"We'd never be too old for presents," Abby said, coming to her safety, better late than never. She nudged Isabel.

Deathly afraid to get near Mabel again, she said, "I'll open it later."

"Suit yourself. Where's Susan," Mabel asked as her eyes followed Isabel's finger to the kitchen. "Right. Go do your teenage things and this old fart will help get everything set up."

She had to know. Isabel usually ran up to Mabel and buried herself into her arms. Then again, she wasn't a tween anymore, she was a full-blown teenager and if she didn't want to be treated like a baby, she had to start acting the part.

Isabel pulled Abby outside thinking fresh air would do them some good.

"I'm freaking out," Abby said. "If they find out and tell my mom, I'm so dead, you don't even know."

"No one's going to find out, just act normal."

"But I don't feel normal. It started out fun, but now, not so much."

Changing the subject, she said, "I wish Sam could have come to my party." They walked through the neighborhood, stopping at a small park in an open space.

"You barely know him."

"I know him enough." And she liked everything about him.

"He seems nice, but your aunt would never let you go anywhere with him." Abby was right. Sam was two years older than Isabel, which made him a freshman in high school. He'd said his mom would lose it, too, if she knew he was dating a girl in middle school. She didn't see the big deal, her mom had been a few years younger than her dad.

The last time they'd met, she was supposed to be with Abby, but instead met him here, in the park, under a tree. They'd met twice already and each time he splayed out a blanket for them to lay on because he didn't want her getting her clothes dirty.

How can boys go from being gross, to being awesome? She found it easy to talk to this specific one. She found his laugh infectious, and his eyes melted her heart. She'd never felt this way about anyone before. The first time he kissed her, she floated on a white fluffy cloud. She wondered if every first kiss with a boy would be the same. Then again, why would she care to kiss anyone else?

Their first kiss, he'd said, "You have to want this as bad as I do. I don't want you doing anything you aren't ready for."

Is he crazy? She wanted him more than anything in the world, lips and all. The tips of his fingers brushed her lips and fire shot down to her belly. She nodded—yes, a million times, yes. The urge to be kissed by him swallowed her mind and she thought of nothing else. Not her dead mom or the ugly truth of her dad, or even her grandpa. All the pain of the past two years lifted the moment he pressed his lips into hers, and she gasped—her first kiss had been everything she imagined it to be.

He looked into her eyes and said, "That was the best kiss I've ever had." His words melted her heart, she was putty in his hands.

The last time they met, she worked up the courage to ask him if she was his girlfriend and if so, what did it mean exactly because when it came down to it, she knew zilch about boys. Zip, zero, nada.

He looked down at her, a smile spread across his face. "I think I'm falling hard for you, Isabel. I hope you feel the same about me."

She nodded, swallowing the lump in her throat.

"Listen, I have something that will help you relax, but you can't tell anyone." He pulled a joint out of his pocket. She'd never smoked, but like every kid in middle school, knew exactly what it was.

"I don't do drugs," she confessed, afraid he'd get mad or worse, not like her anymore.

"I wouldn't ask you to do drugs. I don't do them either."

"Is that what I think it is?"

"If you mean pot, joint, weed, grass, reefer, dope, Mary Jane, or MJ—"

She smirked, "Yes, that."

"It is."

"Another name for a drug."

"It's not a drug. It's safer than alcohol."

She didn't respond. In school, the video they watched said pot was a drug. Why was he lying to her?

"You're going to have to trust me. Everyone smokes."

She eyed him. "That's your reasoning. Everyone smokes so I have to, too?"

"No! Of course not. I just mean, it's safe. Have you heard of medical marijuana?"

"I don't live under a rock."

"Okay, there you go. Why would it be prescribed medically if it wasn't good for you or helpful?"

"Helpful?"

"You can't get addicted to it, Isabel. Just don't smoke too much at a time. People who look stoned out of their mind smoke way too much. I'm talking about taking a couple of hits is all. Here, watch me." He lit the joint and sucked. He pulled his face in and held his breath, letting out the smoke in a steady steam. "See. Do I look crazy?"

You look amazing, she thought. They taught them in school to say no and it wasn't allowed on school grounds. But not wanting to look like a child, she took the joint.

"I knew you were special. Pretty and smart."

"How do I do this?"

He walked her through the steps required. Smoking sounded difficult. She did as he instructed, and it burned her throat causing her to hack out part of her lung. Shook her head, "That's terrible."

He laughed and took it away from her. "You did good. Everyone coughs when they first do it."

There goes that word again, *everyone.* She watched him breathe it in masterfully. "We'll only take two hits each. Now you." He passed it back to her. "This time, try to hold the smoke inside for a count of five and then let it out."

Again, she did as he said, holding the burn in, to a count of four, and coughed up her other lung. He took it from her once more and smushed the burning end on the bottom of his shoe. He placed it in the tissue he had it in and handed it to her. "This is for you when you're alone and want to relax or even have a good time."

"I don't think so! If Susan caught me with that thing, she'd snap."

"She doesn't have to know—hide it."

Isabel's head began to float, and she closed her eyes to savor the sensation. Her lips curved up and her body became lax. A vision of Susan yelling at her popped in her head and Isabel blew the smoke from her joint right into her face. She giggled at the thought.

Crap, crap, crap, Isabel thought as she sat at the head of the table with Mabel and Susan bookending her fuzzy head. She glared at her best friend who sat directly across from her, with Lucas on her right, and had a cheesy grin spread across her dumb face. She had only one thing to do—don't leave Isabel's side and sit next to her at the table. Despite not wanting to like her right now, Isabel couldn't help but smile back at her. An inside joke only the two of them could hear.

With everyone's butts finally in their seats, they dug into all the fixings spread across the table. Burrito bowls were one of her favorite meals and although Susan wasn't the best cook, even she couldn't mess them up.

"This is amazing, Susan!" Mabel said. "I'm impressed."

"Don't be. I stole the recipe from Pinterest," she laughed. "Let's hope it's good. I even seasoned the meat myself." She raised her eyebrows.

"I'm sure it'll be good, I have a very good nose."

If Abby were sitting next to her, like she was supposed to, Isabel would have whispered to her, *What is she, a dog?* Instead, all it took was to look at Abby and they both giggled.

"What's so funny, girls?" asked Susan.

"Nothing," Isabel replied.

"Okay, well we're all here, so dig in."

Isabel filled her bowl to the rim and ate every bite. Too bad for Susan for making such a good meal, because now she'd ask for her to make it all the time.

Doing her best not to say too much, she watched as everyone ate, chatted, and laughed. She didn't have many people in her life, even less family, but somehow managed to have four people at the table who she was certain loved her.

After dinner, she and Abby ran off to her room. Muffled voices followed her. They were talking about her, but she only made out her name. She closed and locked the door behind her, taking a nosedive on her bed. She rolled around laughing. "I can't believe no one noticed."

"Right? I couldn't stop smiling the whole time. Susan probably thinks I'm crazy."

"You are crazy," Isabel confirmed, picked up her furry pillow and threw it at Abby's head, but instead it hit her in the chest.

They both started laughing again.

"I wish I could have been with Sam tonight," Isabel sighed.

"All you talk about is Sam. I think he's too old for you."

"Jealous much," she replied.

"I'm not jealous. I have my own boyfriend and I think it's cool that you have one, too, but we don't even know anything about him."

"Duh. You don't know anything about anyone until you get to know them better by spending time with them. Besides, I know him enough."

"Whatever."

After she opened her presents, they had cake, and everyone

left, including Abby. She had an early game the next morning and wasn't able spend the night despite all her begging. As she lay in her bed trying to go to sleep, she thought of sneaking out to see Sam, like in the movies. She wished for Sam to knock on her window and surprise her.

SIX

MABEL'S SUITCASE LAY ON HER BED WHERE Lucas Dresch left it. He set it out for her before he left for work. One of the hundreds of reasons why she loved him. She was somehow always in his thoughts. She wished she had that way about her. It wasn't that she didn't love him as much as he loved her. She did. She loved him with every part of her and would do anything for him. She tried to plan and do things for him, but somehow whatever she did never amounted to all the little things he did every day.

For instance, he'd packed before he went to work because he knew as soon as he came home they would be meeting her grandma and grandpa for dinner and he wouldn't have time later that night. He knew she needed to pack, too, so he took her suitcase out for her. On the bathroom counter were all the things she normally took with her, including her toothbrush because she always forgot it and they would end up having to drive to a nearby store and buy one. He didn't pack her clothes, but he laid out her phone charger and camera and ibuprofen and all the things she normally forgot.

Her jacket was on the couch, a thin one and a thick one, just in case, because she never knew what to expect with the weather and he always seemed to be prepared. An onlooker might think Mabel couldn't think for herself. When she was with Lucas, it was so easy not to. He made her life effortless and she loved him for it.

She thought of all the things her grandpa did for her, too, and all the things he did for her grandma. Mabel was surrounded by good-hearted men who were raised to take care of their women. She knew nothing less.

If only her brother could have known Lucas and grown to know their grandpa. Pete died at a young age, but she knew if he were here today, he would have been a good man, like Lucas, like their grandpa, like their father.

Love you, Pete, she said under her breath. *Take care of Mom and Dad.*

Her lips curved slightly as she imagined the three of them in heaven together, looking down on her.

When she had finished packing, she dragged her suitcase out to the garage and went back inside to put on her old pair of running shoes; she'd already packed her favorite pair.

Her phone buzzed on the kitchen counter where she'd left it. Before she could say hello, Frankie said "Mabel, where are you?"

"I'm home getting ready for a run. Why?"

"The judge ordered the Wilson girls to live with their aunt. I got a call from my contact and the allegations were founded."

"It's nice to know the system worked and we had a part in it." The Wilson girls were a perfect example of why she did what she did. It didn't always turn out positive, but she took comfort when it did. "Thanks for the call," she said.

"Everything else alright?" he asked, sensing something in her tone.

"I'm good," she said. "I'm just about to go for a run before Lucas gets home."

"Have a safe flight." They said their goodbyes and she headed out the door.

She ran to clear her head, but Isabel interrupted her thoughts. When Isabel had brought up visiting her dad, she thought it would pass. According to Susan, they'd fought about it on her birthday. Mabel never had to convince Susan to keep Isabel from her dad, but she knew her opinion mattered to Susan. After everything Jimmy had done, it'd be careless to expose Isabel to him.

When she'd gotten her ten miles in, she returned to the comforts of her home, showered in hopes of removing her thoughts along with her sweat.

Lucas came home with a big smile on his face, "Hey babe. How was your day?" he asked, excited about going away with her for a few days.

"Don't ask."

Grin gone. "That bad?" She didn't respond. "Okay, well I'll tell you about mine."

She prepped the chicken and he told her about the new guy at work and how he and this new guy had so much in common.

"Sounds like I have some competition," she hinted about him crushing on the new guy.

"In fact, you do. When we get back, Jack and I are going golfing."

She loved hearing about his day. "Sounds like fun." She had told him numerous times to hang out with friends. She worked long hours with Frankie, which left Lucas home alone for days at times.

"You hate golfing."

"Sounds fun for *you*," she corrected. "I'm happy you have someone to stand around with all day and hit balls." She winked and turned to continue prepping the chicken.

He put his hands on her hips and kissed the side of her neck. She could feel him smiling against her skin. "You know, you can play with my balls any time you like."

"Oh, I didn't know we were talking about *those* balls," she said. "In that case," she turned and was about to reach down when she remembered the chicken on her hands. "Can you get salmonella on your balls?" she asked, smiling.

"I don't even want to know what you two are up to," Grandpa said, as he walked through the doorway, setting a pan of pasta on the counter. "But can we have a rated-PG dinner tonight?"

"Oh, John," Grandma smacked him on the shoulder, "leave them alone. They're young and in love," she sang, kissing Mabel on the cheek. "I know we didn't plan for it, but I brought a basket of cinnamon rolls." She held up the basket like Vanna White enticing them with the prize.

"Thank you, Kathryn," Lucas said, followed by a hug. "John," he nodded at her grandpa and shook hands. His face flushed from being caught.

Mabel hugged both her grandparents and soon forgot all about her rotten day. Dinner was a welcome distraction until the last ten minutes.

"Mabel?" Her grandpa raised his voice to get her attention.

She looked at him through furrowed brows.

"Join me on the deck for some fresh air, would you?"

That was Grandpa's secret code for, *Let's talk about whatever's bothering you in my makeshift office.*

"I'm good." Frankly she was tired of thinking about Isabel. She needed this mini vacation she and Lucas were taking. She wasn't going to solve anything tonight no matter how good her grandpa's intentions were. So she took a deep breath, put a smile on her face, and did her best to focus on her family.

SEVEN

LAST YEAR, THIS TIME, ISABEL HAD BEEN grounded for three weeks. One week per violation. First; for not going home as expected. Instead, she'd decided to go home with a new friend to study for an upcoming test. Second; for going somewhere without asking. Susan never got home till five-thirty and Isabel planned on being home by then, so it shouldn't have mattered. Third; for not answering her phone when Susan called. Mind you, she called from work to remind her to take chicken out for dinner, so it'd thaw in time. What were the chances. Oh, and she didn't answer her phone because the battery died. Not her fault the stupid thing didn't charge the night before even though she'd plugged it in.

Today, Sam had asked her to meet him after school. From experience she knew she couldn't. She also knew if she asked, Susan would say no. What is a teenager to do when she couldn't win either way? She decided to have Sam come to her. If Susan came home early, which she never did, Isabel would be dead.

"When did you say your aunt will be home?" Sam asked.

"5:30 p.m. at the earliest. But you have to be gone by five, just in case," she stressed, not wanting to push her luck. She glanced up to the clock on the mantle which read 3:50 p.m.

What would they do for an hour?

He smiled and raised his eyebrow. "Not a problem."

Heat rose to her face causing her to break eye contact. He lifted her chin and leaned in. She held her breath, something she'd noticed with him. He took her breath away every time he touched her and when he looked at her with his amazing green eyes.

He kissed her. By this time he'd given her a hundred kisses in the handful of times she'd seen him. "Show me your room," he whispered in her ear.

She backed away, his words catching her off guard. "My . . . my room?"

His smile curved up, "Yes, Isabel. I want to see your room." The words were innocent enough, but the way he said it shot warning signals to her brain.

What had she been thinking asking him over to her empty house? She had no excuses, no one to blame. She suddenly wanted him to leave.

"What's the matter?" he asked when she failed to give him an answer.

"I . . . I," She what? The words wouldn't come.

It's easy. I want you to leave now. I want you to leave now. See? Easy.

"I want . . ." her face fell.

He stood and put his hand out for her to take. "Show me."

She gulped the urge to cry and took his hand leading him to her room. Why did it feel like a walk of death? She knew why. She may be naïve and uneducated when it came to sex, but every part of her body told her he expected her to have sex with him. She wasn't ready. She wasn't anywhere close to being ready. Kissing was one thing, but this was a whole other level she wouldn't take.

She opened her door, her feet firmly rooted outside her door. "Here it is," she announced, trying to sound like she had nothing to be afraid of.

She followed his eyes into her room and from his eyes she saw a child's room. She should have asked to have her room redone for her birthday. Maybe Susan would still be willing to do it. She was an interior designer after all. She lived for redecorating and making the outdated new again.

He walked in, barely looking around and sat on her purple and white comforter. His eyes met hers, "Come sit next to me."

No. No. No.

"Isabel, I'm not going to bite," he said sardonically.

"Uhm, I know. I . . . it's just that I . . . I forgot all about an assignment that's due tomorrow and I'm sorry, but I need to get it done and," she rambled, but couldn't stop herself once she started. "It's going to take me all night if I don't start it now and my aunt will be mad." He didn't look upset, he looked annoyed.

"You're lying."

How did he know? "I'm not. I really did just remember."

"If you're going to be my girlfriend, you need to be truthful."

"I am."

"You're not." His voice raised a notch and her stomach knotted. "You're still young and I'll give you that, but I'm calling you out on it. Don't lie to me."

She didn't like where this was going. He was now clearly mad and she didn't know what to do. He's much bigger and stronger than her. Her lip quivered and tears threatened her eyes, burning. She felt her throat clench and she walked away while she still could.

He came up behind her, but said nothing, continuing to

follow her to the door. Not knowing what to say, she reached for the knob and opened the door an inch before he reached around her, his palm flat on the door, and shut it.

Paralyzed and unsure what to do next, she waited for him to do something. Wild ideas sprang to mind—*Is he going to hit me? Or something worse, like rape? What if he tells me he never wants to see me ?* He'd say it was all a mistake. She's a baby, too young for him, and didn't know anything. She needed to grow up. That one would be true. She did need to grow up.

He brushed her hair to the side, his breath hot on her neck, and gently kissed her just below her ear. "I'm sorry," he muttered, his voice now low and regretful. "I didn't mean to scare you, but what did you think I was going to do back there?" He turned her around to face him, her back against the closed door. She said nothing, confused. Unsure if she'd read him wrong. "I'd never hurt you," he insisted. "I really like you, and I would never ever make you do anything you didn't feel comfortable with."

"I know." *Did she?*

"Good. Don't make me out to be some bad guy." He moved her aside, opened the door, and was gone.

It's her fault. She jumped to conclusions and now she may have lost him forever.

Knock, knock, knock.

Susan poked her head in.

Why knock if you're just going to let yourself in? thought Isabel.

"Mabel's at the airport and wants to talk to you before she gets on her flight," she said, letting herself in and handing the phone to Isabel.

Isabel rolled her eyes. "I thought you were stopping by on

your way to the airport." Actually, she had forgotten all about it.

"I know, I'm sorry. We were running late and I didn't have time."

"Aunt Susan said you had something to talk to me about." She guessed Susan told Mabel about her asking to see her dad. She hated her aunt for bringing Mabel into it. She only did it because she knows Mabel will back her up with a resounding *no*.

"I do, but it'll have to wait till I return. I don't really want to talk about it over the phone."

"Why not?"

"I wish I had time, but I'm boarding the plane now. I promise we'll talk the moment I get back."

Isabel didn't have anything else to say.

"I'll be back in a few days." She paused, then added, "I love you, Isabel."

Isabel's eyes burned from the tears forming. Before Mabel could say anything else, she handed the phone to Susan.

Her aunt walked out and shut the door again.

Isabel buried her head in her arms and started to weep. Her emotions were getting the better of her and after how things went with Sam, she felt like nothing was going right in her life. What if he was mad at her and never wanted to talk to her again? Her first real boyfriend and she already messed up.

Some time had passed, and when she couldn't cry any more, she dried her eyes and found her aunt in the kitchen pouring water into a cup. Susan turned. "There you are. Would you like some hot chocolate?"

She nodded. Hot chocolate made everything better, warming her from inside out.

Aunt Susan was prettier than Isabel's mom. If Cinderella

had a twin, it would be her aunt, though her mom was no ugly stepsister. She may have been prettier if she'd spent time on herself like her aunt did. Isabel's mom hardly ever wore makeup and she can't recall her ever going to an actual hair salon to get her hair done up.

Susan stirred the chocolate into a cup and said, "I'm doing my best to do right by you, Isabel. All I can think of is, 'What would Robin do.' Your mom was such an amazing mother and at times, I feel like I'm letting her down."

Isabel sipped her hot chocolate, not knowing how to respond. Her mom and Susan were close, as close as two sisters could be.

Susan was an interior designer, which meant, as explained by Susan, improving the interior of a home, office, or room. "The space should be visually pleasing," her aunt said countless times. Her own home, clutter-free, with a designated spot for every single item she owned. She used her home as a model home for potential clients. Whenever clients couldn't make up their minds, she brought them to her home. Nine times out of ten they hired her.

"Color is a powerful tool," Susan once told Isabel when she wore black floral print pants with a colorful floral top. First, Susan laughed at her. Then, she proceeded to tell her how colors effect mood and send messages and blah, blah, blah. In the end Isabel learned all the dos and don'ts of Susan Landry and hoped to god she didn't look like an old person.

She asked, "What happened to Mark? I haven't seen him in a couple of weeks."

Susan looked surprised and spilled her hot chocolate as she set it down. "Uh . . ." she let out what sounded like a half laugh, then cleared her throat. "We went our separate ways." Susan had been dating him before Isabel moved in with her.

Maybe Isabel scared him away? Whatever; she'd never did

like him. He had his own place and traveled a lot, so she seldom saw him to begin with. He gave her the creeps—like stalker creepy.

It didn't take a genius to notice men paying extra attention to Susan. "There are plenty of men who would die to date you."

Her eyes met Isabel's and she cleared her throat again. "I guess we haven't had *that* talk yet have we? I have a lot to learn."

What talk? Her face fell flat when she realized her aunt meant the *birds and the bees* talk. "Max taught me—"

"What?" she demanded, her eyes big. "What exactly did she teach you?"

"Uhm, she asked if you'd had *the talk* with me. You hadn't and neither had my mom. So she did."

"And what talk is that exactly?"

"You know . . . sex."

"My god, Isabel! You just turned thirteen." She rubbed her forehead. "When?"

Isabel shouldn't have said anything. Susan's eyes grew, and she cocked her head like a chicken, saying, *Well? Answer the question.* "A couple weeks ago. Anyway, if you have questions . . . you can ask her."

"Oh, believe me, I will."

EIGHT

ISABEL DUMEL HAD BEEN SPENDING THE NIGHT
at her best friend's house every Friday night for the last year,
only missing two or three nights when one of them was out of
town. No matter how many times she'd done it, waking in any
other bed but her own threw her into a temporary panic. Her
mind played copious tricks on her. Like, did her aunt finally
tire of her and send her away; or had the last couple of years
been a bad dream and her mom would knock on the door to
tell her breakfast was ready; or worse, had her dad kidnapped
her and was now plotting her death.

After saying her goodbyes to Mrs. Schiffer and Abby, she
flung her backpack onto her shoulder and began her short
walk home. The houses in her neighborhood all looked the
same, just different colors. She wondered if any of her neighbors ever pulled into the wrong driveway and tried getting
into the wrong house. That would be hilarious.

Her house came into view. They had company, or Susan had
company. A client most likely. It bummed her out because
that meant her aunt would be working most of the day and
she really didn't want to stay home alone thinking about Sam.
He hadn't called or texted.

She stopped next to the black truck parked in the driveway and peered into the darkened window, seeing nothing but her own reflection. Her dad had owned a black truck, similar to this one, only smaller. This one took up two spaces and she imagined trying to get it into a garage. It probably wouldn't even fit in Susan's three-car garage.

Pushing the house door open, she called out to her aunt, "Aunt Susan. I'm home!" and let her backpack slide off her back to the floor like she'd done every Saturday for the past year. Something felt off. The house didn't smell like cookies like she expected and it was oddly quiet. "Bella! Come girl," she called out. Nothing but quiet.

She wouldn't take her for a walk with a client over. Deciding she must have locked Bella in her room, she started across the living room. She'd peek out back first. Maybe she'd find everyone out there.

The kitchen was empty and the back door closed. Without opening the door, she looked through the window which gave a good view of the empty back yard. What the hell? It wouldn't be the first time she'd come home to an empty house, but never without her expecting it. Susan would have called or messaged—

"Hello, Isabel." An unfamiliar voice said.

She whipped around to find a big man she'd never seen in her life. Her heart leapt in her throat and she couldn't speak. She peddled back pushing herself against the back door. As she did, the floor on the far side of the island came into view. Bella lay there, not moving, blood oozing out of her fur.

Her lip quivered and tears blinded her. She wanted to go to her, check to see if she was dead. Too afraid to move, she stayed put. She managed to wipe the tears from her eyes, and he stood there, watching her with a smirk.

"You don't remember me, do you?" He asked, his voice cool and relaxed.

He did this to her dog. What did he want? Her legs shook, and tears fell from her face onto the tiled floor. "Whe . . . where's my aunt?"

"Which one?"

She had two aunts. *How did he know?*

"Aunt Susan," she whispered.

He shrugged. "She wasn't home when I got here. Hmmm," he shrugged, "maybe your dad shot her, too."

Her heart dropped and she felt dizzy. There were so many things wrong, starting with the fact she had never seen this man in her life. She had always been good with faces and she would remember him. How does he know her dad? *Maybe your dad shot her, too,* his voice sounded smooth with a hint of humor. She didn't find any of this funny. Her dad was locked up for life. Why would he say such a thing?

"What do want," she asked, at last, not really wanting to know the answer.

"You, my dear." He smiled, "I want you."

He took two steps toward her and everything went black.

NINE

ISABEL WOKE FOR THE SECOND TIME THAT morning in a panic, only this time it didn't pass. The dark air wrapped her skin in cold and she shivered. Her foggy mind couldn't make anything out in the pitch-black room. Then the realization came.

He took me! He took me!

Her breathing became labored as it became clear she wasn't safe. She moved her head from right to left but saw nothing but darkness. And it was cold. So cold.

And quiet.

She held her breath, but the only noise was the thumping of her heartbeat, drowning out all other sound.

She didn't belong here.

Too afraid to speak, not even sure she could, she sat up. A sliver of light peeked through from under the door, illuminating a few inches into the room. It felt small and claustrophobic.

Why is it so cold?

The bed she lay on was flimsy, not the soft, fluffy cushion on Abby's. And it stunk, like urine and sweat and bad body odor. Isabel felt around for a blanket, anything to cover with.

Finding nothing, not even a sheet, she wrapped her arms around herself and her whole body shook as she realized she was not wearing the clothes she'd dressed in this morning. She forgot all about the smell of body odor and urine, and whimpered quietly, recognizing someone not only had removed her clothes when she was unconscious, but this person saw her naked. Her lip quivered uncontrollably, rejecting the knowledge that the man who took her had touched her.

He'd replaced her hoodie and jeans with some kind of silky slip, like something she once wore under a dress. She could only assume the silky slip-like dress was not meant for a special occasion. Not one she wanted to be a part of.

Oh god, oh god, oh god! she cried, silently, holding her head to prevent it from splitting open. She racked her brains to recall how she knew the man who'd taken her. Nothing came. She didn't know him. But he knew her.

What if he killed my aunt?

Oh, Bella! He killed my dog!

Her chest thumped to a horrid bass causing her head to pulse to its own rhythm. None of it made any sense. Why would anyone want to kidnap her?

What is that god-awful smell?

She slid from the bed and bent over to sniff the area, pulled back quickly and covered her nose with her arm. The thought of laying on that thing gave her the willies. She stood, afraid to move. The floor felt like cement, freezing like she'd stepped outside in the dead of winter.

Maybe he didn't know her dad or her. He could have learned plenty about her infamous murdering father from reading the paper or online, and a few of the articles mentioned her. If so, he'd been stalking her.

Susan's and Mabel's warning rang through her head. *Be careful. Don't go with anyone you don't know.*

What if she didn't have a choice in the matter?

She reached around to feel a small bump on the back of her head, holding the truth about how he'd drugged her.

She couldn't stand there and wait for him to come back. Her eyes drifted to the glowing light beneath the door and she stepped lightly, placing each bare foot, one in front of the other, on the cold hard floor.

The doorknob rattled from her touch. The back door of the home she had once lived in had a loose doorknob. She'd asked her dad once why he didn't just fix it and he said she'd never be able to sneak in once she got older. He would hear her every time.

The thought occurred to her that whoever took her could be on the other side out of the door. What choice did she have? None she could think of. She turned the squeaky knob, but it failed to turn, and she panicked.

Bottom line, she could be anywhere. And there was a possibility nobody would ever find her. The fog fading, Isabel tugged at her memory, searching for any hint of where the man had taken her.

Hello, Isabel. He'd managed to turn two innocent words into something grotesque and threating. *You don't remember me, do you?* She would know if she'd met him. She didn't see many people with dreads.

Faint voices floated under the door. She scampered to the bed, ignoring the pungent smell surrounding her. Not familiar with her surroundings, she struck her shin on the frame of the bed and yelped. The voices came closer, too muddled to make out. She thought of hiding under the bed, but what good would that do. He'd locked her in the room. There wasn't anywhere to hide.

Just then the door opened and light from the other room flooded the small space. The man who had taken her stood in the doorway, his face hidden by the dark side of the room, but the light behind him outlined his dreads.

"Oh good, you're awake."

Deep down Isabel had known. Hope kept her believing the lies she told herself. This was all a mistake. He'd see it, apologize for his mistake, and take her back to her aunt.

"I want to go home," Isabel cried.

"You are home and you've missed lunch. We can't have you weak." He set a plate on the bed beside her. "Now eat up, you'll need your strength."

For what, she thought, afraid of the answer.

"It's a peanut butter and jelly sandwich," he said when she didn't move. "You're not allergic to peanuts, are you?"

She wasn't, but if she was, what good would that do her. She shook her head.

"You'll soon learn I'm not a patient man, so don't test me."

She looked down at the plate and thought of throwing it at him. She didn't want his food. She didn't want to be there. "I. Want. To. Go. Home," she stressed.

"I already told you. You are home." Frustration edged into his voice, "Now don't make me tell you again. Eat up."

She took a small bite. It tasted just like he'd said, peanut butter and jelly. "Who are you?" she asked.

"Call me Mr. B, like the rest of the girls."

Rest of the girls?

A lump caught in her throat, making it difficult to swallow the small bite she'd taken. She stared at her plate, watching it disappear as he shut the door behind him.

Once, when flipping through channels trying to find

something interesting to watch, she'd landed on a movie about a girl who went with her friend to Paris. It had just been the two of them when men broke into the place they'd been staying and took them both. Susan had walked in right when the screaming started and told her to change the channel, she wasn't allowed to watch something so gruesome. She did as she'd been told but ended up watching the movie from start to finish at Abby's house.

She wondered if Mr. B was like the bad men in the movie. If so, she didn't have a retired CIA agent for a dad who would come save her. No, her dad was locked away, much like her, but most likely better off than she would be. The only one she could rely on was Mabel.

Would she find her in time?

TEN

"ISABEL'S MISSING . . ."

Two words, short and heavy, dropped on Mabel Peters making it hard to breathe. The chatter and noise around her faded, becoming a distant hum. She closed her eyes to stop the merry-go-round, now going full speed.

"Are you alright?" Lucas asked. "You don't look so good."

"I'm fine," she whispered, the words automatic. She was far from fine.

He took the phone from her hand, "John? We're getting off the plane now. What's going on?"

She tried to focus on Lucas' face. They'd both slowed down and passengers started going around them, everyone eager to get off the plane. "I've got her," he replied to John, with worry. "She's going to have to call you back." Her grandpa's voice intensified, but she couldn't make out what he said.

A thousand possible scenarios crashed through her mind. She knew all too well what the words could mean. Her eyes dropped to a little girl with a small backpack. It was pink and sparkled, big enough to fit a couple of her outfits in, or maybe some toys. The little girl turned back and smiled at Mabel, then took hold of her mom's hand.

As they stepped off the passenger boarding bridge into the airport, she wanted her phone back. Her mind remained heavy and weighed down, because she knew from experience what she would learn.

This is what I do.

"Give me the phone," she said at last, the words forceful and not at all how she'd intended, but for god's sake, she didn't have time to freak out.

"Tell me everything," she said, taking a seat away from the gate.

"She was taken some time between 9:35 a.m. and 10:05 am.," her grandpa said.

"Can we narrow the timeline down?" she asked.

"Not yet."

"Susan texted me at," she paused, "at 9:45 AM. She didn't know yet, did she?"

"I'm afraid not. Susan arrived at her house at 10:05 AM and found Isabel's dog lying in the kitchen, bleeding from stab wounds."

"Bella . . . she tried to protect—"

"Looks that way. Susan immediately called 911. Didn't even bother searching the house first," her grandpa explained. She must have been scared out of her mind. "The police showed up within minutes, searched the entire house, inside and out. Isabel was nowhere to be found. She left Abby's house at 9:35 a.m. and by 10:05 a.m., thirty minutes later, she'd been taken."

The walk would take her ten minutes, tops, if she walked like a turtle. "Whoever took her may have been waiting in the house for her," she said.

"Nothing's missing or out of place and there're no signs of a break-in."

"Then she knew her kidnapper. He didn't have to break in,

because she let him in." Him, her? It could have been either. "Do we know for sure she made it inside?" Mabel asked.

"Looks that way. Her bag, the one she'd taken to Abby's, lay by the front door," her grandpa said.

Isabel knew better than to open the door to strangers. It had to be someone she knew, but who? Looking at her watch, she mumbled to herself, "It's been two hours." Isabel's best odds for recovery were within the first two hours. "Jimmy," she stated.

"He's been notified."

"I really don't give a damn. I want to know if he is behind this?" Over 70 percent of abductions were instigated by the child's father or mother, and Isabel's mom wouldn't be coming back from her grave to abduct her child.

"I couldn't say. Where are you now?" he asked.

"At the gate." She'd forgotten her grandpa was picking them up. "Are you here already?"

"Frankie will be there in five minutes."

She stood and Lucas nodded, grabbing both of their bags. With only the phone in her hand, she all but ran to passenger pick up.

"We're coming," she said.

"Mabel?"

"I'm here."

He paused. "Can you do this?"

What he meant was, can she do her job finding Isabel without letting her personal feelings get in the way? The question made her mad, but she knew her grandpa meant well, and he was only concerned about her.

"I won't let her down." She meant every word. Mabel didn't do failing well. She wasn't a sore loser, she just didn't stop until she'd accomplished what she'd set out to do. "I know what's at stake," she continued. "Regardless of whose daughter she is, a child's missing, and this is what I do."

Cold steel bars and cement walls couldn't keep Jimmy out of her mind. Time and again he found a way to slither through the crevices and firmly plant himself into her soul. Her curse was the bond she'd formed with Isabel—for better or worse. The love she effortlessly gave remained a direct line to her childhood. Her compassion—a great strength, and a great weakness.

Once outside, Lucas put his arms around her. "I'm so sorry. I know how hard this is on you." He planted a kiss on the top of her head.

She spotted Frankie pulling in. "He's here," she announced, scurrying down the walk.

Frankie stepped out, hugged her, and helped Lucas put the bags in the back of the car. "Detective Corneal is there along with half the police force in Colorado," Frankie said. A missing child is a priority. Which means anyone in uniform is out helping in some way. "We're going to need help on the inside, and he may be the one to give it to us."

She'd first met Corneal two years back, a lead detective and a decent man. Frankie had his sights on him ever since he learned Corneal planned on retiring at the end of the year. Protecting and serving is in his blood. If he didn't join forces with the two of them, he'd likely do it in some other way.

She asked, "Who's running point?"

Frankie got back into the car and turned the ignition over. The time on the dashboard shouted 12:33 p.m., reminding her of the passing time.

"Detective Mikayla Burton. I heard she's good—and tough. Corneal said she runs a tight ship. Be prepared to create some friction," Frankie told Mabel, "just not too much. I left there an hour ago and things were buttoned up pretty tight."

"Is the FBI involved?" she asked.

"They've been notified, but they weren't there when I left."

"Wait, did I miss the Amber Alert?"

"Nope. Hasn't gone out yet. Not sure what the holdup is."

Questions whirled around in her head.

"Listen Mabel, I'm only saying this because I know you. We have to trust that law enforcement will do their job. It'll only slow them down if we get in their way."

This, coming from him. It was like telling her smoking is bad and then smoking like a train. *Do as I say, not as I do* mentality. "What if it were me missing, would you wait?" she threw back.

"That's a stupid question you and already know the answer—"

"Well, I don't really care whose toes I step on, I'm not waiting another minute."

"I didn't say we *can't* do our own investigation. I'm *saying* we need to stay out of the way. I know you want to go to Susan, as you should, but don't seek information from Burton because she won't give you any and it will only put a spotlight on us instead of Isabel."

"Fine. Who's the Victim's Advocate?"

"Not sure. I'm thinking the FBI will be sending one of their own."

"Where are the police on interviews?"

"From what I know, they've spoken to Abby's mom and she agreed to a search, which I'm sure she regrets."

"Why would she?"

"PD found drugs—"

"No!" she shouted, not believing her ears. Abby's only thirteen, like Isabel. Where on earth did she get drugs?

"Oh yes, and mom lawyered up, refusing to allow Abby to speak to the police. Maybe she'll talk to you, but don't hold your breath."

All three phones went off simultaneously with an ear-piercing tone. The frightening nails on the chalkboard sound meant Isabel had a better chance of being recovered.

AMBER was created and named after nine-year-old Amber Hagerman of Arlington, Texas. Amber was kidnapped on Jan. 13, 1996, while riding her bike with her five-year-old brother. Mabel had been a year younger at the time, nestled safely in her home. She recalled her own dad's words; *Be careful, be aware of your surroundings, don't talk to strangers, yell if someone approaches you, never take anything from a stranger—never, never, never.* No father wanted their child to end up like Amber Hagerman, whose lifeless body was found on the fifth day.

Mabel's father had never known an Amber Alert went out for his own daughter, Melodi. Times like this she found herself aching for the man who had once been the center of her world.

Her phone shouted:

AMBER ALERT El Paso County
13-Isabel Dumel BLN/BLU
Suspect in Ford F150 BLK tinted wnd
Type: Amber Alert

"Wait! There's a suspect?" she shouted.

"The neighbor saw a truck parked in the driveway, one she didn't recognize, but didn't think anything of it because she knows Susan is an interior designer and sometimes has clients view her home."

Hope rushed through her. "What did Susan say about it? Does she know the truck?"

"No. Listen, I'm going to start with Max."

"Max!" Mabel blurted out. "She should be first on the list of suspects. I never had a good feeling about her," she mumbled, mostly to herself.

"So I've heard. Don't let your personal feelings cloud your judgment," he said.

Frankie, freaking Yoda, her Jedi Master. Oh yes, he was strong with the Force. She could totally hear him saying—*That is why you fail*—and she's Luke not believing when all the time Yoda knows all.

"For all we know, she and Jimmy are working together," Frankie speculated.

"I swear if Max or Jimmy had anything to do with her disappearance—"

"Don't get ahead of yourself." This is how her mind worked. It jumped all over the place, sorting through all the information. Frankie had a gift for staying calm and levelheaded. Her, not so much. But her way worked for her. "I'll call the warden and get you a visit with Jimmy."

"Wait, what? Why me?"

He didn't answer and he didn't have to. Jimmy wouldn't talk to anyone else but her.

Frankie put his hand over hers, "You going to be okay with all this?"

She had to be, didn't she?

ELEVEN

J IMMY DUMEL STARED AT THE CEMENT WALL; the same damn wall he'd most likely stare at for the rest of his fucked up miserable life. He should feel right at home being surrounded by hundreds of men just as fucked up as he was. Some more, a few less. Maybe they didn't have Jimmy's anger coming into the shithole, but they sure had it now. He could see it on their faces.

It took all of one day to get a target on his back. Some even put a target on his ass. Let them try it and he'd rip their dicks off and shove them down their throats. Solitary confinement would suit him just fine.

Three months in the hole, with life to go. He rubbed his bald head. He'd grown to like his new look, it made him look more psychotic than he already was.

He heard the faggot guard coming before he rapped on the door. Jimmy turned to see the shift commander, who everyone called Bug, because he had an elongated oval body, short limbs, and beady eyes. He wanted nothing more than to wrap his hands around the Bug's neck and watch his eyeballs pop out of his skull—*pop, pop*—one by one.

On his first day, Bug had told him, *Take off all your clothes, spread your cheeks, lift this, lift that . . .*

Fucking faggot gave him the willies.

"Jimmy, you have a visitor."

"Who is it?"

"How the hell should I know. I was told to come get you."

Jimmy backed up to the steel door with his hands behind his back. He couldn't contain his excitement; the thought of his daughter waiting to see him. Could he touch her, hug her? It'd been too long. Max swore to him last time she'd bring her.

Jimmy tested the chains, now bound to his wrists and ankles. He shuffled down the corridor to a private visiting room. It had to be her. Why else would he get his own visiting room?

When the door opened, a man dressed in a shirt and sports jacket—who looked very much like a pig—stood before him with the warden at his side. What the fuck kind of shit was this? He's already in for life, what more do they want from him?

The cold hard stare of the warden's eyes was gone. He'd never seen this side of him. Bug secured Jimmy's chains to the metal table and walked out leaving him with these two clowns.

"What is this?" Jimmy asked.

"Jimmy, this is Detective Marsel. He's come to tell you some news," the Warden said.

"What news?" he spat.

"Mr. Dumel, earlier this morning, at 10:05 a.m., your daughter was reported missing by her guardian, Susan Landry."

"Is this a fucking joke? Because if it is, it isn't funny."

"I assure you, this is no joke, sir."

Pain, anguish, and misery summed up Jimmy's childhood. Why should his life in prison be any different? He'd taken it all—every insult, slap, or punch—until he didn't. He swore he would never again take it, any of it. Every single person he'd ever known was dishonest and unreliable. Blind, seeing only what they wanted to see, and stupid, believing only what they wanted to believe. He lost all faith in humanity long ago. The single positive thing about prison—he had plenty of time to think. His imagination ran wild and his creativity flourished.

"I'm sorry Mr. Dumel, I know this is hard to take in." The pig pretended to care. "Do you have anyone you need to call?"

Right. Who in the hell would he call? "I need to be alone," he said, leaving any traces of emotion out of his tone or they'd ship him off to mental health. "Please get out. I want to be alone," Jimmy pleaded, not bothering to ask questions because they couldn't give him the answers he sought.

"Would you like to speak to—"

"Do you have a daughter . . ." He couldn't remember his name, "Detective?"

Silence.

Bingo! "I just need a little time is all . . . to pray."

He looked to the warden, then said, "We can give you ten minutes, but then we need to talk."

They left Jimmy alone in the small room. The room, not much better than the pit he lived in, barren, like his heart. Sometimes he wondered if he had a heart because he'd felt nothing but anger for so long. Then he'd think of his daughter and he'd swear he could feel his heart swell. Now it hurt and bled from the inside out.

Chained up like an animal, his hands covered his face, thinking. He needed information and knew how to get it. He swore if Mabel or Max had anything to do with his daughter going missing, he'd kill them—locked up or not.

It felt more like five minutes when the door opened. A duo entered, the warden missing and replaced by another pig, this one in a police uniform. He could almost feel his eyes freeze over, looking right through their rotten cores. Every muscle in his body tightened, taking every bit of energy to refrain from ripping the chain tethering him to the cold steel and wrap it around pig one's neck cutting straight through. He'd laugh when it rolled onto the table. Then he'd make pig two eat pig one's heart, because that was what pigs did.

"Mr. Dumel."

He didn't answer because he'd been dreaming about what he'd do to them.

"Mr. Dumel," pig one said again, sitting across from him. Pig two sat next to pig one. *Oink, oink, oink,* is all he heard.

"No," he heard himself say.

Oink, oink, oink.

"I don't know," he said. "Please take me back to my cell."

They did.

He lay in his rectangular coffin, staring at the same ceiling he'd been staring at for the past month. His first thought— Mabel did it, and he'd kill her. There'd be no taking it easy on her this time. He'd make it simple and slice her throat. He'd never been into knives, they were too messy, but he'd make an exception for her because he didn't want any chance in her living through it.

Urgent to get moving, to do something, anything, he began to pace the small space; four steps north, two steps east, four steps south, two steps west—then start all over again—round and round thinking of Isabel. In his mind she had short blond hair, big blue eyes and the same bony knees she used to dig into his ribs when they played. He loved her laugh, deep and hearty, from the belly—positively infectious. When she laughed, he was putty in her hands.

His cell mate remained in his bed, right where he belonged,

because he knew better than to get in Jimmy's way.

"Henry," he absently called out.

Henry recoiled at the sound of his name. "Yeah, boss?"

"Who got out in the last couple of weeks?"

"I . . . I . . . I," Henry stuttered.

"And don't fucking lie to me."

"Cliff, Ahmed, Gerald, and Roberto . . . that I know of. Why, boss?"

"None of your fucking business." Henry broke eye contact. "I need to get some calls out to them. Find out how I can make it happen."

"It's going to cost you, boss," Henry said.

"No, it's not. It's going to cost *you*."

Henry nodded. The tall lanky man feared Jimmy more than Los Elefantes, Capital 10, R1, and the Night MoFo's. As he should. In the month Jimmy had been locked up with these assholes, no one had touched him. He heard talk of Los Elefantes taking him out, but R1 stepped in and put an end to the supposed hit. R1 wanted Jimmy to join their crew, but he didn't need anyone but Jimmy.

RJD—his gang—Respect Jimmy Dumel. And it included Jimmy and only Jimmy.

"Good. Now do it," he ordered.

Henry jumped to his feet, careful not to touch Jimmy.

"Good boy," he said, patting his head. "Guard!" Jimmy yelled. "I'd like my call now."

Spike, he referred to him as such because of his black spiky hair and mustache, walked over to the cell and asked, "How are you holding up, Jimmy?"

Jimmy shrugged his shoulder. Word traveled fast in this godforsaken shithole.

"Sorry about your daughter . . ." he paused, his eyes stopping on Henry. "We'll get it scheduled as soon as possible. The Commander is tied up right now, but we'll find someone else who can take you down."

Spike walked away talking into his walkie. He had always been decent to everyone, but the way Jimmy saw it, he's just another person in the way of freedom.

Sooner than expected, Jimmy stood with his hands behind his back up against the steel door. They cuffed his wrists and ankles, two guards on either side, and walked him down the corridor while the third guard walked behind ready to take him down. It made him proud to have so much attention.

He sat at a table, shackled with a phone placed in front of him. "Privacy would be nice," he said.

"You have five minutes."

Ruff, ruff, ruff, is all Jimmy heard. *I bet he licks his ass, too. Give me two minutes unshackled and we'll see who wins the dogfight.*

He dialed and at the first ring he dismissed the guard with a hand wave.

"Bradley," Jimmy said after the second ring, "listen closely."

He thought Randy Bradley, his lawyer, sounded tired. Jimmy didn't think the man ever slept and he didn't care, as long as he did what Jimmy asked. "What can I do for you, Jimmy?"

"My daughter's missing."

"I . . . I'm sorry . . ."

"Come see me . . . and I want a visit from Teach." Mabel Peters, no longer a teacher, but the name had stuck. He liked thinking of her that way.

"Ms. Peters? No can do. Not going to happen."

"I don't want to hear what you *can't* do. Find a way and make it happen. Now!"

He let out a puff of air, "I'll do what I can. And Jimmy . . . don't do anything—"

"Don't worry about me. I'm in for life, or did you forget you lost my case? And I want constant updates on my daughter."

His silence meant one thing—he'd do it. Jimmy hung up imagining Mabel sitting across from him. All he needed to see was the look on her face and then he'd know.

TWELVE

THE SIGHT OF TAPE STRATEGICALLY PLACED around the house to keep people out, made it real for Mabel. It hadn't been a mistake. Isabel was missing.

Police cars lined both sides of the road and a huge truck, which she knew housed the mobile command center, took up the driveway. The street where Isabel once rode her bike and played kickball was unrecognizable. Swallowing the lump in her throat, she drove around the black and white vehicles, fighting the urge to plow through the news vans. A part of her said they'd help inform the public, have everyone looking for her, and encourage tips that may lead to finding Isabel. The other side of her didn't have a reason. She simply didn't want Isabel known statewide as a missing child. She didn't want Isabel being another face on a flyer, on TV, or on the radio.

With nowhere left to park, she pulled into a driveway a few houses down, hoping Susan's neighbor wouldn't mind.

With one foot out the door, the cool air hit her in the face. Another foot, and she took in the crispness it offered. *Calm and relaxed,* she told herself over and over, a technique she'd learned long ago. *Focus on finding Isabel. Find Isabel and all will be better.* She looked to the sky for answers. The sun flickered in and out of sight through light fluffy clouds.

Okay, here we go.

As she crossed the street, a K-9 unit drove by. Her watch read 1:41 p.m. Four hours after Isabel had gone missing. She heard Frankie say, "Let them do their job," and she let out a breath.

Making her way toward the mobile unit, a man stopped her. It took her a second to recognize him.

His eyes were soft and optimistic. "Mabel?" he sounded surprised. "What are you doing here?" he asked. "You're the last person I expected to see here."

"Mike," She looked over his shoulder. "I could say the same about you." Her heart belonged to Lucas, it always had. But, like the last time she'd ran into Mike, she couldn't help but notice how good he looked in his uniform. Mike was a handsome man, but it was more than that. He had a heart of gold and she knew it the first time she literally ran into him on her run.

"All hands on deck when a kid is missing." His face turned red, realizing his words.

"Listen, I'd love to catch up, but have you seen Susan?"

He pointed and she followed his finger to the big trailer. "She's in there. They wanted her out of the house while the FBI did their own search."

"When did they show up?"

His eyes settled on her for a few moments before he looked at his watch. "About thirty minutes ago."

"Thanks," she said, ignoring his stare and looking past him.

"You look good," he said, his eyes searched her face for signs of interest.

"Uh, thanks," she replied. Maybe in another life.

His eyes dropped to her hand. "I see congratulations are in order," he paused. "I didn't know."

How could he. They hadn't spoken in years. "I . . . I have to talk to Susan," she insisted.

"I heard what you do now and if you're here to find Isabel, call me with anything. I'll tell you whatever I know."

His last words made her smile. It was good to know he was willing to help her. Then it hit her. What if he only offered his help to get in her good graces and maybe a date, too. The hell with it, she didn't care why if he helped find Isabel.

The door to the trailer opened and out stepped Susan, her eyes puffy and red. She didn't immediately see Mabel, but when she did a fresh rush of tears exploded from Susan's eyes. "Mabel . . . I . . ." she gasped for air, landing on Mabel's shoulder.

With a deep breath, Mabel wrapped her arms around her friend. "I'm here. We'll find her," she said, her voice strong. "We'll find her."

"It's my fault," Susan insisted, wiping the tears from one of her eyes. "I should have been here," she cried and her nose flared.

"Susan, stop!" The word came out forceful. "Don't."

"I wasn't here, Mabel. I wasn't," she was shaking her head, "and if I would have been—"

Mabel pulled Susan close, stroking her hair, "Let's get you cleaned up."

"What? Why?"

"You'll feel better. You need to take care of yourself." She searched Susan's eyes for hints of a breakdown.

"They won't let me back inside the house," she said. Mabel glanced around as if she'd find a bathroom conveniently placed near a tree.

"When you get inside, clean up, okay?"

She nodded.

"Now tell me what happened from the beginning," she said, wiping Susan's tears with her hand.

Her normal flawless skin had a world map drawn in red patches taking up her whole face and neck. "Isabel stayed at Abby's house last night. We'd been fighting about her seeing her dad, but last night before she left, she seemed good," she paused. "And this morning I decided on brunch with a girl-friend," Her voice cracked. "I left a message for Isabel to let her know. I figured she wouldn't answer—you know how teenagers are about staying up late and sleeping in—so it didn't surprise me when she didn't answer. When I came home, I found Bella laying limp and bleeding in the kitchen." She burst into tears. "Detective Burton said Bella probably got in the way while protecting Isabel."

"Where's Bella now?" asked Mabel.

"The vet. She's badly hurt. The Detective said they'd check for DNA."

"Good," she said between gritted teeth. "I hope she made them bleed."

"We don't know who *they* are." Her hands covered her face as she wept. "It's a total shot in the dark, but the neighbor saw a black Ford truck parked in the driveway. It wasn't there long."

"That's good news!" she exclaimed. "Any lead is better than no lead."

Susan shook her head. "My sister relied on me. Me. I'm supposed to be the strong one. And look at me—I'm a mess. How did I screw this up? How did I let this happen? I had *one* job," She held up her finger, "One job and I managed to fuck it up and let my sister down . . . my dead sister. Oh god, what if—"

It hit too close to home. For as long as she could remember, she blamed herself for everything wrong, regardless if she had control or not. Now Susan—a wonderful thoughtful person, who took on the responsibility to raise her sister's daughter—blamed herself for Isabel's kidnapping.

"Susan, I swear to god, if you ever blame yourself again, or even have thoughts of Isabel not being alive—I will slap that nonsense right out of you."

Susan blinked. The tears pooling in her eyes ran down her cheeks. "My god, Mabel, you should be my victim's advocate."

They both smiled.

"I have a job, thank you. And right now, that's Isabel. Now dry your eyes and tell me who may have done this. I need a list of the names you gave the police. Anyone who saw anything."

"I have no idea who," she said, getting worked up again.

"Right now your mind is going a million miles an hour. If you think of anything, let me know. I promise I'll find her." She meant every word.

"I will die if anything happens to her," Susan cried.

Something already did happen to her.

"Stay strong, Susan . . . and positive. You have to think positive." Something she told herself over and over.

Susan looked at the scene around them. "They're watching me like a hawk," she said. "I feel like I should be out there looking for her. She's *not* here. How many times do they need to search the house?"

"They're just doing their jobs. It's good the Feds are here, too, and I hear Detective Burton is the best at what she does. Isabel has a lot of people working hard to find her. Everyone here," she gestured with her hand, "has a specific job to do, and it's not just searching the home."

She nodded. "What are you going to do? Where do you even start?"

"Right here and Frankie is already waist deep in his own search."

She nodded. "Please find her."

"I will," she promised again, not thinking twice about *what if.*

A policeman walked their way with a scowl on his face. What the hell did he want? She hadn't even been there ten minutes and she was about to get kicked out.

"Hi," she reached out her hand and he took it. "I'm Mabel Peters—"

Susan cut her off, "She's here for me," she explained. "She's my best friend and I need her."

"I know who you are," he responded, sizing her up and still looking mad. "Ms. Peters, come with me," he said. She followed as he led her through the front yard.

She kept her eyes forward, fully aware all eyes were on her and thankful the officer walked faster than any normal person.

"Follow me and watch your step." His hand motioned to the small step up into Susan's house. The same little step she'd taken hundreds of times. She kept quiet. Once inside, he said, "Don't touch anything," And continued walking into the chaos.

She didn't follow as instructed, instead she stopped just inside the front door, taking in the action around them. From the front door, the living room was to the right and the kitchen beyond that. The design was open, but with all the uniforms, she couldn't see the floor where Bella had been found.

"Let's go," he encouraged, taking hold of her upper arm and slightly pulling her in the direction he wanted her to go. "Detective Burton wants to speak with you."

Detective Mikayla Burton stood two inches taller than Mabel, had light-brown, shoulder-length hair and dark-brown eyes. She reminded Mabel a little of herself when she was out on a job. Tough, serious, direct—a no bullshit kind of girl. The kind who simply wouldn't take crap from anyone and if you crossed her, she'd put you on your back so fast you'd have no choice but to succumb to her. But, if you had the grit to apologize, she'd buy you a drink.

Burton grilled Mabel on her last contact with Isabel, her whereabouts, and every detail since she woke up that morning at 5:00 a.m. Burton's phone rang in the middle of their conversation and her brows furrowed. "Give me a minute," Burton said, walking away.

No one noticed her standing there by herself, watching and listening, like a fly on the wall. She felt invisible. The busy room buzzed with chatter. Her stomach growled reminding her she hadn't eaten breakfast or drank anything aside from coffee.

She made her way to the kitchen, nearing the spot Bella once lay, when an officer said, "Don't touch that."

Touch what? The blood? Like she meant to step in it or rub her hands all around. She wasn't stupid.

"I'm Mabel, Susan's friend. I just wanted a water. May I?"

"No," he replied, his arms crossed.

"Where's Ms. Peters?" Burton yelled from another room.

"Coming," Mabel hollered.

Burton looked angry. "You didn't tell me you were a private investigator," she accused.

"I'm not here as a private investigator," she lied. "I'm here for Susan, my friend."

Her stare remained fixed on Mabel. She could almost see the gears turning in her head. She met her stare, not wanting to back down and roll over like a dog.

Burton didn't blink. "Stay out of my way. I don't need anyone fucking up."

Mabel bit her tongue, fighting the urge to swallow, break eye contact, or do anything to be less uncomfortable. Mabel knew Burton worked twice as hard as everyone else. "Are we done?" she asked at last.

"You can stay as long as you stay with Susan."

"Actually, I'm headed out."

"That's what I thought," Burton replied and walked away, stopping by an officer who had been watching their altercation. She spoke loud enough for Mabel to hear every word. "If she so much as looks in the wrong direction, arrest her for interfering with the investigation." Nodding, he returned to his original stature, arms crossed, chest out.

She shivered from his icy stare, shook it off, and smiled. "I'm leaving now," she informed him. His cold eyes followed her as she moved across the room.

Isabel had experienced more than her fair share of trauma. How does so much misfortune happen to one family, one person? No one deserved any of this. Mabel feared if Isabel survived—no, *when* Isabel survived—this recent nightmare just might break her.

As she stepped outside, the chaos from earlier had thinned. Many of the police cruisers were now gone, out with their assigned duties. News crew vans still lined the street, but getting out would be much easier than getting in.

Susan approached with a woman, not much older than herself. "Hi, I'm Sheri," the petite lady said, moving a large curl from her face and placing it behind her ear. "You must be Mabel." Her brown eyes kind and gentle. "I'll be Susan's victim's advocate. Will you be staying?"

Mabel shook her head, "I have to go, but I'll be back." She looked at Susan as she said it, hugged her, and noted how Susan's body vibrated against her own. "Call me," she added.

Turning to address Sheri, "It was nice to meet you," she said. Over her shoulder, Mabel's eyes landed on an old, faded brown Buick Regal as it drove by, too slow for her liking.

THIRTEEN

WITH ABBY FIRST ON HER LIST TO INTERVIEW, Mabel would give Burton a real reason to not like her. It took her less than two minutes to get from Susan's house to Abby's house.

She hoped Mrs. Schiffer would be open to her stopping by unannounced. They had crossed paths several times before. Either by Kim picking up Abby while Mabel had been visiting Susan or Mabel herself taking the girls out for the day. Mabel had never found Kim friendly. She'd always been terse, as if she outdid herself simply by looking her way.

Her house looked similar to Susan's, without all the extra bells and whistles added. Mabel rang the doorbell and Kim opened the door.

"Hi Mrs. Schiffer, I'm—"

"Mabel. Please, come in," she said cutting her off. She looked out to the street, stepping aside as she did. "And call me Kim." Mabel barely made it inside before she shut the door behind her. She seemed spooked. But why?

Inside, dark blue curtains were drawn, shutting out the sunny day. A few lamps illuminated the room, providing a strange glow in the middle of the day. Two glasses sat on the coffee table along with a half-eaten plate of cheese and crackers.

"Do you have company? I can come back."

"No, no. My lawyer left ten minutes before you arrived," Kim said while clearing the remains of her prior guest. "Can I get you some lemonade? It's fresh and quite good."

"No, thank you. I came to check on Abby."

Kim moved an imaginary hair away from her face. "I'm worried for her," she admitted, sitting on the sofa, forgetting about what she had been doing. Mabel took the chair to the right. Kim fixated on the coffee table, her mind elsewhere.

The drugs, Mabel thought. What were they thinking? *They*, not just Abby. Anything one girl did, the other most likely followed.

"She must be scared."

Red blotches appeared on Kim's neck down to her V-neck blouse. "Yes, she is. Are you here to interrogate her, too?"

"No one is blaming Abby." And no one is ignoring the fact that Kim and Abby were the last ones to see her.

"She had drugs in her room. *Drugs!* How could she be so stupid? No," she corrected, "stupid is skipping class or coming home after curfew." She paused, "I'm sorry." Tears spilled down her cheeks and she wiped them away. She sat straighter, working hard to keep it together. "That's why our lawyer was here. He said they'll get a subpoena to interview her. I don't want this for her. I told Joe she just needed to talk. It'd be better, wouldn't it?" She didn't wait for a reply. "But our lawyer said no." Eyes wide, she looked to Mabel for answers, or agreement, or permission.

"I don't know what you should do, but in order for me to find Isabel, I do need to know everything you and Abby know. What can you tell me?"

"Nothing. They had a sleepover like they do every Friday night. Nothing unusual or out of the ordinary. They acted the same as always, giggling and talking non-stop."

"Let's start from the beginning, okay." Her voice soft. "I'll tell you what I know, and you fill in the blanks."

Kim nodded.

Mable began, "They met at school at the beginning of sixth grade."

She nodded again in agreement, and said, "And have been best friends since." She smiled at the thought. "Inseparable. As a matter of fact, Isabel has come here every Friday for the last year."

"The girls walk from school to Isabel's house, pick up her bag, and then come straight here?"

"Yes."

"When was the last time Isabel missed a Friday?"

Thinking, her eyes diverted to the table in front of her and then back to Mabel, "I can't remember. It had to be in the summer when Susan took her on vacation . . . oh, and when she got sick in October. But she's been here every Friday since."

"In the last few months, weeks, or days, have you noticed anything different in either girl?"

Her eyes ping-ponged back and forth, searching through memories, coming up empty. "No. Nothing. I'm sorry. They're teenagers; they act weird all the time. Secretive, laugh, get mad . . . nothing stands out." Her shoulders slumped.

"That's okay. I'm reaching here. But if something jumps out at you after I leave, just call me."

Kim nodded.

"Now, tell me everything about yesterday."

"Well, the girls were already here when I got home at 5:30 p.m. Joe didn't get home until closer to six. I started dinner—"

"Did you see the girls when you got home?"

"Yes. I checked on them as soon as I walked through the door. They were in Abby's room and stayed there until I called them to eat around 6:30 p.m."

"What were they doing when you checked on them?"

"Being teenage girls. I don't allow Abby to lock her door, although I tapped on the door before entering. Abby was on her bed playing with her phone and Isabel was sitting at the desk playing on hers."

"Were they talking?"

"Not when I walked in. For all I know they were texting each other. They do it all the time when in the same room."

"Did you get the sense they were fighting at all."

"No!"

"I didn't mean to suggest anything. I just want to know if they had any disagreements."

"No. Not that I know of. They acted normal. And I heard them talking and laughing after I returned to the kitchen. The music was blaring, and I told her to turn it down. We ate as a family like we always do. Isabel was her normal sweet self and Abby was her normal goofy self."

"Did the girls leave your home at any time last night?"

"No."

"How can you be so sure?"

Not intending to do so, she'd offended her. *Think of Isabel, think of Isabel,* she reminded herself. Suggesting she may have imagined the perfection in her daughter was not something Kim, as a mother, wanted to hear.

Her jaw clenched as she mulled of over Mabel's accusation. "I don't know for one hundred percent certainty they didn't leave the house after Joe and I went to bed. Anything is possible I suppose. I did pop my head into Abby's room before I went to bed and they were both in their pajamas and on Abby's bed painting their nails."

"What time was that?"

"Around ten."

"How long did it take you to fall asleep?"

"What does last night have to do with anything? I saw Isabel this morning. She was here, at my house. Nothing happened last night."

"I understand that Kim. I just need to know if anything happened last night."

"Like what? What are you trying to insinuate?"

"I'm not insinuating anything." They stared at one another. Either Kim was hiding something, or she truly didn't see the importance of the time leading up to the abduction. Moving on, Mabel asked, "Tell me what happened this morning?"

"Isabel left here at 9:35 a.m. I know the time because I was making breakfast for the girls. They'd slept in, and Isabel came into the kitchen and said she had to go home."

"Did you notice anything unusual about her?"

"Not at all. She looked like she did any other Saturday morning."

"How's that?"

"Sleepy, tired from staying up too late," she said.

"You mentioned they slept in?"

"Yes. They're usually up by 8:30 a.m., 9:00 a.m. at the latest, and have a bite to eat. I started breakfast late and worried that Isabel wouldn't have time to eat because she always left the house by 9:30 a.m. to go home."

"And you saw her leave your house?"

"I heard the door close as she left. I didn't actually see her walk out, but I saw her walking from the window in the kitchen." Kim swallowed, her face turning a light shade of pink. "I should have driven her home. Why didn't I drive her home?"

"Did you usually drive her home?"

She shook her head.

"Then why would you have today?"

"I know what you're saying, but if I would have, she'd be here."

"She only lives four blocks away."

"That's not an excuse. It could have been Abby. If I would have driven her home, she would still be here," she repeated. "I can't stop thinking how I could have prevented Isabel from being taken."

"You don't know that," Mabel assured her. "Where's Abby now?" she asked, changing gears.

"Her dad took her to get yogurt." She smiled. "His way of making her feel better, like he used to when she was little." She shrugged. "They should be back any minute now. You sure I can't get you something to drink?"

"No, thanks. Can I take a look at Abby's room?"

Her body stiffened instantly. "It's taped up. Abby can't even enter Abby's room." She stood up. Their conversation was over. Kim was a tall solid lady with store dyed reddish brown hair which made her look older than her years.

"Do you know if the girls hung out with any boys?"

"Noah and Sam. The girls went to the movies with them last week. I think Abby likes Noah, but she won't admit to it. I can tell he likes her, too. Isabel likes Sam and from what Abby tells me, Sam likes Isabel."

"Do you happen to know what their last names are?"

"Uhm, Noah Scott and Sam . . . Lawrence, I think."

"How long have they known these boys?"

"Noah goes to the same school as the girls. I'm not sure

about Sam. I only learned about him when they went to the movies."

"Any chance you know where he lives?"

"I don't, but maybe Abby or Noah does. He seemed like a nice kid, even more so than Noah."

"Do you have their phone numbers?"

"I have Noah's, but not Sam's. The police didn't even ask about them, but of course I kicked them out before they could." She skimmed through her phone and read off Noah's number. "Do you think you'll find her?" Kim heaved out a loud breath.

"I do." She stood, ready to find Sam. "If you need anything, don't hesitate to call."

How had she never heard of this boy? Chances were Susan hadn't either. He could be the key in Isabel's disappearance.

Turns out she didn't need Abby or Noah to tell her where Sam lived. All she had to do was give the name to her tech guy, Philip, and he called her back fifteen minutes later with an address.

Philip, a few years younger than herself, fit the definition of a geek; highly intelligent, socially inept, and obsessed with his computer. He avoided all human contact and he didn't make exceptions for her or Frankie. Beyond this, he excelled in all other areas. He was beyond the most intelligent person she knew. He'd been working with Frankie right out of high school with no desire to attend college. Referred by an old partner of Frankie's who had known Philip's dad for years. Going on eight years now he had built up quite the client list, working with several private investigators. He had never given Frankie a reason to question him. If Frankie trusted him, so did Mabel.

With the address in hand, she decided to first make a quick stop at Spring View Veterinary Hospital.

She'd passed it hundreds of times before, but never had the need to visit the place until now. You don't visit animal hospitals if you've never had a pet. Nestled in the southwest corner near a busy intersection, the hospital was covered by overgrown trees and shrubs which outlined the exterior of the building, making it look like a fort.

Her grandma had always been allergic to dogs and her grandpa refused to get a cat. One spring, she'd worked up the courage to ask for a rabbit two weeks before Easter. Confident in the pitch she'd practiced in her room for the last hour, she planned to ask them after dinner and after she'd cleaned up the kitchen by herself. Till this day she's convinced they would have said yes if she would have practiced more. She botched her pitch and they said no in unison.

The front door of the veterinary hospital was covered in a crusty film. Inside, the distinct odor of dog breath, urine, and feces punched her in the face causing her nose to wrinkle. Three empty chairs outlined the small room, one to the left and two to the right. Two ladies sat behind the counter. The short heavy set one sprang to her feet while the other remained paralyzed by her computer screen.

"Hello," the young lady said with a smile.

"Hi," Mabel replied, "I'm hoping you can help me."

The lady looked around searching for a reason for Mabel to be there. When she found none, she said, "I'll do my best."

"Bella, a Labradane, was brought in earlier today . . ."

"Oh." Still smiling, she looked at her screen. "Last name?"

Confused by the question, Mabel didn't respond.

The lady looked at Mabel, smiling, "We have two Bella's today. I need the last name to find the correct dog."

How many labradanes named Bella were there, she wondered. "Dumel," she said, unsure of herself.

"I'm sorry, we don't have a Dumel. We have a Bella Rollings and a Bella Landry."

"That's her, Landry."

She kept her eyes on the screen and her smile disappeared. "And you are?" she asked at last.

"Mabel, a friend of the family. Susan's held up and I was hoping to see Bella and speak to the doctor who cared for her."

"Hey, Monica," she turned to the slightly older woman two feet to her left. "I need your help?" She pointed at her own screen.

Monica didn't smile or acknowledge Mabel. Her long brassy hair hung down to the keyboard making her dead eyes and pointed chin stand out, witchlike. She finally looked at Mabel, "It says here CSPD dropped Bella off and we're only to speak to Detective Burton."

"I'm here for the family because they can't be here." Witch Lady didn't blink. "I'm a friend. Susan would have called, but she's tied up with the investigation."

"Do you think we should call Detective Burton to ask?" the young one asked.

"I don't know. I'll be right back." She disappeared down a hall.

A few moments later a man in a white smock appeared at her side. "Hi, Miss—."

"Peters," Mabel replied.

"Ms. Peters, I was given specific instructions not to talk to anyone aside from Detective Burton." His eyes were kind, his voice low.

Mabel let out a sigh. "Fine, hold on while I call Susan Landry, the owner, so she can take the time from worrying about Isabel, her niece, the missing child, and tell you all what I'm already asking." She had all kinds of patience when it came to children, but she drew the line with adults who stood in her way of solving a case.

"I'm sorry," he said, and she believed he was, but it didn't change her mood.

"Is Bella okay?"

He nodded.

"Oh, thank god. Do you know if they found any useful DNA?"

"I don't, but I can't discuss anything with you. Please, I'm only following orders."

"I understand. Thank you for your time. I'm likely to be the one to pick up Bella when she's ready to go home."

"It shouldn't be a problem as long as Ms. Landry calls and gives her approval." They both stood and he returned to wherever he'd come from.

She called Frankie the moment she stepped outside. "They wouldn't let me see Bella. Any word from Corneal on possible DNA?"

"No, but I'll call him again."

"I'm headed to Sam's house now," she said getting in her car.

"Good. I'm pulling up to Max's."

"Good luck."

"You, too."

Back in her car, she sat with her hands on the wheel and stared at nothing. When she'd lost her dad, she'd wished to go back in time just to see him one more time. Now, with Isabel missing, she wished the same. When time mattered, it raced through anything in its path.

For a second, she saw Isabel crying, broken, but still alive.

She needed to hurry and get to her before it was too late. It would take maybe ten minutes to get to Sam's, the boy who may or may not be linked to Isabel's disappearance.

FOURTEEN

ACCORDING TO MABEL, MAXINE GALLO IS A demon sent from the devil himself. Frankie Dowdy couldn't agree or disagree with her assessment, because he'd never met Max. When it came to anything to do with Jimmy though, Mabel had a flair for the dramatic, which wasn't at all fair of Frankie to say about her, but he hated when she allowed the unworthy asshole to continuously rip her world apart.

Mabel was one of the most compassionate people he knew, yet, she had zero sympathy for Max. The way Frankie saw it, she wasn't to blame for her absentee father. Men like Wilbur didn't deserve to be blessed with sperm. He didn't believe for one second Wilbur didn't know he had a daughter. He's also most likely the reason Jimmy turned out the way he did.

Max lived in a condo downtown. He couldn't imagine living in the busiest part of the city. Frankly, he didn't like people that much to be around them continuously. As Frankie approached the entrance to her building, a couple exited, and he slipped in before the door closed. *So much for a secure building.* He proceeded down a hall which led to an elevator. He'd be up shit creek if it required a key. Inside the elevator, he pressed the button for the fifth floor. A quick ride up and the door opened to another hall.

There were two doors on the top floor. One to the right and one to the left. Max's condo was on the left. An elderly lady opened the door to the right, and he smiled. He loved nosy neighbors. The older the better. He'd always found they love to talk.

He learned right off that Mrs. Hestingburg and her husband were simply enjoying their golden years filling their time as spectators. He bet Max had a love-hate relationship with the two of them. Sweet and surprisingly humorous, but at the same time, big pains in the ass.

Mrs. Hestingburg poured tea in a cup and handed it to him without asking if he wanted anything to drink. "Max needs to settle down, a nice lady like that. If she's not careful, men are going to take her for a prostitute."

He choked on his tea. "What makes you say that?" he asked, between coughs. He loved her already.

"She has people coming and going at all hours. She's a friendly girl. Always partying," she stressed.

"Shirley, stop telling lies. She is not a whore," Mr. Hestingburg blurted out.

"I didn't say she was—you did, the other day—you said, 'That girl looks like a whore.'" Her sweet voice made it all the more laughable. He fought the smile spreading across his face.

"I wasn't talking about her," he defended, "I was talking about her friend. Max is no whore."

"Oh, excuse me for talking about your girlfriend. The detective asked about our neighbor, I was simply being helpful." She shook her head and took a sip of her tea.

Shirley may have been up in age, if he had to guess he'd say eighty something—he knew better than to guess a woman's age out loud—but she was smart as a whip with every brain cell sparking like a thirty-year-old. He wouldn't let her sweet voice and adorable demeanor fool him.

She went on to tell Frankie about her young neighbor who arrived home at four in the morning—too late for her liking because she's a light sleeper and hears everything. She had fallen asleep thirty minutes later and then two of Max's friends came by around 7:00 a.m. and woke her up. They left soon enough.

"Did you get a look at them?"

"Of course. Through the peep hole any way," Mrs. Hestingburg said. "A man and a lady." She pointed at the door.

Frankie followed her finger imagining the old lady standing at the door on her tippy toes. She didn't have glasses on at the time, but he didn't know how well she could see.

"The girl was wearing gym clothes, a brunette. I didn't see her face because of the bag of groceries she was carrying," she said.

"And the man?"

"I didn't get a good look at his face, he wore a hat and was looking down when he walked by. He had dark skin though," she studied Frankie, "not as dark as yours, but I supposed he could have been a lighter-skinned African American." She shrugged. "Maybe even Hispanic . . . I really don't know for sure.

"Do you wear glasses, Ms. Hestingburg?"

"No, I don't, young man! Why you young people just assume all old people are blind is plain rude. My vision is perfect, just like my memory."

"Yes, ma'am," he smiled, "I'm sure it is. I ask everyone I interview. Did you see or hear anything else today? When they left? Did you get a good look then?"

"I was in the shower. I can't be expected to do *all* your job," she grumbled.

"How about you, Mr. Hestingburg? Did you see her leave?"

His face turned red. "No . . . no I didn't, I . . . was . . ."

"Oh, for heaven's sake, George," she said to her husband, then turned her attention to Frankie, "He was in the shower with me," she said. Turning back to her already embarrassed spouse, she added, "The man doesn't care if you take a shower with the person you've been married to for sixty-three years."

Frankie didn't care, but he also didn't care for the visual now planted in his head. "Any idea how long they stayed?"

Mr. Hestingburg shifted his stance, still red as a beet and Shirley continued unfazed, "We had to go to Costco, so after we got dressed we knocked on Max's door. The poor dear had just found out Isabel was missing. I felt terrible for intruding. . . ." She paused recalling, "but we only stopped by to see if she needed anything from Costco. She said she needed to be alone." She shook her head. "I can't blame the poor dear."

Max didn't come off as a kidnapper, but Frankie would keep an open mind. He knew all too well how a good liar can pull one over on the best investigators, even him. He recalled one Mrs. Dupont—a Christian woman, married fifteen years with three children, *mother of the year,* or so he thought. When she'd gone to wake her son on a cold Sunday morning to get ready for church, he was gone, presumed taken in the middle of the night. Six months had gone by and the six-year-old boy hadn't turned up. That was when the Dupont's had turned to Frankie for help. Come to find out Mrs. Dupont was responsible for the death of her son. She'd figured hiring her own investigator would get the authorities looking elsewhere. Little did she know Frankie would solve the case, thanks to her older daughter spilling her secret. Mrs. Dupont had threatened her daughter to keep quiet. According to the girl, she was made to watch while her mom suffocated her little brother and then help dispose of his small lifeless body in a lake across town.

But that wouldn't influence his assessment of Max. First thing he noticed about Max Gallo: her beauty. He wasn't one of those men who gawked at every pretty face or nice body walking by, but he did take note of someone who he found an attraction to and for some reason, Max had his attention. She would never know it though. No one would, because he would ignore every hormone telling him to pursue her.

Second thing he noticed: the bandage wrapped sloppily around her right hand. She did nothing to hide it and he wondered if the DNA taken from Bella would be linked back to Max. Her nervousness blared guilty. But what exactly was she guilty of?

She fidgeted in her seat, stealing glances at her phone every minute or so. Even under the muddled mess—smeared mascara, swollen eyes, wrinkled clothes—he found her lovely.

"Forgive my manners, would you like anything to drink?" she offered, blushing. Was she attracted to him as well? Either way, nothing would come of it.

"Water," he replied, relieved when she disappeared. Nine out of ten times people offered their guests something to drink. If they didn't, he always asked, giving him an excuse to use their bathroom later.

Finding nothing of interest in her living room, he made the short walk to her kitchen and sat on a wooden barstool. "Your place is nice," he said. Her kitchen looked newly redone. Shiny appliances with no food or smudges. She probably ate out and never used them. They were more for show or to remind her she had a home. He loved to cook, but rarely found time to do so. He often ate at John's or Doc's. Maybe it was time to invite everyone over to his place and cook them up a nice meal.

The lack of junk—toys, magazines, books, pictures, art, kid or spouse stuff—reminded him of his place. He never did like clutter and often shivered at the mess he came across in most homes.

When you're not married and don't have kids or dogs, it can get a little lonely at times.

Whoa, where did that come from?

She set a glass of water in front of him and took the stool next to him. "Mabel never mentioned you . . . then again, we don't speak really. I get the feeling she doesn't like me very much." She looked down at his untouched glass and he took a sip. He almost felt bad for her. Almost.

"What makes you think that?" he asked, not sure convincing her otherwise would help him.

"It's just a feeling I get. I suppose if I were in her shoes, I wouldn't like me either." She looked at her phone again. "She's rather close to Isabel and my niece speaks highly of her . . . well she did." She looked at Frankie, "I have nothing against her. I think it's brave what she's done for Isabel. I guess that's why you're here and not her. You're looking for Isabel and drew the short straw."

"Yes and no."

She grabbed hold of his right forearm, her hands soft and cool to the touch, "Please find her," she pleaded, her eyes desperate. "You have to. She's all I have." Her eyes widened. "Her dad. Oh my god, Jimmy! Has anyone called Jimmy?"

"He knows."

"I have to call him . . . no, I can't. I can't *bear* to talk to him," she cried, tears breaking free from her blue eyes.

"How do you know he didn't have anything to do with her going missing?"

"Not Jimmy. There's no way."

She'd only found out about him, and now she's an expert on what Jimmy would and wouldn't do? She must be delusional. Like her brother.

"He could have hired someone to do his dirty work."

She flinched and her eyes watered. "He loves her." She began pulling on a string from her bandage.

"What happened to your hand?"

She lifted her hand and stared at it, as if she hadn't realized it had been injured. "I cut myself," she replied.

"With dog teeth?"

"What? No! The police asked the same thing." She removed the bandage and held her hand out. "You can clearly see this isn't a dog bite."

The gash long across her palm. "Ouch. Get in a fight with a knife?" Bella had been cut with a knife.

"I didn't take her. You'll see, when the DNA comes back. It won't be my blood they find. I would never hurt her, and neither would Jimmy." She glanced at her phone for the tenth time in the last few minutes.

"Are you waiting for a call?"

Her eyes were glued to her phone. "I'm hoping Susan will call. She doesn't like me much, either."

"She's just being protective of Isabel."

She turned in her seat to face him, her eyes examining his face. For a second, he thought she might kiss him, but then she said, "It's not my fault I didn't know I had a brother or a niece. Wilbur . . . he . . ." she turned away, exhaustion taking her over. "I really don't feel like talking about this right now. You're looking for Isabel and as you can see, she's not here.

Feel free to search the place." She gestured. "I need to call my brother. Now, if you don't mind . . ."

"I think I'll take you up on that," he said standing up. When she didn't stop him, he walked into the hall and started his search.

Her voice carried throughout the condo and served as a beacon letting him know where she was while he searched. She had a two-bedroom, and he wondered if she had ever shared her space with anyone else. Her bedroom was warm and welcoming, a white down comforter and several pillows took up the bed. He sniffed the comforter for signs of just washed scent, but there were no signs of detergent. If she'd caught him, she'd think he was a predator, but his nose told him a lot. The bed had been slept in for about a week since it'd been washed, it smelled only of Max, there was no scent of a man or child or anyone else for that matter.

He spotted a picture facing down on her end table and slipped on his gloves. He held it out wondering what made Max cover the photo of her and Isabel at the park, with their tongues out, clearly enjoying themselves. Was it guilt or sadness? The park was only a couple of blocks down from her condo, which meant Isabel had more than likely been to her place.

He snapped a picture of it with his phone and continued his search. He looked in every nook and cranny in every room and found no hint of Isabel aside of the picture. Back in the kitchen he waited for her to hang up the phone.

A couple of minutes passed when she turned and saw him watching her. Her hand to her heart and wide eyes told him she didn't realize he was still in her place. She hung up and said, "They won't let me talk to him."

"I'm sorry," He was, for her sake. "They have rules to follow. Upsetting an inmate can't be good."

"I guess you're right. I feel so helpless." Near tears, she covered her face with her hands and wiped the emotion away. "Is there anything else you need?"

His queue to leave, but he wasn't ready just yet. "One more thing . . . you had visitors this morning." It wasn't a question.

She froze.

"Your neighbor saw them. Who were they?"

"Oh, yes. It seems so long ago." She closed her eyes to clear her head. "Shirley and George are nice, but they are quite the couple, aren't they?"

He agreed with her, but she was stalling.

"Uhm, Thomas and Gina stopped by on their way to breakfast and asked if I wanted to join them. I stayed out too late last night and was still tired, so I passed. Gina brought some groceries with her. We're supposed to have dinner tonight. I'll have to call and cancel. What does my friends visiting me have to do with anything?"

"I didn't say they did."

She swallowed, her brows furrowed, "You think I had something to do with Isabel's disappearance?"

"Everyone's a suspect in my book. I don't mess around when it comes to kids missing." His gut told him she had some experience with the law in her past. "I'll need your friends' full names and contact information."

"I already gave it to the policemen who came by earlier. They really don't need you questioning them, too. What are they going to think?"

"They're the least of your worries."

Her mouth dropped. "What's that supposed to mean?"

"Your niece is missing, remember."

"I told you everything I know. I'm not throwing my friends under the bus."

He began to lose patience. Who was she protecting? "I don't have time to fight with you about this. If you care as much as you say you do, you'll cooperate."

"I already have." She gestured to the door.

He handed her his card. "Call me if anything comes up."

"I'll do that." She shut the door on him.

He looked at Mrs. Hestingburg's peep hole and then over to Max's door. Whoever came by this morning, purposely kept their faces hidden. Max's neighbors had a clear view of anyone coming and going, unless that person didn't want to be identified.

FIFTEEN

"YOU CAN CALL ME SHANDRA," A LADY WITH ratty looking hair said. "I'm Mr. B's right hand, so you have to listen to everything I say and do everything I tell you. If you don't—you pay."

Isabel's first thought was to cry. Then she understood what they had wanted from her all along—money. She'd been kidnapped and Susan was expected to pay a ransom to set her free. For the first time she felt a shred of hope sweep through her. She swallowed, her mouth dry, and said, "We have money. My aunt will pay, whatever is. Have you spoken to her?"

At first Shandra looked confused, then her forehead relaxed and her eyes brightened. A smile swept across her face. "Honey, you aren't ever going to see your aunt again. But thank you for the tip."

Her heart pounded a million miles an hour and she swore she'd pass out any second. She fisted her hands digging her nails into her palms. It served two purposes. To keep her hands from shaking and to convince herself this place, Mr. B and Shandra, were not real. Right now, she would be out with her aunt having lunch, or the mall first, then lunch. Sometimes they went to a movie or bowling.

"Now, listen up," she grabbed hold of Isabel's chin and it began to tremble. Their eyes met and she let go. "I'm responsible for you and the other girls. You work anywhere? Like a McDonalds or something."

Isabel fought the tears threatening and shook her head.

"Figures. You're just a baby." Her eyes surveyed Isabel from head to toe. "You probably never went a day without a silver spoon in that mouth of yours." The tears she'd been holding rolled down her cheeks. "You're nothing more than a product, you hear me."

For some reason, this lady hated Isabel. She tried to remember the last time someone had treated her this way and she couldn't recall one single instance. This lady was plain mean. Mr. B scared her, but right now she wished he'd come back and tell Shandra to go away.

"I'm talking to you," she said, her hand landing smack on Isabel's wet face. It stung and she slid back against the headboard with her knees pulled up, making herself as small as possible. "Men will pay to have sex with you!" she shouted. "You're not any different than anyone else in here, you hear me?"

She didn't want to be here. In a hurry to get out, she scrambled to the door, but found it locked. Disappointment rushed over her even though she'd known it would be. Screaming and banging on the door, she begged for someone to come and let her out.

Shandra yanked her away and she fell back hitting the bed with her legs and falling back onto the place she'd tried to get away from. Shandra's fist came down, landing on her eye. The pain hurt like nothing she'd felt before. "Stop screaming," she shouted, hitting her over and over again. Isabel tried to protect her face, curling into the fetal position. She felt every blow, fist, and every scratch as Shandra clawed at her. This crazy lady would be the one to kill her.

"Don't fucking cry, I ain't no babysitter and I don't put up with any shit, you hear me?" she shouted, stopping for two seconds for Isabel to stop fighting. She froze and closed her lips tight to keep in any sound that may come out on its own free will.

Don't cry, don't cry, she told herself.

But the tears kept flowing. How do you tell your brain to stop sending signals to your eyes?

"Sit up!" Shandra spat. "And look at me." Another slap, hard, but not like her fist. Isabel covered her face to cover the pain and the tears. "I told you!" she spit out.

Isabel sat up, slowly peeled her hands away and looked at Shandra with hate and fear.

Satisfied, Shandra continued with her lesson. "You make the money, I collect that money. Every cent of it, too, and if you even try to steal, I'll know. You think it's bad now? You'll be begging me to stop. You hear me?"

Isabel nodded.

"Good. You have any questions?"

She had a hundred questions, but she shook her head.

"You ever have sex before?"

Oh god, oh god. Her lip quivered and she bit down on it to keep Shandra from seeing it. She'd seen what sex looked like on TV and once she accidentally landed on a sex site on her phone. Two people were naked and . . . and she didn't even want to think about it. It frightened her so much she exited out as fast as she could.

"Well, have you or not?"

She looked down and shook her head.

"That's what I thought. The Johns will pay big money to take your virginity," she laughed, and Isabel flinched.

Rape. That's what they would do to her.

I'd rather die!

"It ain't as bad as you think. After the first few times, you might even enjoy it."

All the blood seemed to drain out of her, and she became lightheaded.

Shandra looked at the clock on the wall, the time read 2:36 p.m. "Come on, I'll introduce you to the rest of the girls. You'll stay with them until you're all called for tonight."

This may be her chance to get away. The second she unlocked that door, Isabel would make a run for it.

"You have to be ready by 7:50 p.m. tonight. The girls will show you what you need to do. If you're late—you'll pay. You think I'm mean, wait till you meet the rest. Us girls need to stick together. And I know what it takes to do what we do."

Isabel followed closely behind Shandra, wiping her eyes and taking a deep breath. *You can do this,* she told herself. *You have to, for now.*

The door opened and Shandra turned, blocking her exit. "Don't even think of trying to get away. There's nowhere to go, every door is locked with men and guns on the other side. No one gets out. Prove your worth and you'll earn your privileges. It won't be handed to you on a silver platter."

Isabel, shoulders slumped, deflated. All hope slipping away.

They walked into a room, three or four times as large as the tiny room she'd been locked up in. It contained an old desk centered near the wall to her left. On the other side of the desk was another door, closed and most likely locked. She wondered if another girl like her was being penned up behind one of the doors. She could see two hallways on either side of the room.

Shandra stopped in the middle of the room. "There are two bathrooms down here. One through there" She pointed to her right, down a small hallway, "and the other is over there," she pointed in the opposite direction to her left. "The one on the left is yours to share." She led her to the right, past the bathroom she had pointed out, then a sharp left to another door. She used a key to unlock it and pushed the door open. The room was the size of a large living room, with six beds and five girls sprawled out. They all lifted their heads when the door opened.

"This here is the new girl who'll be sleeping in the other room. I expect each of you to keep her in line and show her the ropes." A few of the girls seemed bored and turned away. The other two nodded and gave Isabel a look of compassion. "Come," she ordered, locking the door behind them.

They're prisoners, thought Isabel.

She led Isabel back into the open room with the desk. "There are two more rooms on either side." She pointed, "There and there. You were already in one and the other is none of your business. And don't touch Mr. B's stuff or you'll pay." She led her to the left corner, "That's the bathroom you and the other five girls are sharing." She used a key to unlock another door to her right and motioned for Isabel to enter. Much like the other room, it had six beds and five girls. She assumed the sixth bed, in the corner, was meant for her.

"Girls! Listen up. This is the baby. I expect you all to show her the ropes. If she screws up, I'm blaming each and every one of you, and you know what that means." They all nodded, but none smiled. Isabel always smiled when meeting new people, an automatic instinct she didn't have to think about. Now, she kept her mouth clamped shut. "Looks like your bed is over there," She pointed to her right, "I'll leave you to it." She left them, closing the door, and locking it behind her.

I'm a prisoner, she thought, *like my dad.*

Afraid to speak, she walked over to her assigned bed and laid down, glad to see it didn't stink like the other room. The girl in the bed next to her said, "Don't touch my stuff." She looked older than all the others. Her messy dark brown hair just touched her shoulders. Her eyes were cold and dark, in a mean girl sort of way.

The mean girl sat on a hot pink and white zebra striped comforter with a fuzzy pillow placed in the center of her bed near the top. All the girls had their own style of bedding, except for Isabel. Her bed had an ugly green cover with a flat yellow stained pillow. It didn't matter, she wouldn't be here long enough to want anything more.

She thought of Shandra's words and what she had to do to earn money.

"I think I'm going to be sick," she said, without thinking. Her stomach turned and a cold rush ran through her, her mouth watered even though it'd been dry ever since she ate the sandwich Mr. B had brought her.

"Don't you dare throw up in here!" warned the mean girl. "Go to the bathroom, now." She pointed to another door Isabel hadn't seen.

She darted across the room, barely making it to the toilet in time to puke out the sandwich she'd eaten.

"And clean up after yourself," she heard another voice shout.

She wanted to brush her teeth but didn't have a toothbrush. Flushing the toilet, she looked around the bathroom. It was cleaner than she expected it to be, aside of the makeup and hair supplies filling up the countertop next to the sink. She washed her hands, taking longer than needed, and rinsed her mouth out. She felt better, but her head was pulsing again. She looked at the girl in the mirror staring back at her.

What am I going to do? she asked the girl in the mirror. She had no one to talk to. It's as if everyone hated her. Sitting on the edge of the tub, she let the tears pour. Once they started, she couldn't stop them and soon she was sucking in air trying to breathe. How did this happen? More important, why? She'd talk to Mr. B and tell him he had the wrong girl. She wasn't who he thought she was.

He knows my dad is in prison. And he knows my name.

She tried to clear her mind and think back to her dad's friends. He had to be one she'd met and forgot about. But why would he take her? Then she thought about her aunt. Susan would have reported her missing when she came home and found Isabel gone . . . and Bella dying.

Oh, Bella.

They'd all be looking for her. She just had to hang on until they did.

My phone!

What had they done with it? If she could get to a phone, she could call her aunt. No, 911, or even Mabel. Mabel would come get her. A glimmer of excitement spread through her. If she couldn't get out, she'd get to a phone.

A knock on the door caused her to jump. "You ever coming out?"

"One more minute," she replied, her voice hoarse. There were two doors in the bathroom. One led to the shared room and the other to the large open space. Her hand touched the knob and her heart quickened. Shandra had said all the doors were locked, but she had to try. But if it did open, then what? She hadn't seen any windows except in the bedrooms. She had to try. She tightened her grip and turned. Locked.

"Ha, she just got here and she's already trying to escape," said a voice from the other room.

Would they tell?

She left the bathroom with her head down, not wanting to face any of them.

"It's about time," A girl with short blonde hair and blue eyes glared at her. "This isn't the Broadmoor, Baby," she spat, bumping her shoulder as she did, "We *all* share this bathroom." She slammed the door closed.

"Sorry," she said in a low voice, too quiet for anyone to hear.

"Don't worry about her," said another girl. This one was dark skinned with large lips and long dark curly hair. "She's just mad because now she's not the baby."

Isabel nodded, returning to her bed. Laying down, she faced the wall, and hoped to be left alone. A couple girls chatted behind her about their life, she assumed before they were taken and held as prisoners.

A room filled with five other girls, yet she couldn't have felt more alone. Change never bothered her, she was used to it. She'd changed schools three times. Making new friends came easy. Talking to adults never made her uncomfortable, until now. The two adults she'd met since getting here were like no others she'd ever met. Even her dad's friends, who could be loud and obnoxious, didn't scare her like Mr. B and Shandra.

She must have drifted off, because she woke to the dark-skinned girl with curly hair shaking her. "Hey, wake up."

She rolled over and saw all the girls standing by their bed.

"It's dinner time," she added. A man rolled in a cart filled with food, like something you'd see in a hospital. He parked it between two of the beds and left. Like robots, each girl took a tray and returned to their beds to eat. Not hungry, she still obediently took a tray and sat down on her bed.

The girls ate in silence, Isabel picking at her food. When a girl returned her tray to the cart, Isabel copied and set her still full tray, back on the cart. The girl looked at Isabel's tray, "You need to eat. Take it back and eat it all."

"I'm not hungry."

The girl huffed out and looked around the room to the other girls. "Tell her. She needs to eat."

"She's right," said the curly head girl. "If you don't eat, none of us will get anything to eat tomorrow."

She took her tray back and sat back on her bed, taking her plastic fork and forcing herself to eat the meat and potatoes she was served. The only positive is they were not served very much to begin with. The food was bland and tasteless, but she ate it all.

The door opened several minutes later and in came Mr. B. He wore a smile and said, "Girls, how are we doing this evening?"

"Fabulous Mr. B," said the tall blonde.

"Never better," added a black girl.

Each responded, their face brightening up at the sight of him, smiles spread from ear to ear.

"Good to hear it." He looked at Isabel who hadn't responded. She was about to speak when he said, "If I could borrow this one for a few while the rest of you get ready. You have one hour before show time." The girls stared at Isabel. Did she get them all in trouble for not responding? Mr. B sauntered over to her bed and put out his hand for her to take. "Come with me."

She hesitated, afraid of what might happen. His face appeared calm and inviting, but he was the one who brought her here and he couldn't be trusted. She stood and took his outreached hand. It was warm and soft.

"How are you adjusting to your new life?" he asked, his voice rough, but pleasant. He took her to the room she'd started out in.

She wanted to tell him he made a mistake, but she couldn't. What if he beat her? She licked her dry lips and swallowed, saying nothing.

"Sit down," he said, motioning to the bed. She did and he sat next to her. She faced the wall not wanting to look him in the eye, but she sensed him facing her. "Look at me," he said, as if reading her thoughts. She trembled, but turned her head, the rest of her body stiff. He grabbed her by the shoulders and turned her toward him. "There. You and I are partners, so you're going to have to get used to me sooner or later. Did Shandra tell you what is expected of you?"

She thought she did, but still had no clue. "She doesn't like me," Isabel admitted. The words meant for her inside thoughts, slipped out. She stiffened, remembering the beating Shandra had given her, and afraid of what Mr. B may be capable of. He'd certainly hurt her ten times more than Shandra ever could.

He lifted her chin to meet his eyes. "Don't worry about Shandra. She's envious of you because you're extra special and she knows it."

"I . . . I don't know what you mean."

He put her hair behind her ear dragging his fingers across her jaw line. "You, my dear, are my favorite. But, shhhhh," He put his finger over her mouth, "don't tell the others. Beth, Tiffany, and Charlotte tend to get jealous. Now don't you go playing their games." He laughed. "There is plenty of me to go around."

What does that mean?

"Oh, and if you do good tonight, I'll have a surprise for you tomorrow." He teased.

"I'll get to go home?"

His lighthearted demeanor faded. "You *are* home. The sooner you get that through your head—well," he took a breath, "you have no reason to go back to your old life. It's not like you had a real family." Tears came to her eyes and she froze, expecting him to hit her. Instead, his expression turned soft and he wiped away her tears with his thumbs. Taking both of her hands in his, he said, "This is your home now. *We* are your family and I will do whatever it takes to make you happy. You know that, right?" Not believing, she kept quiet. "You will soon enough." He stood up. "Business first. I was told you are a virgin." She gulped. "This is great news. My clients will fight over you and ultimately, the winner will pay top dollar."

She wanted to tell him he was a bad man and she didn't want to be a part of his games. She looked at the door, wishing she could run through it and be free.

Mabel, please hurry, she pleaded, closing her eyes, knowing full well the trick never worked. Why do they say, *Make a wish*, when you blow out your candles? She'd done this very thing every year for as long as she could remember, and not once did her wish come true.

SIXTEEN

S AM LAWRENCE'S SHOWY DISPLAY MAY WORK
around other people, but it did not sit well with Mabel.
She smelled a snake the moment she shook his clammy hand,
with his gentle eyes holding hers as he pulled her in for a hug.

"You must be Mabel Peters," he said.

What kid used a person's first and last name?

"Yes." she replied as she wiped her wet hand on her pant leg.

"Isabel talks so much about you! It's good to finally meet
you."

He looked like the rest of Isabel's friends, grungy, hair
unkempt, but in the 'it works' sort of way. His facial hair
fought to make its way out on his upper lip and chin, but not
enough to begin shaving daily.

He made her uncomfortable, which not many did. It was
easy to see Sam was different than most kids. *He's just a kid,*
she reminded herself, trying to shake the creepy feeling she got
being around him.

"I'd like to talk to you about her," she said, breaking his
embrace.

"Yes, ma'am!" he said. "What would you like to know? I'm

an open book." His mom stood there, silent. He caught Mabel looking her way and said, "Mom, can you get Ms. Peters whatever she wants?"

Without missing a beat, "Sure. Uhm, what would you like to drink?" she asked Mabel. "We have—"

"Just water please," His mom nodded and disappeared into the kitchen. Did she always wait on her son? Her quick response said, *She sure as hell did.* Mabel wondered if Sam's crude behavior was the derivative of his father.

"Please, have a seat," Sam directed Mabel into the living room making himself comfortable on a bulky chair, she took the couch sitting nearest to him. He didn't flop himself down like most kids would, instead he sat with a straight back and his hands on his thighs. His light-green eyes watching every move Mabel made. "I'm guessing you're here because Isabel's gone missing. She told me you work with missing kids. Are you a cop?"

For a second, she thought of lying to him. He needed some fright shoved down his throat. Then she noticed his eyes flick toward the door and then back to her. The motion quick, but she caught it. "No, I'm not. I work for a private security service. How did you and Isabel meet?" she asked, taking control of the conversation.

He leaned back in the chair and brought his leg up, crossing it over the other. "We met at the mall in the food court. We ended up talking . . . well, I spoke first and she couldn't resist my charm." He smiled and flashed his straight brace-free teeth as if Mabel would fall in love with him on the spot.

"How long ago was this?"

"I don't know. Let's see . . . three weeks ago, I guess." His eyes looked to the door again and back. Was he waiting for his dad to come home?

"When did you see her last??

His responses had been quick, almost practiced, until now. "Am I like a suspect or something?"

"Why would you ask that?"

"Isabel's like no other girl I've ever met. I like her a lot. What can I do to help? I'll do anything."

"You can answer my questions. Should you be a suspect?"

"Don't they always look at the boyfriend?"

"You just answered your own question, didn't you? When did you see her last?"

"This is such bull!" he shouted. "I wouldn't hurt a hair on her head."

"Why won't you answer the question?"

Mrs. Lawrence walked in. "What's going on in here?" She handed Mabel a glass of water and set down a platter of cookies and fruits on the table.

"Mabel here is treating me like I had something to do with Isabel's disappearance, Mom" he cried. There's the kid in him, no longer acting like the adult he clearly was not.

His mom glared at Mabel, "I think you need to leave."

"Your son assumed he's a suspect. I don't work for the police. All I want to know is when he saw Isabel last. I'd also like to know where he was this morning between the hours of eight and eleven."

"She works for a private security service, Mom. She might as well be the police," Sam said in a whiny kid voice.

"It sure sounds to me like he's a suspect."

"Mrs. Lawrence, I'm going to be blunt with you. Since I *do not* work for the police, I can't tell you whether your son is suspect or not, but I can guarantee you they will be questioning your son soon. It'll be in his best interest to talk to me, or the police, about everything he knows, as minor as it may seem. If your son has nothing to do with her disappearance, then he has nothing to worry about. Either way, he needs to talk."

"Then what's your role in all this?" she asked.

"As your son said, I work for a private security service who finds missing children. I also know Isabel personally. His interview with me won't be his only one. The police will want to talk to him too."

She looked at her son.

"I don't want to talk to her," he said. "I'll talk to the police."

"There you have it. I'll see you out," she said escorting her to the door.

"Okay, then how about you? Can you tell me where your son was?"

"I'll talk to the police, too," she said.

Mabel stepped outside and caught a glimpse of the same brown Buick she'd seen drive by Susan's. She was being followed. Turning around, she said, "If you lie for him, it will only make matters worse."

Mrs. Lawrence closed the door in her face.

By the look of it, Doc was having a party. Not a happy party, but family and friends who found a way to support each other no matter the circumstances. And Doc's house was the one place they all ended up when times were tough.

Eight hours since Isabel went missing. Each hour sucking away hope, but Mabel refused to allow each passing minute to drain her optimism of finding Isabel.

The front door opened, and Lucas stepped out.

Sticky and dirty and not caring one bit, she fell into his embrace and laid a wet kiss on his lips.

"I missed you," he gushed.

"Mmhmm," she replied, kissing him, not daring to let go. For a moment, everything in the world was right again.

"I brought you some clothes if you want to change," he said, leading her into the house. She still wore the same long sleeve and khakis she had put on early that morning. Thank heaven for Lucas. He took such good care of her.

She looked around the room, "Where's Grandpa?"

"Bathroom. You know old men and their bladders."

On cue, her grandpa stepped into the entrance. He smiled when he saw her. "Mabes!" he said with relief in his voice, hugging her, like he always did. "You look tired. Have you eaten?"

Skin and bones, he always said. She shrugged. "I'm okay."

He continued to assess her for signs of despair. "How's Susan?" he asked.

"A wreck. I've kept in touch throughout the day. Her family's there now, which is good and bad. They can be overwhelming at times."

"That's understandable. What she needs is you. A friend who just listens and doesn't judge."

"What she needs is for me to find Isabel. I can't do that at her house."

"Then you need to eat. You have to keep up your energy."

It'd be easier to lie and say she ate, but she never lied to him. "I will." And she would, but right now she'd come for information, not for a visit. "How did the search go?"

"From what I gather, the police don't think she's anywhere near Susan's house. Do you have any leads?"

"The boyfriend's sketchy and I don't trust Max or Jimmy, so there're two more. Frankie's working Max's alibi. The neighbors swear she was home, but she had some visitors around that time."

"And the police? What do they think?"

"I don't know yet. I'm hoping to get some insight from Corneal. Oh, I ran into an old acquittance." He shook his head, and she continued, "Mike, a policeman from Weld County. I ran into him at Susan's house and he offered to help any way he can."

"Is he trustworthy?"

"I think so, but to be honest, we haven't spoken in a couple of years."

Lucas caught her eye, smiled and winked, making her chest flutter. Such a small gesture made her head spin, her heart leap, and everything else tense. She batted her lashes in return, her body coming alive. She flushed remembering her grandpa was standing eighteen inches to her right. She took a deep breath trying to clear her mind. She snuck a glance at Lucas, and he smiled ear to ear. He knew what he did to her. Even at times of despair he had a way of making her come alive.

"You two will be alone soon enough," her grandpa said.

Purposely not looking at her grandpa, she walked away. It was getting late and she and Frankie needed to touch base. Neither of them planned on turning in anytime soon. Sleep would not come easy for either one of them.

She found Doc and Donna first and greeted them with hugs and kisses. Then she continued her search for Frankie, finding him in Doc's office on the phone. As she closed the door behind her, he hung up his call and jotted down a note. Good news she gathered from the excitement in his eyes. "That was the warden. You have a visit with Jimmy tomorrow at 9:00 a.m."

Not exciting. "You're kidding me? On a Sunday?"

"I can be persuasive," he smiled. "We want to get to Jimmy before Max does. The warden said she's visiting him on Monday. She hardly knows Jimmy, yet she's convinced he had nothing to do with Isabel's disappearance. I don't buy it."

"I'm glad you're coming around."

"Bet your ass I am—he'd do it to set you up."

"You think he could have sent Max to do his dirty work?"

"Not sure yet. She said you don't like her."

"I don't," Mabel confirmed, taking the chair across him. "What else you got?" she asked, her chin in her hand. She caught herself and sat to full attention to keep focused. She didn't have time to be lazy, Isabel depended on her, and so did Susan. She found it hard to breathe, but this wasn't about her. This was about a little girl whose life depended on her, and Isabel's chances of survival and recovery went down with each passing minute.

"I'm hitting the streets tonight to find out what I can. Someone saw something. I just need to find this mystery person who knows more than they're willing to admit to the police." His eyes were laser focused. She admired that about him. His ability to keep his head straight no matter the situation.

She wondered if he'd always been that way. Frankie and her grandpa had been friends, serving together in the Army, along with Doc. The three of them kept in touch and remained friends. She'd known them both for as long as she'd lived. They were like family. Especially Frankie, whom she referred to as an uncle.

She imagined Isabel on the streets, doing the unimaginable, and shook her head to get the image out. Surely, Frankie could see her chest rising and falling. She fought hard to hide her emotions, but her nostrils flared and her eyes began to sting.

"You alright?" he asked.

She nodded. "I'm fine." Her stomach growled. "I haven't eaten all day." Her grandpa was right, as usual. She needed to fuel her body.

He gave her a stern look and walked out, returning with a turkey sandwich, no fixings. She took a bite and then another. By the time she took her last bite she felt a hundred times better.

"I'm coming with you," she said, taking a sip of the water he had set on Doc's desk without a coaster. Doc would kill him if he'd seen.

"No. It'll look better if I go alone."

It'll look better because he was a man looking to have sex with a young girl. The turkey sandwich she just scarfed down turned in her stomach.

Just then, she recalled the Buick. "I think I'm being followed," she blurted out.

"What?" he roared. "Who? When?"

"An old, faded-brown Buick Regal, like late '70s or early '80s old. I've seen it twice. Once leaving Susan's and again leaving Sam's. It could have been there when I left Abby's . . . actually it had to, how else would they have known I was at Sam's."

"Did you see it when you went to visit Bella?"

"No . . . not that I noticed anyway."

"I don't like it."

"I'll keep an eye out. If I see it again, then we know for sure. It hasn't been close enough to see the plates or the person inside. From a distance, a man appeared to be behind the wheel, but I'm not 100 percent."

"Maybe we should stick together then."

He meant well, protective as always, but she didn't need a bodyguard. "I can handle him, or her."

"I know you can. I'm sorry, you're right. It's a habit."

"Apology accepted. Now, where is everyone else going to be tonight?"

"Your grandpa and Doc are visiting as many hotels as they can." She hated involving her grandpa, but he wouldn't have it any other way. He'd slowed down a smidge in his old age, but remained energetic and in good health.

"Good. Lucas and I are both stopping at Susan's first, then he will keep an eye on Sam's house and I'll drive around to all the hot spots." He nodded, halfway out the door. A surge of adrenaline shot through her.

SEVENTEEN

ISABEL DUMEL STOOD AGAINST THE WALL LIKE A police lineup, only they were a buffet to the men looking at them like they were pieces of meat. She kept her eyes on her bare feet to avoid eye contact with any of them.

"I'll take that one," the man with brown leather shoes and gruff voice said.

She held her breath.

"Jackie, you're up."

Isabel let out her breath and sucked it back in. Her turn would come soon enough.

"One."

"One dollar?" brown shoes asked.

"What are you, stupid? One hundred."

"You should charge extra for stupid questions, boss," said another man. He had a nasally annoying voice.

Brown shoes laughed. "No problem. For a moment I thought something was wrong with her."

"I don't have all night. You want her or not?"

"No sense of humor? Okay, here." Brown shoes stepped

forward. "Let's go beautiful," he said to Jackie and she left their lineup to follow him.

"I want the young one," a soft voice said.

Isabel tensed. They were all young, but she was the youngest.

"She's going to cost you," laughed the man doing the selling. "She's the calf in our herd. You're getting the best veal right there."

Tears streamed down Isabel's face, falling to the dirty floor in a splash. Her body began to tremble, and she feared she'd get a beating for it, but she couldn't contain the fear she felt.

"I want her," soft voice said.

Maybe he'll be kind to her. Maybe he'll just talk, get to know her, and not expect anything aside of her company. Maybe . . .

"Five."

"What? That one just sold for one."

"I'll take her," a deep voice said and Isabel's trembling body tensed instantly.

"Sold," laughed the seller.

"Wait a minute, I called her first," soft voice argued.

"Boys, boys, there's no need to fight over her. You can both have her."

"Me, first," said soft voice. "Here's your five, and you can bet I'll be getting my money's worth."

"Whatever. You have fifteen minutes."

"Yeah, yeah." He grabbed Isabel by the arm and yanked her to follow. All the hope drained out of her and she followed him, just as Jackie had.

The seller laughed. "Next."

"I'm Dan," soft voice said, shutting the door behind him. "Oh boy, you're a young one alright. I've never tried one as young as you. How old are you anyway?"

She had yet to look at him. He wore brown cowboy boots, jeans, and a huge buckle.

"C'mon now, look at me," He lifted her chin with his chubby fingers. "We don't have all night, baby doll." His light blue eyes lied, they looked kind, but she knew he wasn't going to be kind to her at all. He kissed her on the lips. "Mmmmm, your lips are so soft." He ran his fingers up her arms, over to her face, and back around to her bare back. "I could get used to this."

Pikes Peak. Beautiful, breathtaking, difficult, commitment. These are the words she used to describe the 14er. The trees beautiful, the view breathtaking, the climb difficult, but she was committed and persevered one step at a time. She'd done it! All thirteen miles to the 14,115-foot summit, 7,400 feet and thirteen miles from their starting point. Pikes Peak via Barr Trail has the largest elevation gain of any trails in Colorado. She felt exhilarated, accomplished, and proud.

She was there now, in her mind, hiking with Bella as Mabel nudged her along. The fan blowing air was a breeze rustling through the aspens. She liked how the leaves trembled in the wind. The smell of the room and of the man crushing her was the hardest part of the trail. She did it before, she could do it again. The pain was her legs and body wearing down, tired from being pushed. She could do it. When she fell, she got back up. When she couldn't breathe, she used the oxygen in her pack.

She made it. On top of the world, with Bella licking her face.

Wet and hurting, she curled up in a ball and cried. She only had a minute before another man came to her room, only to do it all over again.

The dark-skinned girl had told her not to think, not to feel, not to fight. It's only your body, she had said. They can never take your spirit because your spirit is elsewhere. The other girl spent her time at the beach, the sun warming her skin, the sand rough on her feet. Isabel had never been. The girl said she loved the beach and always wanted to go back. And she did, every night between the hours of 8:00 p.m. and 5:00 a.m. Nine hours at the beach. Some days she swam with dolphins, other days she worked on her tan.

Isabel didn't have a beach, only the mountain. She tried hard to leave her body, to not think, to not to feel, and after a few men, she learned not to fight.

It hurt.

When it hurt, she pictured Bella turning back to make sure she was following. Bella helped her to keep going, to follow close and not fall behind. Bella zigzagged in and out of the bushes, stopping only to mark her territory.

When the night was over, she cried and cried. Dying, slowly.

EIGHTEEN

FRANKIE DOWDY LEFT WITH HIS EYES WIDE OPEN. He'd hoped to see the brown car Mabel saw twice, but there were no suspicious vehicles lurking around. There were no doubts in his mind Mabel could handle herself, she'd proved it time and time again. Still, he found himself caught in the grip of disgusting thoughts hidden in the back of his mind.

What if this time is different?

What if you aren't there and she dies? Like Helena . . . like Raven.

He'd never spoken of either one, ashamed. It'd been thirty years and the images he'd formed in his head haunted him every day since. He did what he did because he couldn't save his daughter. Ever since, he'd sworn to save as many as he could in her name.

Once, he'd had a family of his own—one he certainly didn't deserve, but they were his. Now, all he had was his adopted family. John's family. Mabel was part of that family, like a daughter in a way, and he'd do anything to keep it that way.

A left on South Nevada would lead him toward Max's condo. He hadn't planned on paying her a visit tonight but wondered what he'd catch her doing on a Saturday night. She'd failed to give him her friend's information which suited him fine because it gave him an excuse to drop in.

He passed her condo on the right. She lived above a fancy restaurant and other small businesses. Compared to his earlier visit, the block looked very different, busier. And all the weirdos were out.

Parking a few spots down from before, he dropped a handful of quarters into the parking meter and verified the machine gave him two and a half hours. Then he set his watch to go off fifteen minutes before his time expired to avoid anything that could place him near unpleasant individuals. When you go looking for trouble, you had to cover your ass.

Times like this, he put aside his morals and became the person no one else wanted to be. The person no one else could be.

One of two things will happen tonight—either he'd severely bring harm to the bad guys or he'd take them out entirely.

He slipped on his light jacket and locked John's car. The small breeze had a nip in the air, enough anyway for him to get away with the extra layer to conceal his vest, two guns and a knife. The fewer people he freaked out, the better. As a large black man, he attracted plenty of unwanted attention without even trying.

Screams came from the park across the street and his head jerked up. Shouting could be heard, but from his vantage point he couldn't make out what was happing. Looking both ways, he crossed the street and made his way toward the noise. Halfway there, a group of kids came into view, yelling and goofing off. Deciding they weren't worth his time, he strolled down Tejon Street which proved entertaining. In the two blocks to his final destination, he walked past noisy, unruly bars, people smoking pot, guys selling drugs down an alley, a couple having sex in that same alley, two policemen—one holding a prosthetic leg, he couldn't make this shit up if he tried—and on the corner of Max's condo, he ran into a prostitute in plain sight.

"Hey, big boy," said the lady with a god-awful blonde wig that had seen one too many nights. She sported loud makeup with thick, tar-like eyelashes. Lady Gaga, he thought, a much uglier version. Ugly Lady Gaga stomped on her cigarette with her seven-inch platform.

"No, thanks," he replied.

"I didn't offer you anything," she responded, in a husky voice. He ignored her and kept walking. "But you *can* make me an offer," she called after him.

He spotted a group of men nearby, watching her—her pimps. If he gave her money, they'd take it without a second thought. Slipping into a bar at the end of the block, he asked for a cup of water to go. The bartender turned away not willing to waste his time on a someone ordering water.

Frankie shouted, "Hey, man!" and the asshole turned to see Frankie laying out a bill on the counter. He slithered over and looked at the ten-dollar bill, deciding his time was worth the ten. He put the bill in his pocket and filled up a to-go cup with ice water.

What an asshole.

"Change your mind, big boy?" she asked. "I promise to make it worth your while."

He handed Ugly Lady Gaga the cup of water.

"What's this?"

"Water," he said. "Take it."

She looked down and saw a fifty-dollar bill on top. "Okay, how do you want to do this?"

He kept his hand on hers and the cup. "I'm not buying

anything. This is yours, not the men watching you across the street."

Her eyes darted to the men watching intently. "I don't get it."

"I know it's not much. But I didn't come here to buy sex. You seem like a nice enough lady who could use some help." He turned and walked away.

Standing in front of the call box, he reached for Max's button, but thought better of it and pressed another.

"Who's there?"

"Mrs. Hestingburg? It's Frankie, from this afternoon. May I come up? I have a couple more questions." He had none.

"Frankie?"

It was close to nine and she sounded tired. He wondered what time old people went to bed.

"Come on up," she said after a few seconds.

He found her door open. Peeking in, he let himself in. "Mrs. Hestingburg," he called out.

"Come on in. I'm in the kitchen putting some tea on. Hope you don't mind decaf. If I drink anything else at this time of night, I'll never get to sleep."

"Decaf is fine."

He found her in the kitchen like she said. Mr. Hestingburg appeared, from what could only be the bedroom, wearing only his boxers. He jumped back at the sight of Frankie and covered his junk. Another image he didn't need.

"Uhm . . . when . . . why?" he stammered, not sure what to say.

"Good evening, Mr. Hestingburg. Sorry to bother you at this hour, but I'm under a bit of time constraint when it comes to finding Isabel. The longer—"

"I understand. You startled me is all." His saggy cheeks

flushed. "If you'll excuse me." He walked back where he'd come from.

"He's always been a shy man. Not sure why. He has no need to be if you know what I mean." She winked at Frankie. "He should be proud."

His face felt hot. This is not what he came for, but exactly what he gets for dropping in unexpected. "Since we spoke this morning, did you think of anything else that might be relevant to Isabel's disappearance?" he asked, as she set a cup with a tea bag inside. The cup read, *Grandpa, no matter how hard life gets, at least you don't have ugly grandchildren.* "I like the cup," he commented, holding it up.

"My daughter bought it for George a few years ago." She smiled and poured steaming water into his cup. "Oh!" she exclaimed, pulling out a drawer and handing him a spoon. A strained look came over her as she filled her own cup and sat next to him. Something was on her mind and if experience told him anything, she had more to say. Every witness withheld information. Rather it be because they thought it insignificant, or didn't want to get anyone in trouble, or felt they were meddling in other people's affairs. He'd give her time to get her thoughts together.

"Do you think Max did something?" she asked at last. "The police came by earlier, but they seemed satisfied with her being home." She scrutinized him. "You seem to have your own thoughts on this. Max is a wonderful lady and she works with foster kids, for god's sake."

"Ma'am, do you know how many times I've heard similar logic in my line of work?"

She shook her head.

"I'm proving her innocence, too."

Satisfied, she smiled, and her eyes lit up. "Ah, yes. What

can I do for you?" She sat back, and he imagined every muscle relaxing.

"The friends from this morning, have you seen them visit before?"

"No, I don't believe I have. She has so many, I couldn't say for sure. I'm sorry." She sipped her tea, keeping her eyes on him.

"How about the one with the groceries? Max said she was one of her best friends."

Her eyes went up, searching her memory. "I didn't get a good look. Like I told you, the bag covered her face. I suppose she could have visited before. I'm sorry I'm not much help."

He smiled. "It was a long shot." He was wasting her time. "Can you call me if you see them again?"

She pursed her lips. "I don't like lying to Max. She's been so good to me."

"You said Max was home and that leaves her friends. She wants to find Isabel, too, and I need to know their whereabouts when Isabel was taken."

"I suppose I could call you. I always wanted to be a detective like in those mystery books. How I love Agatha Christie."

He handed her his card, something he should have done earlier. "I need your phone number, so when you call, I know it's you."

"Oh yes," She pulled open a drawer and sifted through the mess, finding a self-addressed envelope. "Here, take this," she said, ripping the corner off and handing it to him.

"Thanks," he said, glancing at the typed address and phone number, then placing the torn paper into his wallet.

"My daughter made them for me," she added. "She moved to Europe a few years back and thought it would be easier for me to write. I don't use computers or any of those fancy phones."

"Thanks for the tea. I better get going."

She followed him to the door, "Goodnight, Frankie," she said pushing him out. "Please call before you visit next time."

"Yes, ma'am," He turned to shake her hand, but she surprised him with a kiss to his cheek. He felt the heat rise to his neck and face and he hurried to get away. He felt her watching him as he knocked on Max's door.

"She's not there. She left an hour ago."

She stood behind him, close enough to plant another kiss on his cheek. He stepped back, "I appreciate your help, but please don't leave your door open like that." He pointed to her open door. "You never know . . ."

"You sound like my boy," she scolded. "Of course, he only visits a couple times a year and feels he has the right to tell me how to live my life."

"I'm telling you as a . . ." he paused, her blue eyes sparkled from the light overhead.

She blinked, bringing him out of his trance. "Well go on, spit it out."

He wanted to say friend, though she felt more like a mom. She reminded him so much of his own mother. He grinned at the thought.

"What's so funny, Frankie? Do I have spinach in my teeth? George is always telling me when I do, bless his heart." She picked at her teeth.

"No, no, nothing like that. You remind me of my mom, that's all." His cheeks flushed.

"I do?" she asked. "I don't know if you've noticed, but you're a black man and I'm . . . well, I'm white," she whispered the last part. "Did your mom not tell you?" Her whole face lit up.

"You see, that's the kind of shit my mom would say."

She slapped him in the arm. "Don't use that language with

your mother, young man!" She smiled again.

He liked her. He liked her a lot. He led her back to her door. "Did you see if she was by herself or if she left with anyone?"

"She was definitely by herself."

"Any idea where she went?"

"No idea. She wasn't dressed up like she is most times. Just jeans and a t-shirt. May have just gone out to meet a friend. She didn't look like she was going out to a festivity, if you know what I mean." She winked.

"Like for work?"

"Oh no. She dresses very nice and conservative for work. What a beautiful young lady she is. I can always tell when she's going out to a festivity because she's dressed more provocatively. Half the kids dress that way these days. You know, like the girls do in Vegas. George and I went there once when our youngest insisted on getting married there. We went to a show and had to walk down the strip and George gawked like I'd never seen before. I had to lay one on him. I gave them girls a piece of my mind. How on earth do they walk in those shoes? My feet hurt walking in *my* shoes and they're made for walking." He automatically looked at her feet, buried in furry slippers. "You know, the ones you get from the Walking Company. They're the most comfortable you can buy. Anyhow, the girls wore skirts way too short, high heels, and shirts way too low." She demonstrated how high or low with her hands.

Frankie knew exactly what she was talking about. It was obvious she didn't venture out of her condo at night. If she did, she'd see the same thing on the streets below her.

"She's too pretty to be dressing like that," she continued. "There's no reason for it. I told her so."

He believed it. "What'd she say to that?"

"She tried to convince me that was the style in the clubs.

What clubs? Strip clubs?"

Frankie snickered. Mrs. Hestingburg was too much fun. He could talk to her all day. "Thank you for the additional information. I really need to get going. Lock the door behind you."

"Always do. Bye, son."

He couldn't help but smile as he walked away.

When Frankie stepped out onto the street, Ugly Lady Gaga no longer worked the corner. The men keeping a watchful eye on her were gone too. He could have taken a right to his car, but he had work to do. And he really wanted to run into the two pimps from earlier. Something told him they would lead him to Isabel, or at the very least have information that would lead to her. It wouldn't come easy, information never was, but he was prepared to do whatever he needed to retrieve it.

Left it is.

He rounded the corner and found the men waiting for him. No surprise there. Frankie Dowdy attracted the crazies. He wouldn't be a pawn in whatever game they were playing. Instead he crossed the street, took a left, then a quick right down an alley further away from people. Three kids were smoking pot and he told them to get lost. As the boys ran out of the alley, the two pimps entered.

"You're not a very smart man, are you mister?" The skinny black man wearing a track suit spoke first. He raised the joint he'd been holding between his thumb and pointer and inhaled, his eyes staying on Frankie. His droopy lids told his story, along with his tattoos. A few on his face, one poking out of his hideous suit, and the now visible one on his palm. The one on his palm looked like tally marks, like something you'd see on prison walls to count the days incarcerated. If he had to guess, he'd bet the tally marks were either how many people he'd killed or had something to do with pimping.

Skinny Black exhaled and the smoke came out of his nose and mouth simultaneously.

"What can I do for you gentlemen?" Frankie asked, keeping his eyes on their hands.

"You can take the service you paid for and go be a good citizen somewhere else."

"You're mistaken. I never paid for any service. Now, I have somewhere to be." Frankie took a step forward knowing he had nowhere else to be except right where he stood. They stole Ugly Lady Gaga's money and they needed to be taught a lesson.

The big one, Big Ugly, made a fake move toward Frankie. What is this, fifth grade?

"Option two it is," Skinny Black said, holding his two fingers mimicking a gun to his temple.

"You're going to shoot yourself?" Frankie asked smiling. "Be my guest," he added, as he threw a knife at Skinny Black's shoulder hitting him in the brachial artery. He had a strong throw and the knife stuck straight out, halfway through his arm. He could have aimed for his axillary artery, where he'd likely bleed out too fast and die before he could get the information he needed. That wouldn't work for him, he needed him to bleed slowly. An injured man could speak, not a dead man. Although, he guessed it'd be a fifty-fifty shot with Skinny Black because he was stoned out of his mind.

"Fuck, Fuck, Fuck!" Skinny Black shouted, pulling the knife out.

In the meantime, Frankie's on Big Ugly. He hit him with his forearm right on his Adam's apple and down he went like a rock hitting the pavement. Not waiting for him to protect himself, Frankie struck him in the chest knocking the wind out of him and causing him to do an uncoordinated crunch. While Big Ugly's head was lifted slightly off the ground, Frankie punched him on the side of the head. The blow did exactly what Frankie hoped. Big Ugly was out, sleeping like a baby.

The action happened so fast, Skinny Black was still holding his arm jumping around in pain. Frankie dragged Big Ugly behind the dumpster. For now, he wasn't his concern.

He grabbed Skinny Black by his track suit, feet swinging freely, and shoved him up against the alley wall. "Stay," he demanded, but Skinny Black had his own agenda and tried to free himself. Yanking him back into place, he then punched him in the face and broke his nose. "Stay and maybe I'll let you live or run and die before you find help."

He fell into a slump against the wall, now bleeding from his nose and shoulder.

Frankie picked up his knife and wiped it clean on Skinny Black's pants. "Now we can talk," he said.

He tilted his head back, as if looking up to the stars, but kept his eyes on Frankie. "I'm bleeding out here," he said, desperate, one hand covering his bleeding nose and the other his wounded shoulder.

"Answer my questions first."

"Fuck you!" he said, spitting blood at Frankie.

"Wrong," Frankie said sticking his thumb into the man's wound. He let out a howl and Frankie covered his mouth. "I don't plan on killing you, but I doubt anyone will miss you if I do. My guess—you're just a bottom bitch working for the real boss." He squirmed, mumbling under Frankie's hand, but he held his hand tight over his mouth. If he was working for someone above him, they'd be checking in. He didn't have much time. "Tell me what you know about a blonde teenage girl who went missing from her home earlier today." He removed his hand.

"I don't know about any girl."

Frankie caught a flicker in his eyes. "Wrong," he said again, pushing his thumb in harder. It hurt like hell, he guessed, but his thumb served pain and slowed the bleeding. "Where can I find her?" Frankie asked. "The girl," he said again. "Where is she?"

"I told you, I haven't seen the bitch," he argued.

"Suit yourself," he said, pulling his gun out and aiming it at Skinny Black's head.

His hands shot up, "C'mon man, I told you." He slurred his words. Frankie pressed the gun in harder. "Okay, okay. I may have heard about the girl, but I don't know anything." Frankie didn't move. "I don't even know if she's the same girl."

"You have others?"

"Not me. I work with mature bitches."

"Who then?"

"You're going to get me killed," Skinny Black said.

"I'll kill you myself and you're running out of time."

"I heard they're moving her, but I don't know where, I swear man."

"Who has her?" Frankie raised his voice.

"I don't know his name, but he's a big black fuck with dreads."

"I'm a big black fuck!"

"He's a pretty boy. I only seen him once on my circuit."

"I'm a pretty boy. You talking about me?"

"No man! His name is Bradley or Brandon or some shit like that."

"Where can I find this Bradley or Brandon?"

"He's everywhere and nowhere, man."

"Where were they moving her and when?"

"I don't even know if it's the same girl. He likes them young. But I heard she was going out this week. He trains them first, then ships them off to bigger cities. My guess would be Denver or wherever there's a demand."

"If you're lying to me, I'll find you and I'll be your fucking worst nightmare."

He nodded, understanding. Moving quickly, Frankie removed Skinny Black's jacket and ripped it, tying a tourniquet around his upper arm and gave him the rest to hold to his nose. He pulled the man's phone from his pants pocket and dialed 911.

"Tell them you were attacked and need help."

He shook his head. He didn't want any legal medical help, it would put a spotlight on him.

"Suit yourself," he said, setting the phone down, taking out his own, and snapping a picture of Skinny Black. He then did the same to Big Ugly, who began to move around.

Time to go.

He found a homeless man a few alleys over and traded jackets with him, making sure to take all his property with him including his ammo. He tossed his cap in a nearby dumpster, he'd find another. When he was in the clear, he pulled up the two pictures he'd just taken and sent them to Mabel, along with the names, Bradley or Brandon, description: big black man with dreads.

The sirens went screaming past Frankie Dowdy as he ducked into a pub two blocks from Max's condo. Max sat at the bar, seemingly alone, although it was packed, shoulder to shoulder.

The music was turned up too loud and the place smelled of beer and sweat. A tall, pale, skinny cowboy started hitting on her. He looked out of place and a bit young to be in the bar.

"Go find someone else to hit on," Frankie demanded over the blaring folk rock coming from the band not fifteen feet from where they stood. He shoved the cowboy aside and took the seat next to Max. The cowboy stood behind Frankie momentarily stunned but walked away.

"That was rude," Max said, slurring each word.

"I'm sorry. Were you planning on taking him home tonight?"

"Maybe," she said, taking a sip of her drink. "What's it to you?"

"Why don't I walk you home? We can talk there." If he stayed, he'd likely get in another fight. He never had to look for one, they found him.

"We've talked enough." She looked at him through long eyelashes. "I just want to get drunk tonight." She emptied her glass. He imagined the gold liquid sliding down her throat, warming her insides. Then she said, "Buy me a drink, Frankie. I want to have a drink with you." By the looks of it, she'd had too many already.

"Only one," he agreed. "Then we go."

She smiled and batted her long eyelashes. Batted isn't the right word though, because the movement was slower than she intended. If her eyelashes could talk, they would also come off as a drunken, seductive, and flirtatious slur, and say, *I need to close my eyes and keep them that way, maybe throw up, either way, put me to bed . . . by myself.*

He held up his hand, getting the bartenders attention. "Two Johnnie Walker Black Rocks."

The bartender glanced at Max. "This is her last one," he said to Frankie.

"Good man," she told Frankie when he handed her the drink.

"Better enjoy it, it's your last," Frankie replied.

"So I've heard." She held her glass up to salute and gulped it down in one swig before Frankie could meet his glass to hers.

He frowned. "Here's to finding Isabel safe," he said, holding his glass up, then taking a sip. "You didn't enjoy yours," he added.

"Oh, I did," she said wiping her lips with the back of her hand. "Thank you, Paul," she called out to the bartender. "See you next time." She slid off the stool and fell into Frankie's arms.

Paul witnessed her clumsy performance and rushed over in time to see her clenching to Frankie as she fought to stand on her own.

"Wow. That was close," she laughed.

"Sorry about your niece, Max," Paul said in a gruff voice. He sized Frankie up. "Are you going to be good walking home?" His tone apprehensive, his dark eyes equally concerned. This Paul guy was clearly into Max.

"What do you think? Just look at my friend. No one will mess with him."

"Right . . . I guess not." He examined her. His head tilted down and to the side as a man from the other end of the bar hollered, *bartender*. He motioned to leave, but first added, "Take care then."

"Hey," Frankie said before he could get away. Paul turned back, his attention on Frankie. "I'd like to talk to you tonight. What time do you close?" He offered his business card and Paul took it, turning it over.

"We close at two. If you come about two thirty, we can talk."

With a nod, he gulped his drink down. It warmed his throat

and chest as it went down. "Let's go", he said to the drunk woman still in his arms.

Max stepped back, clumsily, and he held her steady. She would have never made it out on her own. Not without falling and bumping into everything and everyone as she exited.

"You are quite the gentleman. Mabel never told me. Of course, we don't talk."

He escorted her the two short blocks to her building, pleased they'd made it with no further problems.

NINETEEN

A S SHE STUMBLED HOME WITH FRANKIE, Max's mind wondered. She had lost count of how many drinks she'd had, and still, the image of Isabel remained clear. She had thought, *I'll drink until I pass out. Then maybe I'll forget.*

"Last one," Paul had said in a firm tone.

He said last one, the last time he poured me a drink, she thought. *Paul, the bartender, has a big-time crush on me. I wonder if he means it this time. Probably not.*

She had watched him serve other patrons less drunk than her. The loud buzz of the crowd made her head pound, as people fought to be heard over the music.

Tonight she had come alone, as she often did. The pub was sort of her hang out. She always sat in the same spot and ordered the same drink. He didn't know it, but Paul was like family to her. When you didn't have your own bloodline, you filled the dark, empty hole with friends who were really nothing more than acquaintances. Most of them meant no more to her than the t-shirt on her back. As a matter of fact, the blood-red suede strappy heels she'd bought that day meant more to her than any of her fake friends.

She worked hard and deserved to spend her hard-earned money any way she liked. And tonight, all she wanted to do was drink the night away till she passed out. *Maybe tomorrow and the next night, too.*

Isabel.

What had she been thinking? Believing she could have a relationship with her. She'd made peace knowing she wasn't meant to love or be loved. Then Isabel comes along making her believe she had it all wrong. Making her question her whole life.

It's not like she ever wanted kids—god no—she could never bring a child into this world. But she'd thought about adopting one or two. Then she'd remember her own childhood and her decision became clear.

Learning she had a niece was the single best thing that had ever happened to her, and now none of it mattered.

Max puffed out air and gulped back half her drink.

She could count the number of highs in her life on one hand.

Her mom, one.

Her first foster family, two. Although . . . she probably shouldn't count them because her foster mom died of cancer and Max ended up back where she started. So it kind of canceled itself out.

The Murphy's, three. Wait . . . two. She's still on two. Mr. and Mrs. Murphy were the nicest people ever. They had a daughter, Candice, two years older than Max. Everything had worked great until Candice turned into a little drug addict. Long story short, Max got blamed for the drugs and the nice couple sent her away.

Her job, three.

Jimmy, three point five. She was still undecided. The first

words out of Jimmy's mouth when she first met him—well, after he said, "*Who the hell are you?*"—were, "*Stay the fuck away from my daughter!*" Then he went on to tell her if she so much as dared touched a hair on Isabel's head, he'd kill her. "*Don't let these walls fool you,*" he'd said.

It was things like this that made her think Jimmy was in no way capable of hurting Isabel. He'd die for her.

The lady who had been sitting next to Max paid her tab and left. A skinny kid slid into the seat and stared at her. She ignored him mostly, only stealing a glance. He wore a cowboy hat and boots. *Maybe he was lost.* He started talking and she had wished he'd disappear. She took another mouthful of her drink.

That's when *he* showed up. Franklin Dowdy, the last man she expected to see tonight and one of the finest looking men she ever laid eyes on. He gave the impression of a protector, a family man, a great lover . . . a man who would put her first.

She reminded herself: *Anyone can give a good first impression. And anyone can pretend to be someone they're not.*

It was light out when she'd first entered the pub. Now it was dark out, as she stumbled back to her place. Cherry wasn't at her usual spot. She'd met her the first night she moved into her condo. Cherry was only sixteen then. Max tried to get her into the system, but she refused.

She needed another drink. *Like father, like daughter,* she thought.

According to Jimmy, Wilbur was an alcoholic. He'd given it up the day Jimmy's mother committed suicide.

What a screwed-up family she never knew she had.

"Are you doing alright?" he asked, when she fumbled with

the keys. "I can do that." Frankie took the keys from her and opened the door. Just then he placed his hand on the small of her back, to lead her, and his touch sent flames through her shirt. She imagined him ripping it off and closed her eyes to savor the thought. The whole room begun to spin.

He caught her again with his strong arms, pulling her into his hard chest. She turned to face him, her eyes still closed, waiting for the room to stop spinning.

You had too many drinks, she lectured herself. The spinning wouldn't stop anytime soon. *Just kiss him.*

She did, sloppily. With her eyes closed and her world spinning, she found his mouth, his lips, hot and wanting her. She opened her eyes to take in the sight.

"Don't," he whispered, leading her to the couch and positioning a cushion underneath her head, because that's the kind of man he was. "I'll get you some water," he said. But first he made sure she was comfortable.

The idea of being taken care of felt good. She closed her eyes and floated above the clouds, her mind drifting.

"I'm going to be sick!" she cried, moving too fast toward the bathroom. He followed and grabbed hold of her hair as she puked out her brains.

TWENTY

A STORM BREWED INSIDE, AND MABEL YEARNED to release it. She needed answers, or better yet, for Isabel to walk through the door, unscathed. The truth wouldn't come easy and she'd have to work harder. No rest.

Frankie came across two deadbeat pimps he thought might be a link. She'd sent the pictures and names he had taken to Officer Mike. He seemed happy to help and said he'd get back with her soon. Soon couldn't come soon enough.

She worried they'd find Isabel too late and dead. Or they'd find her, and it would still be too late because whoever took her had taken her innocence. Either way Isabel lost.

Positive thinking wouldn't do Mabel any good. She had to think the worst. Whoever took Isabel did it for a reason and she'd guess it wasn't to allow her to live out her happy teenage life. Unable to cry and feeling helpless, she swore to not stop until she could look into the deep blue eyes of Isabel Dumel.

At Susan's, Lucas and Mabel beelined to the front door ignoring the microphones shoved in their faces. The public demanded answers and the police weren't talking.

The door opened and shut quickly behind them. An agent

had let them in. Immediately Mabel thought the worst. They found Isabel's body, but it was too late.

Pieces of Isabel were everywhere, the girl who'd already experienced more than her fair share of misery. The entrance where she had greeted Mabel hundreds of times, the couch where they watched movies, the table where they ate dinner, the pictures they'd taken together, Bella's bed where Isabel curled up with her best friend . . .

"Where's Susan?" she asked the agent. He pointed to her bedroom.

As she got closer, crying could be heard. Quickening her step, she opened the door to find Susan on the floor.

"What happened?" she asked. Susan looked up and burst into loud unearthly cries. She hung onto Mabel, pulling her down with her. "Susan, what is it?"

The look she gave sent shivers down Mabel's spine. What was it she didn't know? She got up to leave. If Susan couldn't talk, she'd get the agent to. As she neared the door, Susan said, "I can't do this."

She'd seen it before. A mom or dad blaming themselves, the guilt so heavy it suffocates them. "Susan," she said, carrying her name out longer than needed. She glanced around the room and spotted a prescription bottle on the end table. Her heart began to race. "What are you doing, sweetie?" She knelt next to her. Expecting to see a handful of pills in her hand, she was relieved to see her holding a picture instead. It was Isabel, the night of her birthday.

"What if it's all my fault?"

"What?"

"Just listen. We've been fighting more than usual. This whole thing with her dad. I don't want to fight with her anymore about it."

"Then you won't. I know what you're thinking, and you need to get those negative thoughts out of your head." Susan sniffled and shook her head, not believing. "C'mon," she helped her up and sat on her bed. Isabel visiting Jimmy in prison was the least of her worries at the time. The bottle of pills bothered her now. She picked it up, afraid she'd find an empty bottle. It looked full. "What's this?" she asked.

"My mom picked them up for me. She thought I needed something to help me sleep."

It'd probably be a good idea, but Mabel would never take them, how could she tell Susan to. Susan needed Isabel, not a magic pill to help her forget for a night. She had grief written all over her face and it simply wouldn't do.

"I told you I'll find her," Mabel said. "Do you believe me?" It wasn't a fair question, but she needed Susan believing.

"I'm trying. God knows I'm trying."

"Mabel," Lucas called. He stood just outside the open door.

She looked to him and back to Susan. "Lucas is going to stay with you." Susan nodded. Just then she wondered why no one else was around. "Where is everyone?" Mabel asked, growing frustrated. She should have never been left alone.

"My mom was feeling ill and my sister drove her home."

Mabel knew all too well how selfish her sister was. The youngest in Susan's family, but not too young to know better. Mabel bit her tongue. Badmouthing her family wouldn't bring Isabel home.

"And the victim's advocate?"

"The agent sent her home. He said I'd have another arrive any moment."

"How long ago was this?"

"An hour." Mabel sealed her lips tight, to keep any negative thoughts quiet. "I'm fine," Susan countered, her shoulders slouched, eyes droopy and red. She was not even close to the definition of fine.

Mabel stood, ready to fight someone, anyone. Lucas grabbed hold of her hand and pulled her into the hallway. "Are you going to be alright?"

She paused. "Yes," she said at last. "I have to be."

"Just go. I'll stay with her."

She peeked into the bedroom. Susan sat upright on the edge of her bed staring at her small TV with a black screen. "Okay. We'll stay here tonight, but don't expect me home anytime soon." She went to Susan and sat next to her. Without saying a word, she hugged her, then walked to the front door with Lucas following.

The first time Mabel had met Susan, she didn't like the vibes she'd given off. Susan had come off as one of those ladies with her nose in the air, judging everyone but their perfect selves. Mabel hadn't earned her trust yet and she'd probably given off her own bad vibes because truthfully, she partly blamed Susan for not protecting her sister from Jimmy. Surely there were signs.

But they'd grown close over the last couple of years. Now she needed Mabel's help more than ever.

Lucas kissed her softly before opening the door with the agent watching. "Be safe," he said. He took her hand, turned it over and planted a kiss dead in the center. A small gesture, he'd done the day he proposed to her. *My heart is in your hands, today, and for the rest of my life,* he had said. Since then, he did it often. Each time, her heart beat faster, just like it did now.

She smiled, and said, "I love you till the end of time." She opened the door, turned and smiled at him one last time, missing the brown car as it drove by. If she'd been watching, like she should have, she would know for certain someone was watching her.

In her car she let it all out. Every bad word she could think of came out of her mouth. On the outside she must have looked like a crazed lunatic and she couldn't care less, because every crummy emotion ran through her like poison. In the past she used a punching bag, ran or sparred, but today she didn't have time for any of it.

Furious she'd spent the last ten hours chasing dead ends and mad as hell Isabel was still out there. She hadn't said anything to Susan, but she and Frankie had spoken about the possibility of Isabel being trafficked. Trafficking had become a concern in Colorado. A sin no longer reserved for other countries. It happened in their own backyard. The thought sent shivers from her ears to her toes. If Isabel were trafficked, chances were slim to none she'd still be in the state.

She knew all too well what traffickers did to young girls. The last case she and Frankie had worked took weeks to solve. They were able to bring the girl home, but she wouldn't use the word "saved" because she knew the girl would relive those days, weeks, and months for the rest of her life.

Calming down, she began to think clearer.

She hated Jimmy, but even he wouldn't do this to Isabel. The boyfriend could definitely be a pawn, grooming her and leading her to his boss. And it's possible Max had something to do with this, but she didn't know exactly how yet. It didn't sit well with her that Max conveniently came into Isabel's life just six months prior. Not to mention she tried too damn hard to get close to the her. Hell, she worked in foster care, a structure where children are the most vulnerable. Isabel didn't exactly fit that mentality, but maybe somehow Max took advantage of her.

TWENTY-ONE

S HE WASN'T THE FIRST LADY FRANKIE TENDED to as they prayed to the porcelain gods. Some of the jobs he'd done were far worse than holding the hair of a puking lady.

Mabel would love this, Frankie thought.

He'd held Mabel's hair once upon a time. They were celebrating their first job together, a success. It was partly his fault. It was his idea after all and he could hold his liquor. Mabel, on the other hand, could not. They still laugh about it . . . well, he does. However, Max was remarkedly further along in her drunkenness.

After Max seemed to have nothing else in her, he swayed her to brush her teeth, certain she'd thank him in the morning. Then he made her take three Advil and carried her to bed, tucking her away for the night, clothes and all. He only bothered to take her shoes off.

In all her drunkenness, Max attempted to pull him down and kiss him again. Her lips were wet and soft, and she tasted of peppermint. His head swam as he inhaled her sweet scent. She was one beautiful lady, mascara smeared and all, and he wanted her, but he'd never take advantage of a woman, drunk or not, and that wouldn't change tonight.

It didn't take long for her breathing to become heavy. He never understood why people drank until they passed out. He experienced being all-out drunk once in high school and that was it for him. He swore to never do it again. After high school, he joined the Army and never drank more than one or two. As a big man, one or two never affected him, and he wanted his mind clear and sharp.

He scanned the room for the laptop he'd seen on his last visit. Before it had lain on her bed, now it was nowhere in sight. He searched her office and continued to look around her living space, at last finding it on the kitchen counter.

He called Mabel to catch her up. She picked up on the first ring. "Guess where I am?" he asked.

"A strip club," she replied.

"What gave it away? The loud music or the girl moaning in my ear?"

"What kind of strip clubs do you go to?"

"Can we get off strip clubs? I'm in Max's condo."

"Close enough." *Ouch!* She really did hate her.

Ignoring her jabs, he explained Max was dead asleep in the other room where he put her after he'd found her in a pub, wasted. Mabel made sure to get her *T* in, sounding like a teenager. "And before you say anything, no, I didn't have sex with her."

"I hate to say it, but you sound like a guilty man." Her sense of humor replaced her hostility toward Max.

"Ha-ha. I have her phone and computer," he explained. "Hold on . . . shit, her phone is locked."

"Good thing you have her finger in the other room," she said, sarcastically.

He walked into the bedroom where Max was snoring. He lifted her silky-soft hand and pressed her index finger against the back of her phone. "I'm in," he announced.

"I bet the computer is locked, too."

"I'll deal with that later. Where are you anyway?" he asked, scrolling through hundreds of contacts in her phone.

"At the mall watching Sam."

"I thought Lucas was going to do that?" Damn, he maybe had 250 contacts in his phone, mostly work related. There had to be over a thousand here. Mrs. Hestingburg was right, she did have a lot of friends. He'd have to download them because there was no way he'd have time to go through all of them tonight.

"He stayed with Susan. It's a long story, so here I am."

"And? What's the punk up to?"

"Not much so far. He met up with a couple of friends, neither of whom are Noah. They're hanging out in the food court talking like teenagers do. I can't shake the feeling there is more to him."

"Trust your instincts," he said.

"Have you heard anything from Grandpa or Doc?"

"Not recently. I last spoke to them," he paused, "an hour ago. They'd knocked six hotels off their list. I'll call again when I'm done here."

"I tried calling fifteen minutes ago and he's not answering. Have him call me, I'm worried."

"Will do." He tapped buttons on Max's phone. "How many contacts do you have in your phone?" he asked, as he continued tapping buttons.

"I don't know. Why?"

"Just guess."

"A hundred, maybe. Why?" she asked again.

"Max has a buttload, and by buttload, I bet she has over a thousand. I'm backing up her phone to our account."

"What kind of person has over a thousand contacts? There's no way she keeps in touch with that many people."

"Maybe they're work related." He finished the download and said, "Done. We'll find out soon enough. Can you call Philip and tell him to decipher the information for us? Did you get anywhere with the pictures and names I sent you?"

"I haven't heard back from Mike. I'll call him after I call Philip."

"Okay, I'm going through her computer now, and then I have a bartender to speak with. Call me once you hear from Mike. Talk to you soon." He hung up before she replied.

He got into the computer easily. It appeared clean aside from one suspicious folder he couldn't access. It required a password and every combination of letters and numbers he could think of didn't work. He had no choice but to take the computer with him. If Max turned him in for theft, he'd deny it and she couldn't prove it.

He stood over her, ignoring the urge to plant a kiss on her lips. Instead, he pulled the covers to her chin and left with her laptop tucked into the back of his pants.

TWENTY-TWO

AFTER HANGING UP WITH FRANKIE, SHE CALLED Philip, the man behind the curtain. He had just read the email and said he'd get on it.

With Philip on her mind, Mabel Peters once again missed the brown car following her out of the mall parking lot. She'd driven all over north-eastern Colorado Springs following Sam and started to wonder if he had made her. She doubted it, because she had grown quite good at tailing. Either he'd made her, or he was lost. Just when she was certain he had been leading her on a wild goose chase, he parked his car in front of a dark brown house, but instead of going into the house, he crossed the street and approached a gray Altima. The night clear, she could see him reach into the car and come out with a brown paper bag. A gun? Drugs?

Her heart leapt when he glanced in her direction. *Shit!* She threw her car in drive, but luckily before she put her foot on the gas, he then glanced in the other direction. He hadn't seen her after all, but he was up to no good. Grabbing her binoculars for a better view, she could make out a McDonald's logo on the bag. He held onto it like he had nothing to worry about. He got in his car and drove away with the Altima behind. When Sam reached the corner of the street, he turned left, and the Altima turned right. With only one of her, she decided to follow the Altima.

The Altima took her to a trailer park. Parking a few trailers down, she waited for the driver to get out. The guy was young but appeared to be in his mid to late twenties. She stepped out, he turned, and a smile spread across his face.

"What can I do for you pretty lady."

She had her hair in a ponytail, dressed head to toe in black. The thought reminded her of another time, but she threw it out of her mind and replied, "I'm looking for Sam."

His smile disappeared. "What did you say?"

"Are you Sam?"

"You're looking for someone and you don't know what he looks like? A pretty lady like you shouldn't be here."

"Is that a threat?"

He took a couple steps closer. She remained next to her car door ready to fight if necessary. Able to see him clearer, his face was covered in harsh lines and acne scars, he had big ears and long legs. Coupled with his dark brown intense eyes, which made her uncomfortable, he reminded her of a jackrabbit. She bet he had a gun tucked into the small of his back. Looking her up and down, assessing, thinking of what to do with her, he said, "Are you his girlfriend?"

"No, but my friend is. I just wanted to talk with him."

"And why do you think I'm him?"

"I got your address from her room," she lied. "She's missing."

The realization hit him, she may be a cop, and he bolted. Quick and like the jackrabbit she knew he was, he moved swift between two trailers and threaded the park like he'd done it before. Good thing for her she ran nearly every day, had been for years, and she was fast. Faster than most. Tonight, she'd met her match. It took some time for her to close the distance between them but then he slowed down a fraction as he looked back to her and she pounced on him sending them both to the ground. She landed on him which softened her fall.

Pulling herself up on all fours she rammed her knee into this groin making him yell out in pain.

"What the fuck is wrong with you?" he yelled.

"Why did you run?" she demanded.

"Fuck you, lady!"

"Wrong answer, asshole!" She pulled out her gun and pointed it at his head, standing over him.

"You're a crazy bitch! I have rights."

"Not with me you don't. Now what were you doing with Sam earlier?" She could see the gears turning in his head. "That's right. I saw you give him a bag."

"I'm just the delivery driver."

"Delivery driver," she thought out loud. "Delivery of what exactly?"

"Screw you!" he shouted, spit flying everywhere.

"How about I blow your balls off?" she asked pointing the gun at his groin.

"Okay, okay," he said throwing his hands up in surrender. His eyes shot down to her feet and she kicked him as hard as she could on his side. He curled up on his right side and moaned.

"Answer my questions or it'll get a lot worse. How do you know Sam?"

"He's just a customer."

"What kind of customer. Be vague again and I'll kick you in the head to knock some of those rocks loose."

"I don't know him. My boss tells me where to go, who to

meet, and what to deliver. I don't ask questions. I didn't even know his name."

"What did you give him."

"Drugs, I think. I don't look. I never look," he said, defeated, pulling himself up to a seated position.

"Who's your boss?"

"I can't tell you. If I do, kill me now."

"Look at me," she said squatting down to his eye level, the gun aimed at his head. "You're giving drugs to minors. What do *you* think he'll do with it?"

He didn't respond, his eyes dead.

She pulled out the picture of Isabel and showed him. He looked at it.

Nothing.

She knew from the lack of his reaction he had never seen her before. She reached behind him, finding a gun tucked into his jeans along with an extra magazine. She felt his pockets and found his wallet. "Adam Fuentes," she read, "twenty-five years old, one-hundred and seventy pounds, five-eleven . . . oh and lives here, in this mobile park, #227. Nice to meet you Adam. Ever sell drugs to minors again, I'll shove them down your throat."

She left him sitting and ran back to her car. Driving away she called Corneal and asked him to run a plate, LFA739. She learned the car was registered to Janet Fuentes, his mother, who had the same address. No record.

Regretting her decision to follow Adam opposed to Sam, she drove away angry.

TWENTY-THREE

FRANKIE DROVE AROUND THE STREETS OF Colorado Springs looking for something or someone, stopping every now and then to talk to the locals. He showed the picture he'd taken from Max's bedside table. Who knows, someone might just recognize Max, too.

No one had seen Isabel, but one creep told him where his friend goes for sex. According to this friend, some had to be minors. He'd said they worked out of a home but didn't know where.

Closing time for the pub neared and Frankie had yet to find anything concrete that would lead him to Isabel. He parked in his same spot and walked the streets around Max's condo and the pub. Drunk young men and women exited the bars. He caught sight of one lady getting into a car with a man, the lady appeared to be in her late twenties, early thirties. Not Isabel or a kid. The alleys were empty, no one smoking, no one doing deals or having sex. He'd been doing this job for a long time and someone scared everyone away. Was it him or Skinny Black?

As it neared two-thirty, Frankie walked into the pub and was hit by a funky stale odor. The lights were turned up, two men sat at the bar, separately, and a couple of workers were cleaning the floor. He took a seat at the end and Paul's head popped up, ready to tell him they were closed.

When he saw who it was, Paul said, "I'll be right with you." Then he turned to the other two men, "Jack, Tony, time to go man."

One held up his drink in salute, then poured it down his throat. "Thanks, Paul. See you tonight," he said on his way out.

The other man didn't move. "Tony? I said time to go," Paul repeated himself, giving Tony a nudge.

He stood up, swaying. "I . . . I don't think I can drive man," he slurred.

"Not my problem, call a cab," Paul said, becoming more and more agitated. He grabbed Tony's drink, put it behind the bar and walked away.

"Hey! Give it back." Paul ignored him. "Dude, seriously?" The man stood and stumbled into the table behind him.

"Fucking drunks," Paul grumbled. "Sit your ass down," He pointed to the stool and Tony did as he ordered. Paul picked up the phone and called a cab.

"Rough night?" Frankie asked.

"When are they not? This is my dad's bar and he asked me to run it for him when I turned twenty-one. At that age, who wouldn't want to run their own bar?"

Me, thought Frankie. Even young and stupid, twenty-one-year-old Frankie had never liked bars.

"Eleven years later and I'm stuck doing the same damn thing day and night." Paul shook his head. "How's Max? Did she get home okay?"

"Sleeping like a baby."

"Babies don't drink themselves stupid."

"No, I guess they don't."

"What did you want to talk to me about anyway?"

"I'm trying to help Max find her niece."

"Oh right, your card says you're a private investigator."

Something like that, he thought. He nodded.

"What does this have to do with me?" Paul asked confused.

"How long have you known Max?"

"Is she a suspect?"

"Nah, nothing like that. I'm interviewing everyone that knows Max. It's often someone the victim knows."

"Then I'm a suspect?"

"Just answer the damn question."

"Four years. Since she moved in down the block."

"Have you ever met Isabel?"

"No. I work in a bar, remember."

He felt like punching the guy in his snotbox. "Has there been anyone with Max you didn't like or trust?"

"Besides you?"

He reached over the bar and grabbed Paul by the shirt, pulling him up on the bar. "I've had enough of your smart-ass mouth—"

"Dude, I'm tired. It's been a long day. Give me a break," he cried.

"I could say the same." His eyes burned a hole through Paul's skull.

"I'm sorry." Paul spotted lights just outside the entrance. "Tony," he shouted, still laid out on the bar, "your ride is here."

Frankie looked up and saw Tony watching the show, "Need help, Paul?" he asked stumbling around the stool.

"No, I'm good. Do you have money . . . for the cab?"

Frankie let go and sat back down.

"I think so."

"See you next week then," he said, composing himself as he pulled his shirt down. "Look, I don't know anything. Max comes in here once or twice a week, usually by herself and orders one to two drinks and leaves. Guys hit on her all the time, but she mostly ignores them. I saw her outside the bar a few times with other people, friends I'd guess. She's always coming or going.

"Anyone you know?"

"No. She talks about family and work, but never friends. She told me she has a brother in prison, she'd just met her dad and then he died, and she'd lost her mom at a young age. She's had a tough life, growing up in foster care and all. I think it's cool she's helping the system that helped her."

"Tell me more about the men trying to pick her up."

"Oh wait, there was this one guy. He looked a little like you, but not as big." Paul's cheeks flushed.

"He's black?" Frankie asked.

"I think so."

"It's not hard to tell," he said sarcastically.

"I know, but this guy had lighter skin."

Big Ugly? "Is he ugly or good looking like me?"

Paul made a face. "Good looking."

Not Big Ugly. "Okay, so why does this guy stand out to you? Were you into him or something?"

"No man, but he had facial hair and dread locks."

Dreads? "That's it? There are plenty of guys with facial hair and dreads." Frankie said.

"In the past four years of Max coming in here, I never saw her with a man. I figured she was a lesbian. She noticed this guy though."

"Did they leave together?"

"I don't think so. He left, she finished her drink and left maybe five minutes after. I guess they could have met up. He looked . . . I don't know . . . like a player. I sure hope she didn't get involved with him. I never saw them together again."

"And how long ago was this?"

He searched his memory, "Uhm, it's been a while. Oh! He wore a light brown leather jacket, so the nights were getting colder. Maybe September."

"If you see him again, call me. You still have my card?"

He pulled it out of his back pocket and showed Frankie. "Sure thing."

TWENTY-FOUR

SUICIDE, AN UNSPOKEN THOUGHT.

Isabel Dumel had seen it on TV and heard adults talk about it in hushed tones. Before today, she never quite understood the idea—Why would someone want to take their own life? Before today, she thought, *Could life be so bad that there was no coming back from it?* Was it so bad, that time skipped you and all the pain, and misery, and anger festered? She was no stranger to any of it, but before today, time never failed her.

Now, she knew her life would be forever changed . . . if she made it out alive. There was no coming back from this. Time was the least thing she needed. What she needed was a way to end her life—because now she knew, this was the easiest way stop the pain and shame she felt—and she would do it without a second thought.

What would Mabel think? The strongest woman she knew. Her role model and mentor, the one person she knew who fought her way to freedom.

She was not naïve. She knew she was not the first thirteen-year-old to lose her virginity. Not even the first to lose it unwillingly. Knowing this brought zero comfort. She's a statistic now, a number.

What would her aunt Susan say? Her dad? Tears streamed down her face. Everyone would think she's a whore, a prostitute.

She swallowed the lump in her throat. It hurt, but crying wouldn't save her. She should be sleeping, like the others. The room was medium sized, much too small for six girls to share. A couple of the girls were heavy breathers and one snored. Her swollen eyes felt heavy and tired. Her body hurt, but no longer felt like hers.

With as little movement as possible, she scooted out of the bed and headed toward the window.

"Don't bother," a voice came from the dark room.

Isabel turned, but she couldn't make out which bed the voice came from.

"The window. Don't bother trying to escape," the girl said, faintly. Isabel made out her silhouette.

"I wasn't. I just wanted to see if it was light out," she explained, thinking of the man with an afro who last threatened her about trying to escape.

"Don't bother with that either." The girl stood next to her and pulled back the curtain. "See, the goddamn windows are blacked out. You can't see shit. And in case you didn't notice when we came in, we're underground."

"Then why the window?" Isabel asked.

"To mess with your head." The girl flicked a lighter and the flame bounced off the blackout out window, which was sealed with wood or dirt or who knew what.

She nodded. "I'm Isabel," she said for some reason.

"No real names here, Barbie. Your name is now . . ." she paused, "that'll do. No doubt you're a barbie. Where'd they find you anyway?"

Tears sprung to Isabel's eyes and her lip quivered uncontrollably.

"Hey, we can come up with a different name."

"It's not that. I . . . I want to go home."

"Don't we all. Come, sit with me. We can talk for a while, but we really need to get some sleep. They work us hard."

"How can you sleep?" she asked, not moving.

"I've been here for nine months. You get used to it." She shrugged. "I stopped fighting after the first week when I realized I wasn't going anywhere. I'm telling you sweetheart, no one gets out. You're here to stay." She looked her up and down. "You're not like the rest of us. You were chosen for a reason. I could tell right off you were special to the big boss and there's no way he's letting you go."

The words cut through her. Is this how it would end for her? She wouldn't go out again. She couldn't. If she didn't end up finding a gun or something useful to end her life, she might just die with one of those monsters. She shivered, thinking of it.

Wiping the tears that had formed in her eyes, she said, "Who is he?"

"Mr. B? Don't ask me his name, none of us know."

Isabel picked at the thin blanket which probably hadn't been washed in weeks, if ever. "He's the one that took me from my home."

"Damn, Barbie, you are special," she said.

"Stop saying that!" Isabel shouted. *What does that even mean? Why her?*

"Keep your voice down. You don't want them coming in here, do you?" This girl acted like it was a game, so sure of herself.

She'd spoken to her before, but couldn't recall her name.

"What's your name . . . or fake name?"

"I'm Jackie, you know like Jackie Kennedy. Don't you think I look like her?"

She did, actually—a little anyway, from what she could see of her face in the dark room.

Jackie shrugged. "I usually wear a wig. The men like the fantasy." Isabel closed her eyes in disgust and held her breath to keep from screaming. "I figured if I was going to be forced to be here, I was going to be someone else. It helps to remove yourself from what's happening. Like it's not really *you* doing all the horrible things that are expected of you. You know, Jackie's doing it, not me."

Now that sounded like something she could do. Be Barbie. Barbie was the prostitute, not Isabel. She nodded. "Do you have a wig for me?"

"Thing is, you actually make a good barbie just the way you are," she said.

"No. I need a disguise."

"Okay, I get it. I'll help you when we wake up. Now get some sleep. Goodnight, Barbie."

No, not a good night.

"Night," Isabel responded and crawled under the green blanket. She closed her eyes and tried to not think.

TWENTY-FIVE

M AX GALLO CAME TO, AWARE OF HER DRY
mouth and throbbing head. Every time she made a
promise to herself that next time would be different, it never
was. After one, she started to loosen up, after two she felt good,
relaxed, happy—but more than that she entered the danger
zone of stupid drunkenness where she'd either be too friendly
or be a full-fledged bitch.

She recalled Frankie putting her to bed—or was it a dream?
She opened her eyes afraid she'd find him watching her. He
wasn't and she couldn't help but feel a little disappointed.

I kissed him! Oh my god—she touched her lips—*I can't believe
I kissed him.* Never before had she been so brazen, even in
her worst drunken state. The butterflies in her chest brought
a smile to her face. His hands were strong, and surprisingly
soft. *Did we have sex?* she wondered. Her body told her no.
Her head felt like it was going to explode. A glass of water
and bottle of Advil called out from her nightstand. She took
four followed by all the water. In retort, her stomach recoiled
and fought back, sending her running to the bathroom. Her
head pulsed in perfect rhythm, quickly rising to a crescendo of
crashing rocks as she spewed the contents of her stomach into

the toilet. Sprawled out on the throne, déjà vu came over her and a meme her friend had sent her once popped in her head, a dog praying to the porcelain god.

Feeling the worst had past, she huddled into a ball against the wall with her legs pulled up to her chest. Only then did she notice she wore the same jeans and t-shirt from the night before. It could have been worse, she could have woken up naked.

She pulled herself up, in spite of her hangover, and got on with her original plan before all hell broke loose.

TWENTY-SIX

THE NEXT MORNING, MABEL WOKE TO pounding on the front door. After realizing she wasn't in her own bed and the reason why, she trampled over Lucas and ran to the door only to find Susan had beat her there. Detective Burton asked to come in and Susan stepped aside.

"Ms. Landry," Burton nodded, then walked past Mabel bumping her without a word. She realized she was dressed only in Lucas's shirt and Susan was fully dressed for the day and smelling freshly showered.

"Can I get you coffee?" asked Susan.

"I'll do it," Mabel offered and scurried off into the kitchen. The two rooms were open making it easy for Mabel to hear everything said.

"The Feds are on their way. They should be here any minute. Do you have somewhere private we can talk?" Mabel took the jab and pressed start on the coffee maker. She didn't worry about impressing anyone but preferred to look a little more presentable for the FBI. She hurried back to the bedroom to change. She closed the door behind her and smacked Lucas on the butt, who still lay in bed asleep. "Get up. Burton's here and the FBI is on their way."

He rubbed the sleep from his eyes. "Did you even sleep last night?"

"Not much," she said, throwing on a clean pair of jeans and a t-shirt.

"Why aren't you out there eavesdropping?" he asked, pitching his legs over the bed and sitting up. He took one look at her and added, "Ah."

She squeezed her feet into her Nikes without untying them and caught him staring. "What?"

He held his arms out. "Come here."

She couldn't bring herself to comply, to take time to enjoy the warmth of his arms. Isabel was out there somewhere, and time didn't stop for her to take breaks. "I have to get back out there," she said, leaving him to go brush her teeth.

The routine mechanical. *Wet toothbrush, open toothpaste . . .* If the Feds were taking the time to come over, what did they have? *Squeeze toothpaste . . . too damn much, too damn much—Fuck it.* It couldn't be good. Her stomach felt sick. *Wet it again, brush, brush, brush—back first, left side, right side . . .* She had almost three hours of sleep. Three hours too long, but she knew if she didn't get a little her mind would be too tired to think. *Front, top, and at last, finish with the bottom.*

Lucas walked in. "Babe?"

Brush, brush, brush . . . has it been two minutes?

"Babe?"

Brush, brush, brush . . .

He grabbed her by the shoulders—not hard, but firm—and held her there. A blurry Lucas appeared in the mirror and she blinked away the tears. "I'm fine," she warned. *Brush, brush, brush, spit, tongue, blah,* she hated this part, *rinse, spit, rinse, spit.* She put her toothbrush away and started for the door.

He caught her before she escaped and held her tight. Instinct told her to fight, but she didn't want to fight, his arms felt too good and it wasn't Lucas she was mad at. She wanted him more than anything, but the guilt was too much. Her tears broke free and rolled down her face.

Taking her face in his hands, he lifted her eyes to meet his. "I love you, Mabel, and you're the bravest person I know. You're going to find her."

She nodded.

"Now go out there and do what you do best—Find Isabel. Don't worry about Susan or anyone else. It's Isabel who needs you most."

A sense of relief rushed through her. Four simple words, *don't worry about Susan,* removed the small boulder from her shoulders. Mabel had been through all this before—only on the other side, with kids she'd never met before.

She'd witnessed it firsthand. A mother's world shred to pieces—by police, family, friends, neighbors, media, and people offering help—until she had nothing left. A mother trusted no one because everyone was to blame—the uncle who showed too much interest, the cousin who had showed up unexpectedly, the pastor, the teacher, the clerk, the neighbor, the friend's dad and maybe even the husband, or brother, or grandpa. The lack of trust becomes every mother's nightmare.

Mabel could see Susan headed down this path at a rapid rate, but Mabel wouldn't find Isabel by Susan's side, so she kissed Lucas on the lips and told him she loved him.

Back in the kitchen, coffee had already been served with Burton on the far end of the counter and Susan to her left and two men stood opposite the ladies on the other side of the counter. One she recognized from the previous day. Susan turned to the sound of Mabel as she approached and held out her hand for Mabel to take.

"We didn't get far," Susan exhaled and continued, "I asked

them to wait for you. I need you next to me," she explained, squeezing Mabel's hand. "Here," She slid a cup towards her, "I poured you coffee."

Mabel guessed Susan was stalling, afraid to hear what the Feds had to say. "I'm here now." She glanced at Burton who kept her eyes on the tall slender agent dressed in a dark blue jacket and light blue shirt. The agent fixated on Mabel, glowering like she was to blame for the current situation. The agent took his eyes off Mabel, moving to Susan, his face visually softening. He opened his mouth to speak, but Susan spoke first.

"Mabel, this is Agent Younge," she said pointing to the agent in the dark blue jacket. "And with him is Agent Radburn. He was here yesterday." They both nodded to Mabel.

She knew Radburn was head of investigations in Colorado Springs, but wondered why Younge was here, who appeared to be above Radburn in the pecking order of the FBI.

"Ms. Landry, our initial investigation, led by Agent Radburn, consisted of a neighborhood canvas with an expanded search, roadblocks, and other resources looking at any vehicles coming in and out of your neighborhood around the time when Isabel went missing. The black truck your neighbor saw leaving your house was caught on camera from a home security system a few houses east of you." Mabel's heart skipped. "It was reported stolen on Friday."

Damn.

"We've been looking at other angles as well. One, in particular, raised some red flags."

Get to the damn point!

He continued, "We have reason to believe the person or persons involved are part of a sex trafficking ring—"

Susan grabbed hold of Mabel, her eyes protruding from her head, tears erupting.

He said sex. They had information and leads. Most likely names, even places they were watching.

"I lead a multi-agency task force. Our primary goal is to bring Isabel home. This is a collaborative effort with federal, state, and local law enforcement. We have access to all the subject matter experts and intelligence. We worked last night on a strategic plan. In the meantime, I'd like you to go on camera, talk to the media, we want every person in America looking for Isabel."

It's about time, Mabel thought.

Susan whimpered and Mabel stood frozen with her arm held tight around Susan's shoulders. Thank goodness Detective Burton decided to pipe in, because even if Mabel could ask questions, she would be told to stand down and let the big boys handle it.

"Susan, this really is good news. We now know where to search and we won't be wasting any more time on places she won't be. As with any missing person, time is against us and same goes with trafficking. When Agent Younge said everyone is working to find Isabel, he isn't joking. We have partnered with surrounding states—the airlines, buses, trains, you name it."

Mabel learned all she was going to learn. She had to get out of there and couldn't do it with them there. As if they read her mind, Agent Younge said, "We best be on our way. We'll call you with any updates, so please stay here where we can find you."

Mabel shut the door behind them and hugged Susan, now sobbing again. "Susan, I'm sorry to leave you, but I have to go."

"I know, I know. Go. Bring Isabel back to me."

TWENTY-SEVEN

B Y THE TIME MABEL MADE IT TO DOC'S, THE time was creeping up on 7:00 a.m. She found Frankie in Doc's training room.

"Hey," said Frankie when she walked in. He puffed under the strain of bench pressing too much weight.

"Hey, you. Need a spot?"

"Sure."

Comfortable silence came over them allowing Frankie to finish his set. Sitting up, he said, "You're here early."

"Yes, well, I was woken up by Burton banging on the front door, then the Feds came soon after," she replied. "Burton's a pretty lady, why don't you talk to her? Maybe you can win her over with your charm."

"Sure, because that's what I do," he said laughing, adding more weight.

"Did Under Armour finally call you to team up with them?" she smiled.

"Ha-ha," he replied with a smirk.

"No, really. I like the Rock and all, but they could use a fresh face." He pumped out another set. When he finished, she added, "The Feds confirmed Isabel is being trafficked."

He sat up and wiped his face with a towel. "Doesn't surprise me."

"I think Isabel was being groomed."

"The boyfriend?"

She nodded. "Isabel's smart, but a girl her age interested in boys, especially one who says all the right things, has disaster written all over it. There's something about him."

"What do mean?"

"He acts . . ." She was about to say *he acts too grown up for his age*, but the word, *acts*, is what bothered her. He's acting, playing a role he's been trained for. He's manipulative. "I can't explain it. I just don't get a good feeling from him."

"We'll keep an eye on him."

She nodded. "I'm going to take a quick shower and then we need to go."

"I'll be ready."

With the possibility of Isabel being trafficked, Mabel needed to change her thinking and trust the professionals who dealt with human and sex trafficking daily. Frankie had told her last night the man he spoke to said he planned on moving them in a week.

He trained them first . . .

They made the short drive to Jimmy's new home—the Colorado State Penitentiary in Canon City. The flawlessly clear sky made a perfect day for a drive, but the day was far from perfect. First, she had to talk to the man she thought she'd never have to face again. Second, Isabel wasn't with her.

Just before they arrived, Mabel's phone rang. "Hello," she answered.

"You're not going to believe what I just learned," Mike said.

"Please let it be good news."

"One of the detectives went out to pay Max a visit bright and early this morning and she's gone."

She furrowed her brows, sure she'd heard him wrong. She looked at Frankie as she replied, "What do you mean, *she's gone?*"

Frankie mouthed, *What?* and she put her finger up, *Hold on.*

"Like vanished," Mike responded.

Frankie's irritation grew.

"Mike, hold on a sec," She pressed the speaker button on her phone, "I'm with Frankie, you're on speaker."

"Start from the beginning," Frankie ordered.

"I just got in twenty minutes ago for a meeting and all of a sudden Burton gets a call from one of the detectives she sent over to Max's and according to him, she's not home."

"Okay . . . why is this important?"

"She vanished, no one knows where she is. They have a team searching her condo now, but no one has seen her . . . well since you brought her home last night."

"Fuck me!" Frankie blurted out. "I left her sound asleep."

"Her neighbors vouched for you. The old lady saw you leaving, alone. But watch your back; Burton is out for blood."

Frankie clenched his jaw. The news put a wrench in their investigation. "I have nothing to hide. Thanks for the call, Mike."

Mabel added, "Keep us posted."

"You didn't hear it from me."

"What the hell are you up to?" Frankie mumbled under his breath, deep in thought.

Her mind ping-ponged back and forth. She needed to keep

a level head. Before they left Doc's, Frankie had shown her the picture he took from Max's condo. She hated to admit it, but Isabel looked truly happy. At the moment, Mabel secretly hoped Max had nothing to do with Isabel's abduction. God knew the girl needed more people who loved her in her life and Max just put a huge target on her back.

What or who scared her away?

Unless . . . *Jimmy.*

Frankie pulled into visitor parking and killed the ignition. "Don't hold anything back," he advised. They'd agreed, Mabel would go in alone. "You won't get another chance to speak with him." He watched as she made her way to the front gate.

With every step her heart beat faster. She couldn't help but wonder if she had put a bullet in his head when she'd had the chance, if Isabel would still be here. With Wilbur gone, there's no way he would have been able to raise Isabel on his own. Knowing he was rotting away in a cell brought some reprieve.

Inside, she handed her driver's license over to the guard. The room was well maintained, not at all like the movies. Aside from a slight odor, the place didn't make her want to barf.

She was searched, a little too well, and led through steel gates and corridors. The calls from the other inmates went in one ear and out the other, but their eyes left her feeling naked. Still, the prison wasn't the worst place she'd found herself.

They came to a large open space where she immediately spotted Randy Bradley, Jimmy's lawyer. *What the hell is he doing here?* After shaking his hand, they were led along empty cells, stopping in front of one at the end.

Jimmy laid on his back, dressed in red, staring at the ceiling. *Red.* What an odd color for an inmate. Wasn't red an angry color?

She watched him for a second, noting he'd put on some muscle and his head was now bald. A chair had been positioned in the middle of the hallway directly in front of Jimmy's cell. She sat with nothing more than a thick glass partition separating her from a serial killer.

He sat up, faced her, and smiled. Her pulse quickened as she imagined ripping his head off and tearing him to shreds. His smile disappeared as quickly as it had come.

"Teach," he said when the two guards walked away. He paced, back and forth, back and forth. His eyes remained on her. Back and forth, back and forth. She had the sudden urge to bang on the glass like a kid at the zoo, but she maintained her glare without saying a word.

He broke the stare down first, turned to Randy and said, "Give her some space, would you?"

Randy's presence slipped her mind. He did as Jimmy ordered and sauntered over to the guards, who stood ten feet behind her with their arms crossed. Jimmy smiled, proud of his authority over his defense attorney.

"Wipe that smile off your face or I'll do it for you," she barked.

"Teach, Teach, Teach—oh, how I've missed you. You always were fun," he cooed. "By the way, you look like shit," he added.

"I could say the same about you. Although, the cage complements your persona. You find a girlfriend yet?"

"Why, you offering?" He replied between gritted teeth.

She despised him. "I have better things to do with my time than waste it at the zoo."

"Fuck you! I called you here to look you in the eye."

"You called me?" That would explain why it was so easy to get a visit and why his lawyer was present. "I don't think so. I came on my own free will to find out what the hell you did to your daughter."

"The hell you did!" he scuffed. "I think you're behind this.

As a form of retaliation or something."

"You sure you didn't miss my beautiful brown eyes? Tell me, Jimmy, what do see when you look into them?"

He studied her for a moment, then said, "You didn't do it."

"Good, we agree on something. Now, you going to tell me which ex-convict *you* sent to take her?"

He laughed. She could almost see the wheels turning in his head.

"Where's your sister, Jimmy?" she asked, amazed by how much he looked like Max. She hadn't seen it before because she hadn't seen Jimmy in two years, but with his head shaved, she could see they had the same features.

His eyebrows rose in surprise. "What's that supposed to mean?" he shouted, slamming his fist into the unbreakable glass.

The guards appeared, ready to take him out. Jimmy stepped back with his hands up. Wow. What the power of prison did to a person. She didn't think he could be trained, but here he was with his head bowed, hands up, relinquishing the power he didn't have. Mabel waved the guard off.

"Max disappeared. Poof." She gestured with her hands. "Don't you find it strange? Almost like she's hiding something . . . or someone."

"Fuck!" he moaned, not wanting the guards to come back. His body tensed and his face turned red.

"You two are close. Is she responsible for this?"

He ran his hand over his bald head and pursed his lips. "How would I know, I was in solitary confinement." She wanted to ask for what, but really didn't care. He deserved every bad thing that happened to him. "Randy?" he called out. The short man with glasses and neatly trimmed sideburns appeared before him. "Why didn't you tell me Max was missing?"

"Uh, I didn't know. I hadn't heard . . ."

What a joke, she thought. This man was not lawyer material. He had no spine.

"Find her," Jimmy demanded.

She wondered how this weak man planned on fulfilling Jimmy's demand. His best bet was Mabel, but her priority was Isabel. Unless by finding Max, she found Isabel.

He looked at Jimmy, choosing his words, "I will." He nodded and walked back to the safety of the guards with his tail between his legs.

"If she's alive," Jimmy told Mabel, "she won't be for long."

She never wished death on Max, but she sensed if she didn't find Max before whatever goons the lawyer sent, the next time she laid eyes on her, she'd be a corpse.

TWENTY-EIGHT

J IMMY DUMEL COULDN'T BELIEVE SHE CAME. He last saw Mabel in court and swore then if he ever got out, he'd kill her with his bare hands. It only seemed fair. If she would have died the first time, he wouldn't be in this predicament. But here he was, two years later, locked up for life, like an animal.

"I heard from the grapevine you're some kind of private eye. Are you looking for my daughter?" he asked, breaking the silence growing between them. If she didn't do it, like she said, he needed her to find his daughter. For the life of him he couldn't figure her out, so he'd have to be careful. "You say you *care so much*, what have you been doing since she disappeared?"

"I don't have to explain myself to you."

"Maybe not, but I'm asking as a father," he said.

"Ha! You call yourself a father just because you have sperm. No, Jimmy, you're no father, you're nothing but a killer."

He ignored her attack and continued, "What have you done to find Isabel? What are the police saying?"

"I'm not one of your thugs, Jimmy. I don't work for you."

He clenched his jaw and considered how to respond. He

could play her game and attack her right back—did he need her that bad? Or could he swallow his pride? With his thumb under his chin, he rubbed his nose with the side of his finger up and down, thinking. He'd been through an anger management class when he first arrived. Maybe it helped him now. He relaxed.

"If you care about Isabel, like you claim, then we need to work together," he said.

She scoffed, shaking her head. "I'm here for her and only her."

"No one will tell me anything," he continued. "All I can do is sit here and do nothing!"

"You think I would actually help you?" she spat.

He bit his lip, holding back. "Do you want to know what I know or not?"

She blinked.

"I had nothing to do with Isabel's disappearance and I don't know anything about Max. She may be my half-sister, but I never had a relationship with her, and I never asked her to come visit me."

"That's it?" she probed.

"I think she's a prostitute."

She laughed. "Makes total sense," she nodded and continued, "When she's not finding a home for orphans, she's working the streets. God! You must be losing it in here. I may not like her, but really? A prostitute?"

"Shut up and listen for once and maybe you'll learn something! You don't know everything. One of the prisoners who got out recently paid for sex with her just a few weeks ago."

She scoffed, still not believing. "I need a name."

"Roberto Dominguez. But he didn't refer to her as Max, he called her Angel."

"How do you know he wasn't feeding you a load of shit?"

"Roberto did time for soliciting a prostitute and second-degree assault. When he got out, he didn't want to get caught again. He learned of a man who ran a business, sort of a mix between an escort agency and a brothel, completely under the radar. He was given a book with pictures of the women, like some kind of menu. He had it all from age, gender, race, you name it. This was his first-time having sex in eight years, so he asked for the best and was willing to pay for it. 'In that case,' the man told him and pulled out another photo showing him a picture of Angel, or as we know her, Max."

"Did you ask Max about this accusation?"

"Hell no. What she does is her own business. Until now." He could see she didn't believe one word out of his mouth. He was wasting his time. He'd have to deal with Max on his own.

TWENTY-NINE

M ABEL LEFT THE PRISON DUMBFOUNDED. SHE didn't trust Jimmy one bit. He had certainly never given her any reason to. He also had nothing to gain by lying to her. She recalled the desperate look on his face. The only way to know for sure was to find Roberto. With luck, he'd lead them to this mystery man and possibly Max.

In the car, she told Frankie everything. He didn't seem quite as surprised as she had been. He turned the ignition and said, "Where can we find this Roberto?"

"Old Colorado City. He lives with his sister, Elena Dominguez."

Frankie dialed Philip, "Find me the address to Roberto Dominquez, Colorado City, sister Elena Dominguez. The house should be listed under Elena. Roberto was released from prison in the last couple months." He listened, throwing in a grunt here and there, hung up, and turned to Mabel. "He'll look into Roberto. He's sending over the information from Max's phone. None of the numbers are repetitive aside of her work number, a couple of her coworkers, the prison, Isabel's, and Susan's. He went through the calls coming and going in the last six months and he found something."

"What?" she asked, her heart speeding up.

"A pattern. One number, each week, called in and out and then suddenly stopped. Then another number called in and out for a week, then stopped. This has been going on for the last few months."

"Burner phones."

"Has to be."

Mabel thought about it. "What about this last week? Were there any calls around the time Isabel went missing?"

His phone beeped, "Let's find out," he said opening an email. They had yet to drive out of the parking lot, the ignition still running. "Look at this," he said pointing to Friday, two days prior. "She made three calls while at work to the same number and once more that night." He swiped up. "Look," he handed her the phone. "According to Philip, the phone number of the week, was called daily. Like every single day."

What the hell? she thought, trying to decipher the information. If Max was truly a prostitute, did this mean she did it willingly? Or was she working under fear? "Do you think she's being trafficked?"

"I don't know, but it's possible. Her silence could mean one of two things. She knows something and is afraid, meaning the same men selling her are the same men that took Isabel; or she had something to do with it and is on the run."

"So which is it?" Mabel asked, more to herself. She tried to put herself in Max's shoes. If she were being trafficked, free to live another life but owned just the same, she would run the first opportunity she had. What did they have on Max to keep her quiet? On the other hand, if she were involved, why put a target on her back and let them take her niece?

"Well, what do we know for sure?" He counted on his fingers, "She's related to Isabel," he said, holding his thumb out.

"And although most children know their abductor, the chances of it being a female relative, aside from the mother, are low."

"She knew the person, or persons, and opened the door for them." He added his pointer, counting off. "Max disappears after her niece goes missing and she only met Isabel six months ago."

"Isabel knew her attacker. She could have opened the door to a number of people."

"Or, the attacker could have been waiting for her inside the house. Maybe he or she didn't have to break in. What if Susan left the door unlocked?"

"Are you saying Susan may be involved?"

"No. But you know as well as I do, you have to look at all angles and sometimes it's the one you least expect."

"Max disappearing could mean she's a victim, too."

"We can't say for certain until we have more information." He started the car and pulled out of the parking lot at last.

She looked at the prison thinking what a tragic life Isabel lived.

Is she alive? Either way, she'd find her. If Max had anything to do with . . . she hated thinking about it.

How can one family be so evil?

THIRTY

THE THING ABOUT SECRETS: SOONER OR LATER someone will talk. Frankie told her everything about his night. Mabel imagined the streets of downtown Colorado Springs speaking in hushed tones. The secrets of Ugly Lady Gaga, who didn't say much and didn't have to. The fact she was there, on that corner, was enough. Finding Max two blocks away from where she lived, drunk, in a pub she frequented. Learning she never showed interest in men until Dreads walked in. The idiots who followed Frankie into the alley who saw him as a threat, and they were right. Last, finding stillness in the heart of the city.

Someone knew something. All they had to do was find this someone and get them to talk. People were more apt to talk to private investigators than the cops.

Downtown is where they would find the answers to their questions. As they neared Cimarron Avenue, Frankie switched lanes to take the exit, then pulled over a few blocks later to drop her off at the corner of S. Cascade. "You start here, and I'll start on the other end, near Fillmore. Meet me in the middle," he said.

She nodded. The distance was just over three miles. As he drove away, she took in her surroundings. The Women's Pro Rodeo Association—she'd never been—was directly in front of her. Across the street from there, to the west, stood a credit union; catty-corner was a bank, and to the south, the visitor center. People walked by, dressed in their Sunday best and suddenly she felt out of place. She crossed the street toward the visitor center, wondering if traffickers hung around these kinds of places to snatch the out-of-towners.

As she crossed the street, the sun wrapped her exposed skin in warmth. When she reached the other side, a goth girl bumped her shoulder as she went by. If she hadn't done so, Mabel probably wouldn't have given her a second thought. She turned to see Goth Girl stride down the street with a purpose. Her posture rigid as she walked and her head volleyed side to side as if she were looking out for someone. Goth Girl took a right on the next street and Mabel followed her nearly six blocks. She crossed the street once again and disappeared inside a thrift store.

What was so urgent in a thrift store on a Sunday? Maybe she was late for work. Mabel jogged across the street after her, ignoring the honking cars who sped by. An old lady approached the entrance and Mabel quickened her step to hold the door open. The lady scowled at her and entered the store.

Her heart fluttered when she spotted Goth Girl looking through racks. *Not an employee,* she thought. The girl looked in the direction of the entrance but paid no attention to Mabel and the old lady. Instead, her eyes continued to skim the store.

Who is she looking for?

Mabel casually glanced through clothes and made her way closer to the girl. Like Mabel, Goth was not shopping. She, too, went through the motions. She had to be waiting for someone. But who? On a typical day she wouldn't care or even notice, but her gut told her there was something off about the girl and to wait with her for whomever was supposed to walk through the door.

She was a young girl with jet-black hair that just reached her shoulders. Her hair was wavy, but her bangs were straight and touched the tips of her long black eyelashes. Thick eyeliner made her light blue eyes pop and her black lipstick and spiked dog collar topped off her goth look.

There were only a few shoppers to begin with and all, except the old lady, were looking through children's clothes.

The door chimed and Goth's eyes widened as a man entered the store. *Secrets*, thought Mabel, as the man looked straight at the girl, paused momentarily and scanned the area. He looked back at the girl and gave her a nod, subtle but noticeable to someone watching. Slowly he made his way to the girl and Mabel moved in for a clearer view. They'd done this before. No one in the store, aside of Mabel, paid any attention to the scene playing out.

No hiding, in plain view for anyone to witness, but nobody did, because everyone had their own lives to worry about.

This kind of ignorant behavior made corruption possible. Not that the average person was to blame. She took a deep breath and reminded herself to stop thinking so much. At some point, she had to learn to shut it off. If she didn't, those she loved were the ones to suffer.

The man walked down the aisle, passing the girl, but not before bumping into her as he did. She'd seen it before, on TV, the bad guy or sometimes good guys, passing information onto another. Goth shoved a piece of paper into her front pocket and the man was gone, in and out in under a minute. The girl watched him leave and put back the pants she had been holding.

"You're about the size of my niece," Mabel said holding a

shirt up to the girl. "Do you think she'll like this?"

The girl froze, her light blue eyes wide, her pupils dilated. She shrugged and walked out, again in a hurry. Did she have a home? Or live on the streets?

Mabel hurried after her, but the store clerk yelled out for Mabel to stop. She had forgotten about the shirt in her hands. Tossing it on a table filled with knickknacks, she pushed the door open. She caught a glimpse of the girl at the end of the block. The girl looked back, saw Mabel, and broke into a sprint. She was fast, but Mabel was faster.

It didn't take long to catch her. "What are you running from?" Mabel asked.

"Please," she begged, skittish about who might see her talking.

Mabel pulled her into the closest store, an auto shop, and said, "I'm not going to hurt you."

Tears sprang to Goth's eyes and she wiped them, visibly mad at herself for showing any kind of weakness. "Please don't take me in," she spoke fast.

"I'm not who you think I am."

The man behind the counter, with a receding hairline, shouted, "Hey, I don't want any trouble. Take it outside."

"Walk with me," she told the girl, grabbing her by the arm. "We need to talk."

The girl obliged and Mabel wanted to scream. Nothing about the situation was right. The auto shop man turned a blind eye even though the girl was clearly afraid of Mabel. A little kindness wouldn't hurt, would it? Then she thought of Isabel. Taken from her home. Someone saw something, they just turned a blind eye, like the auto shop man.

"Can I buy you lunch or a soda or something?" Mabel asked.

"I can't be seen with you," she said. "They'll think I'm talking to the police." The girl's blue eyes darted around, never quite holding eye contact.

Mabel turned and said to the auto man, "We need your help."

"Help? What kind of help?" he asked.

"My friend is in trouble and needs somewhere to hide out."

"I don't want any trouble," he repeated.

"Someone's following her. Just give us five, ten minutes max."

"You stay you buy something," he responded.

"Fine, but we need to stay out of sight."

He looked around the store. "How about I call the cops instead?"

The girl cringed.

"That won't be necessary," Mabel replied.

At last, he looked at the girl and asked, "Is she bothering you?"

"No," the girl said. "She's helping me."

He grunted. "Five minutes. If you get caught back there by my boss, I'm fired."

"I understand. Five minutes," Mabel promised.

He led them to a small space filled with rows of inventory, much neater and cleaner than she had expected.

When he left, Mabel glanced at her watch. "What's your name."

"What do you want?" Goth asked, completely ignoring her question.

"To help you and . . . maybe you can help me, too."

"I don't see how I can help you."

"How long have you been on the streets?"

She shrugged.

"Where do you sleep?"

"What's it to you," she replied.

"I'd like to help you, but you need to tell me how. What do you need?"

"Money," She looked her straight in the eye for the first time.

"I can't just hand you money . . ."

"Times up then, gotta go."

"Wait. Have you seen this girl?" Mabel held out her phone and Isabel's face smiled back at them. A picture she'd taken on their last hiking trip.

"She's pretty," she replied. "She run away?"

"No. She was taken . . . we think."

The girl still had the photo. "I don't know her, and I would remember if I've seen her."

"Are you sure?" Mabel pressed.

"I'm sure!"

"I think she's being trafficked."

"I don't know what that means."

"Used for sex, sold for labor. Forced to work the streets or kept somewhere and men come to her. Do you know of a place, where she may have been taken?"

The girl looked away, "No." Mabel spotted track marks on her hands. She guessed if the girl removed her jacket, she'd have them up and down her arms.

"Come with me. I can find a place for you to stay."

"I don't need a place to stay, I need money."

Torn on what to do, Mabel pulled out a fifty and handed it to her.

Her eyes widened in surprise. "You have more?" she asked.

"What do you plan on doing with it," Mabel asked.

"I'm hungry and I have friends who haven't eaten in days."

"What did the man in the thrift store give you?"

"You need to leave now," the auto man demanded. "My boss just called and he's on his way."

"One more minute," said Mabel. "What did he give you?" she asked again.

"An address."

"For a job?"

"Yes."

"Can I see it?"

"For another fifty," she said.

Mabel pulled out a hundred and handed it to her. The girl smiled. Mabel didn't let go, "First the note."

Goth girl pulled it out and handed it to her, yanking the hundred out of Mabel's hand.

The note read, *528 Night Owl Drive, 7:30 p.m.* Not wanting to trust such important information to memory alone, she used her phone to take a picture of the torn paper. Handing the note back along with her business card, she said, "Call me when you see this girl."

Not if, but when. The girl looked young, too young to be turning tricks.

"Why haven't you answered your phone?" Frankie accused. "You know the rules. I drove all the way here and looked all over the thrift store for you, and guess what? You were nowhere to be found. Then I see you're a few blocks away. Do you know the things that went through my mind?"

He'd pulled up behind her as Mabel left the auto store, heading north. She opened the door and got in. "I hope you know how crazy you sound right now," Mabel replied. They tracked each other for protection and Mabel didn't need protecting at the moment.

"Fuck crazy, Mabel. You know the rules."

She wanted to argue, but knew he was right to an extent. They had agreed. If one of them wasn't where they were supposed be, then call or text the other to let them know. She hugged him. "I'm sorry I didn't message you. But I have a lead." She smiled trying to lighten his foul mood. "I followed a girl here and got this address from her." She pulled out her phone, messed with it and handed it to him.

"What's this?" he asked.

"The girl I followed is a prostitute and her pimp gave her this address. She's supposed to be there at 7:30 p.m. tonight."

He studied the address. "You think Isabel will be there," He pointed at the phone, "tonight?"

"I don't know, but we're going to find out. I showed the girl a picture of Isabel and she didn't recognize her. I don't trust her denial."

"And she just handed this over to you?"

"Not happily, it cost me." She suddenly wondered why he came to her. "Why are you looking for me already? I thought we were meeting in the middle?"

He rubbed his head. "Philip called with the address to Roberto Dominquez."

Everything is starting to come together!

She no longer felt a million miles away from Isabel. They could be heading in the complete opposite direction as Isabel, but she preferred to think they were inching themselves closer. The day was still early, and they didn't have to be at Night Owl Drive until 7:00 p.m.

The car had yet to move. Eager to get moving, she said, "Let's go."

"Look at this first," he said as he clicked at his phone and then handed it to her.

She looked at a spreadsheet, with no idea what it all meant.

"It's the detailed information from Max's phone," he continued.

Yes! The information she'd been waiting for. This would tell her for sure if Max had anything to do with Isabel's disappearance.

"It's all separated by calls, notating the questionable ones."

"My god, it's like a web of stories. Bless you, Philip!" She couldn't believe her eyes. He had phone numbers with names, addresses, dates, and times, all attached to a call, text, or email. Damn, he was good. Her eyes focused on one text that read, *13 oz meat, 23.5 EA #2.* She showed him, "What does this mean?"

"You got me. It looks like she either eats a lot of protein or she works part-time at a meat market."

I doubt butchers text this kind of information. Then again, she knew nothing of the meat business. *What was the name of that company where you buy—*

"Omaha Steaks!" she shouted.

"Yes," Frankie replied.

She imagined Max in a yellow truck driving around town selling meats and seafood. She tapped her fingers on her temple to think. There had to be more to the texts than Max working at a stupid meat market. The texts were similar with different numbers, then stopped abruptly a week ago. There were secrets here to be found, she just needed to put it together, like a puzzle.

At last, Frankie said, "First, we visit Roberto, then we go back to Doc's and brainstorm. We can use someone not so close to it all."

She agreed. The temperature was rising fast and the car was heating up. She imagined a thermometer, the mercury expanding and rising in the tube as it heats up. That was her brain, all the intel they'd gathered rising and soon her head would explode unable to hold more information.

Frankie parked in the driveway of a little white house, on a street where all the houses looked the same. The only distinguishing feature was the paint. There was a brown Buick parked in the drive. Could it be the one following her? It looked oddly familiar.

A woman stepped out dressed in a yellow top and black pants. "Can I help you?" she asked, her voice edgy.

Mabel smiled as she neared the front porch. "Hi, are you Elena Dominguez?"

"Who's asking?"

"I'm Mabel and this is Frankie."

"And? What do you want with me?"

"We're friends of your brother, Roberto."

"I doubt that," she replied. "Him maybe," She pointed at Frankie. "Did you do time with Roberto?" she asked.

Frankie stepped out and put his hand out. "I did. I got out before him and thought I'd see how he was holding up."

"He's holding up fine and doesn't need whatever problems you bring with you."

"Oh, no, ma'am, I'm clean. Roberto is a good man and I wanted to see if he needed anything. There's too much temptation on the outside and when we get clean inside, we tend to stick together."

Her features softened. "Do you like biscochitos? I just made a batch. Come in and I'll make some coffee."

"Thank you," Mabel responded. When the lady turned for them to follow, Frankie whispered in Mabel's ear, "They're delicious." He had a huge smile on his face. She'd have to trust him because she'd never heard of it, but it sounded like a bread.

The screen door creaked when she opened it, the house was cool and smelled musty. The furniture appeared old, but in good condition. In the kitchen Mabel pulled out a wooden chair and sat, Frankie did the same. Elena set a plate of cookies in front of them and put water to heat on the stove.

"These are delicious," Mabel said. The cookie light and flaky, with cinnamon sugar sprinkled on top. There were little brown seeds inside that tasted like licorice.

Elena beamed, proud to share her good food. "Thank you. I got the recipe from my mom, God rest her soul. She was a good cook and I feel I don't hold up to her quite yet. My brothers fought over everything she had and all I wanted were her recipes."

"How many brothers do you have?" Mabel asked.

"Three. Roberto, Jose, and Antonio. It's just me and Roberto here, the other two live in New Mexico where we grew up." She poured water in two cups and set two canisters on the table along with creamer. "I don't know how you like it, so help yourselves." She sat down and took a bite of a cookie. "What do you want with Roberto?" Before they could answer she went on to say, "He's asleep. He found a job working the night shift, so he doesn't get in till six in the morning and he sleeps most of the day."

"I hate to wake him," said Frankie, "but it's important. I have to admit, I was never in prison and I only know your brother through another inmate whose daughter is missing—"

"And you think Roberto had something to do with this girl?"

"No, no, nothing like that. But we're hoping he might know someone else we can talk to."

Elena audibly let out her breath. "I don't know. He just got out a few weeks ago and—"

"Please, Elena," Mabel uttered. "This girl just turned thirteen and she's in danger. Every minute that goes by is another minute she's out there. We don't think Roberto had anything to do with it, but it's no secret your brother pays for sex."

"He would never hurt a child . . ."

"We know, but he can possibly lead us in the right direction. You have our word, his name will not be mentioned to anyone."

She thought about it for a minute and stood up. "Follow me. He isn't going to be happy to talk to you two and I'm not about to tell him why you're here. You can do that yourselves."

They followed her through the living room, down a short hallway and through the closed door on the left. "Roberto, wake up," she said. "You have visitors. Roberto," she put her hand on his shoulder and shook him.

As he roused from a heavy slumber, he muttered, "What do you want," but instead it came out, "Wha wa."

She turned, "He's a heavy sleeper," she explained. Giving him a good shake, she raised her voice. "Get up. You have company."

He rolled over and opened his eyes, startled to see two strangers staring at him. "What the fuck, Elena! You just let cops into my room."

Elena started to explain, but Mabel took over. "We're not the police. I'm Mabel and this is Frankie. We're private investigators working a case for a missing girl and we're hoping you can help us."

He was clearly upset, and she didn't blame him, she would be, too. "I don't know nothing about nothing," he exclaimed. "Hand me my pants, will you?" he demanded. He could have been talking to her, but she didn't care to see him get dressed.

"We'll be in the living room while you get ready," Mabel said. She turned just in time to see Elena throw his pants at him. She gave Mabel a look like she knew hell would come later.

Frankie took the seat closest to the door and Mabel sat in the only chair next to the kitchen. Roberto was forced to sit on the love seat furthest from the front and back door. They often had to prevent a perp from escaping. Of course, he could always go out the window in his bedroom. It wouldn't be the first time someone tried and failed.

Two minutes passed before Roberto entered the living room, hair a mess but thankfully dressed. Irritated, he stared down Frankie.

"I'm not here to measure dicks," Frankie said. "Have a seat so we can get this over with and we'll be on our way."

Always so subtle, thought Mabel.

Roberto sat. "Who did you say you work for?" he asked. He looked just like his sister, if she grew ten inches, gained a hundred pounds and cut her hair short.

"We don't work for anyone in particular." Mabel handed him a picture of Isabel and Max.

"What am I supposed to do with this?" he asked.

"Just look at the damn picture," Frankie shouted.

Mabel gave him a look to let her handle it. They weren't there to brow beat him. "Have you seen the girl before?" He looked down at the picture quickly and shook his head no. "Look again. We know you haven't been out long, but we also know you like the ladies."

"How about the little girls?" Frankie added.

Goddammit, Frankie, let me handle it. He had his way and she had hers. Roberto's eyes looked scared. "I've never had sex with a minor."

"How do you know, do you ID them before?" Frankie couldn't help himself.

"Listen," Mabel said, "we just want to find her. We're not the police and you're not going to jail. Now look at the picture carefully, she may have changed her identity."

He studied the picture and Mabel hated to think what went through his mind. "I don't know. I don't think so . . . but I know her," He pointed at Max.

"Her name is Max," she kept her face expressionless.

"Nah, her name is Angel. I hooked up with her a couple weeks ago. I tried to find her Friday night, but she was preoccupied at the time."

"What do you mean, preoccupied?"

"I don't know. I figured she was with another man who paid for her all night. I don't have that kind of cash. She's expensive, but worth it, if you know what I mean." He smiled showing yellowish teeth and Mabel shivered.

"You went back for her?" she asked. He nodded, which meant he knew where to find her. "Where did you go?"

"I'm not telling you that! What do think I am, dumb?"

"No, Roberto, we don't think you're dumb. Angel is missing, too, as of this morning," Mabel explained.

"I wouldn't worry about that. Some men like the women all weekend. If someone rolling in dough hired her, then don't expect to see her for a while. You know, like *Pretty in Pink*, shit. I have to say, if I had millions, I'd probably do the same."

Frankie rolled his eyes. Mabel knew he was beyond his limit in bullshit and he would beat the man until he told them what they wanted to know. She didn't have much time to get it out of him peacefully.

"We didn't come here to bring trouble, but we're not dumb either. I suggest you tell us what you know."

He looked at her and then Frankie who conveniently had his hand on his waist to signal he had a gun and wasn't afraid to use it. He scratched his head thinking. "Ah, fuck it. Elena," he yelled out. She poked her head out of the hallway. "Grab me my wallet, will you."

She disappeared and was back in under a minute and handed him a thick, dirty, brown wallet. He opened it up and searched through cards he'd shoved inside. "Here it is," He reached out to Mabel and handed her the card.

"Colorado Springs Medical Group, Doctor Brady," she read. Roberto shook his head and made a gesture with his hand to flip it over. She did, and her body relaxed. They were another step closer to finding Isabel. "3750 N Cascade," she said.

He bobbed his head up and down.

"Who's the boss?" asked Frankie.

Roberto sucked in his lips as if to prevent the name from slipping out. He let out a breath, "I'm not positive, but there was a black guy there both times I went." His eyes darted to Frankie. "Smaller than the both of us and he looked like a kid himself. I'd say nineteen, twenty. He had a afro, thin mustache and facial hair, but not a lot." He looked down, "There were girls there, too, but I didn't have anything to do with any one of them. The second time round I hooked up with a lady that had to be in her late twenties or early thirties. I swear."

Mabel's heart sped up and her throat tightened. This could be it.

Frankie stood up, "Thank you for your cooperation," He shook Roberto's hand and held it. "If I find out you touched a little girl, I'll be back for you," And he let go.

Mabel could see Roberto's Adam's apple move up and down. He nodded at Frankie.

Frankie got up to leave, but Mabel remained seated. She

stared at Roberto, wondering what was going through his mind. Frankie was staring at her, but she kept her eyes on Roberto.

"Don't you have something else you want to share?" she asked.

"No . . . I . . . I don't know what you mean."

"I think you do. Why are you following me?"

He stood up with nowhere to go. Frankie pushed him back down on the sofa. "Start talking."

"Jimmy told me to."

No surprise there. Jimmy must have known she'd figure it out this morning after he gave her Roberto's name. Did that mean he trusted her now?

"But he called earlier and told me to stop," he added.

"Take my advice, don't do anything Jimmy tells you to. He's a murdering psycho in for life." She got up and walked out with Frankie following.

As they walked to the car, Frankie mumbled, "Mother fucker!" and shook his head.

Mabel wanted to drive straight over to the address Roberto had given them and demand to see Isabel. But it didn't work that way. They needed a plan. They now had two different addresses, and a whole lot of information to decipher.

At Doc's she sat on a stool at the kitchen counter. Doc walked in and kissed her on the head. "Hi, Mabel. Did you two eat yet?"

"I'm fine," she said glancing up.

"Speak for yourself," said Frankie. "I'm starving!"

She glanced at her watch and the time read 1:30 p.m.

Already? Her stomach growled and told her she needed to eat despite her not wanting to take the time to do so.

She was grateful when Doc opened the refrigerator and pulled out meats and cheeses. "What do you make of this?" she asked, turning her iPad around so he could see it. She pointed to one of the texts.

"Looks like steak prices to me," he said.

"That's what we thought, but I'm not so sure."

"Why are you asking?"

"It's a text from Max to all these random numbers."

"Let me see," He grabbed the iPad and scrolled through the list. "Hell, if I know." He looked at Frankie "What do you make of it?"

"My gut says Max is into some weird shit and she has something to do with Isabel missing."

Personal feelings aside, Max seemed like a nice enough person, but who sent texts like this? She turned to see her grandpa coming down the hall. He dragged his feet as he walked, something he never did before.

"How's it coming in here?" he asked. He kissed her on the cheek and took the seat next to her.

"Philip sent over the information from Max's phone."

"And?"

"And it looks suspicious."

"You'll figure it out. You got your brains from me." He smiled and she couldn't help but return one.

"How was last night?" she asked. Frankie'd already filled her in, but she asked anyway.

"Eye opening. You wouldn't believe the number of young girls out there." He shook his head. "We found one hotel and two apartment buildings."

"Most of them were not much older than Isabel," Doc

added. "I'm guessing a couple were younger . . ." he paused, "Wait a minute, what if the 13 represents an age? Look here," He pointed to *13 oz meat* on her computer screen.

Baffled, she responded, "Max is a pimp?" First Max is a prostitute, now it looks like she's pimping. Which was it?

"No . . . I don't know. Maybe." He paused, thinking, and then added, "I think *13 oz meat* stands for thirteen-year-old girl . . ." he paused again, "and *23.5 EA* could be the time, like 11:30 p.m."

"I don't get it. How do you get 11:30 p.m. out of 23.5?" she asked.

"Military time," her grandpa replied.

"Exactly," Frankie said, excitement in his voice. "This one says, *15 oz meat, 21.00 EA #4.*" He looked at her as he said what she didn't want to hear. "Fifteen years at nine o'clock."

Her eyes closed voluntarily as she struggled to control the feeling taking over her body. The touch on her arm, brought her back.

Her grandpa removed his rough hand from her arm. "Look, they do most of their business at night and the ages range from eight to twenty-six, but most of them are between nine and sixteen. They all end with double zeros or five before EA and none of them above 23.5."

They were both right. Her not wanting to believe didn't change the awful truth staring back at her. "What does *EA* stand for? And the number following the pound sign?" she asked.

"Not sure," they said at the same time.

"That one's a mystery," Doc added.

"It could be the location," Grandpa suggested.

"I'm going to be sick," Mabel stood up and took a deep breath. "If this is what we're all thinking, then Isabel *is* being trafficked and Max *is* behind it." She closed her eyes and swallowed hard. Deep down she hoped they were all wrong.

"Didn't you say Max works in foster care?" Doc asked.

She nodded as his words sucker punched her in the gut. "Max has access to hundreds of kids." She felt the blood drain from her body. "I swear if Isabel is being trafficked because . . . She's going down." Mabel said under her breath.

"Let's not get ahead of ourselves," her grandpa said, putting his hand on her shoulder. "We're guessing here; it's all a shot in the dark."

"And a damn good one," she added, her hands on her face. "God, I'm freaking out," she said. "We need to get this information to the Feds and Burton. Right now, they have more resources than us."

"I agree," Frankie said. "I already sent it to Corneal. Don't forget we still have the address you got from the girl."

"What address," her grandpa asked.

"It's a long story, but we have another lead."

"Great!" he said.

While they had been talking, Doc made sandwiches. He put a platter in the middle for them to take, along with a few other sides and drinks.

"Every time I think of food, Isabel pops in my head." They all stared at her. "I mean, is she eating and drinking? Is she warm, or is she crying and afraid?"

Frankie set half a sandwich before her. "Eat," he demanded. "We have a long day ahead of us."

She did, otherwise she'd never hear the end of it.

Did traffickers kill their money makers? she wondered.

THIRTY-ONE

WITH ONLY THREE HOURS TO THE MEXICO border, Max Gallo stopped. She couldn't do it. She left thinking of herself only. She'd convinced herself there was nothing she could do, she had no choice. But she did have a choice. She could save Isabel for the cost of her own life.

Now, parked in front of Martha's supermarket in Vaughn, New Mexico, she couldn't put the car in drive. In her forty-two years of life, she'd never once given up hope.

Hope. A desire for something good to happen.

Why would it? In the past year, she'd done nothing good. And now, here lies the question eating her up. Would running away make it any better? She couldn't honestly say it would and that went for the life of those around her. The guilt over the last six months had already been killing her slowly.

Truth?

She left because she couldn't handle it, everything coming at her at once. Brandon. Isabel. All those kids. How could she live with herself? She should have run the first time Brandon made her have sex with other men.

She should have left when Brandon made her send children

to him. It had all gotten out of hand. Then she met Isabel, and everything changed. And now, he has taken it all away, like he took everything else.

A little girl, about four, caught Max's attention. She had jet black hair that ran halfway down her back in waves. She looked straight at Max and wiggled her little fingers. She had the longest eyelashes and biggest eyes Max had ever seen. Her lips moved as she tugged on her mom's dress who struggled to load groceries into the back of their SUV. Max gasped when the mother handed the little girl a doll she'd just bought. The little girl hugged the box and pointed to Max, her lips moving. The mother turned her attention toward Max. Startled, Max sat up and wiped her eyes. A tap on the window. Unsure what to do, she bowed her head. Another, harder, knock. Figuring the lady would never leave, she rolled down her window.

"Can I help you?" Max asked looking into the dark pools of the little girl's eyes.

The woman spoke broken English and responded, "*Mi hija* asked I check on you. *Estás bien?*"

"I'm fine."

"*Estás perdida?*"

She didn't know what to say. She spoke a little Spanish but couldn't remember what *perdida* meant.

"Uh, you lost?" The woman nodded.

"No," replied Max, shaking her head. "*Es bonita.*" Max smiled.

"*Sí. Gracias.*" She smiled back, worry spread over her. She grabbed her daughter by the hand and led her away.

Max watched as the mother-daughter duo drove away and imagined her mom doing the same. Memories flooded her mind, memories she hadn't thought of in far too long. Her mom did the best she could raising Max on her own. They didn't have much money, but her mom always found a way to put food on the table and keep her entertained. She didn't have many toys, but she remembered her fourth birthday, when her mom had surprised her with a Baby Alive doll. It wasn't new, she'd probably got it from Goodwill, but it was hers. She could still feed it, change it, and bathe it. Her mom made diapers and clothes by hand so Max could change her and dress her. She hadn't thought of her doll in years, but seeing the little girl with hers brought back buried memories. After her mom died, she never saw that doll again.

What am I doing? Oh my god, what have I done?

Before she could change her mind, she turned on US 54 E, and headed back to do what she should have done long ago.

THIRTY-TWO

EARLIER TODAY, GOTH GIRL HAD LOOKED fourteen, maybe fifteen. Now, as she walked up to the house on Night Owl Drive, she looked like a twenty-something hooker. Makeup coated her young face and she wore five-inch gold platforms and a tight black dress with the neckline plunging down to her belly button. Mabel had to look hard to be certain she was looking at the same girl.

"That your girl?" Frankie asked.

"Yeah, she looks like a—"

"Prostitute," Frankie finished for her.

Mabel let out a breath. A big white bald guy with tattoos and piercings opened the door and waved the girl in. He looked like the muscle, the bouncer, or security guard. "That can't be who she's meeting."

"Nope. This is a whore house."

"Are these girls trafficked?"

"My guess—this is a legitimate whore house. It's better than a car or alley for them, so they do it."

"It's disgusting!" she said wanting to take the words back. Goth Girl, whose name she didn't even know, was homeless and didn't do this because she chose to.

"I'm calling Burton," she said. Just then a white SUV pulled into the driveway and two black men stepped out.

"What the hell?" Frankie shouted. "He's one of the two fuckers I took down last night."

Mabel grabbed the binoculars from Frankie and looked closer. "He's half your size. Couldn't have been a fair fight."

"You should have seen the other guy." He grunted.

"What do you want to do?" she asked.

"Call Burton. We stay put until backup arrives."

Burton was tied up, but promised to send officers. They didn't have to wait long.

A cruiser pulled up and Frankie cursed, "Son-of-a-bitch! It's going to take more than two men to take that place."

She nudged him. Four more cars pulled up and parked around the block. Mabel watched as men swarmed the house, the first two officers went to the front.

"Now that's what I'm talking about!" Frankie shouted, slamming his fist into the dash. An officer headed straight for them and Frankie rolled down his window.

"Did you call this in?" he asked.

"Yes, I'm Franklin Dowdy and this is Mabel Peters."

Mabel watched the police file out of the house with men and women and girls in handcuffs. When Goth Girl came out, Mabel felt a pang of guilt shoot through her. She was just another person to let her down.

"Hey, that's Ugly Lady Gaga!" Frankie pointed at a woman accompanied by an officer. He'd told her all about the incident, her hooking in front of Max's apartment and him getting into it with her pimp.

"I bet she's not even eighteen." She sighed, thinking of Isabel, the one person she hoped would walk out the door.

She never did. Grief washed over her.

THIRTY-THREE

THERE WERE RULES EVERY GIRL HAD TO FOLLOW. First; do as you're told. Sounds simple until you're told to do something unimaginable. Second; don't make eye contact unless told specifically to do so. Easy enough, she didn't want to see any of the men who worked there, especially the customers. Some of the harder rules made it impossible to live; don't talk, fight, scratch, scream, or cry. If you did, you were beaten or worse. There's always worse. And the most difficult rule of all; don't try to escape. Isabel had already been beaten, sexually abused, and didn't care if they killed her; so how much worse could it be.

Jackie warned her not to do anything stupid, but she couldn't live another night like the one before. So when they filed up the stairs she hid in a closet. When the hall was quiet, she opened the door, right into Mr. B himself.

"Well, what do we have here?" he asked.

"I . . . I got turned around," she lied.

Disappointment spread across his face and his big hand landed on her cheek, blood spraying out of her mouth and nose. "Now look what you made me do."

Tears rolled down her face and before she knew what was happening, he grabbed a fistful of her hair and dragged her across the room. She needed the bathroom earlier and didn't go, a decision she now regretted. The sweats they'd given her to wear were now drenched in urine. When he realized what she'd done, he picked her up by the arms and threw her against the wall.

"Davis! Get in here and take care of this mess."

A man she'd seen earlier ran into the room with eyes wide. "Yes, boss." His eyes landed on the heap against the wall. "What should I do with her?"

"Strip her down, clean her up, and put her on the wall."

"Yes, boss." This must be a thing, because he didn't argue. Mr. B left and Davis said, "You shouldn't have angered the boss. It's never good when the boss is angry." His words came out soothing, but Isabel felt nothing but shame. He led her to a large bathroom with a shower and told her to take her clothes off, but not before locking the door behind him. She did as he said, because she didn't want to think anymore. He followed her into the shower, and she imagined she was elsewhere.

When he had his way with her, Davis placed a red cloth over her eyes and tied it around her head. He tied one limb at a time to the leather straps anchored to the wall, making her into a human starfish. Unable to see, she sensed every person who entered the room stare through her. Tired and scared and hungry, she dozed off a few times, to be woken by someone touching her.

The deep gasps of girls told her they were brought to her to see what happens when you try to escape. "Oh, Barbie," she heard Jackie murmur. When a different man came to get her down, she was told she would go right back up after work.

"I don't think I can," she whispered.

"You don't have a choice," he said matter of fact. "Here, take this, it will help with the pain." He handed her a glass of water, which she drank every drop, two pills, and a slice of bread, which she gobbled down.

Jackie ran to her the moment she saw her enter their room. "I told you. Dammit, Barbie, do you want to die?"

Isabel nodded. There was nothing she wanted more.

"God, now I have to worry about you killing yourself. Did you know if one of us dies when we're together, the rest of us pay for it? If you want to hurt yourself, go right ahead, but don't be dragging us into your mess."

Her mess. She did this, because she never listened. Whatever the man gave her started working because she soon felt no pain.

No one would come to save her. She wondered if they were even looking for her. With her gone, everyone's life would be simpler. Maybe this was where she belonged.

THIRTY-FOUR

THE DAYS LEADING UP TO ISABEL'S ABDUCTION

THE MORNING AIR FELT COOL ON HER MILKY white skin. Max opened her eyes, focused on the clear blue sky behind the white tip mountain peaks. She needed an escape. A whole new start, away from her past and present. Where could she go? They'd find her. Sooner or later.

At one point, she thought she could make a difference. Once upon a time, she'd been good at her job. She'd been good enough to move up to supervisor and well on her way to director.

Her buzzing phone startled her. "Shit", she mumbled, glancing at her watch. She couldn't be late. Locking the sliding door behind her, she missed the second call. He'd call until she picked up, so she might as well answer. She didn't need him showing up at her work.

As predicted, her phone buzzed again. "What?" she said into her phone.

"Today's the day." The words came like nails on a chalk-board. "Make it happen," he added.

"I'm already running late to work." It didn't matter what excuses she had, but she tried anyhow. Picking up her purse and keys, she locked the door behind her.

"You want me to do it?" he asked, his voice firm.

No, she didn't. But she didn't want to do it either. "No. Listen, I have to go."

"Maxine," he sang her name, "my beautiful Maxine."

Her skin crawled.

"Aren't you going to tell me you love me . . . like you used to?" His voice was smooth, like it used to be.

"No." The words came out weak and she hated herself for it. She hated him.

He started to laugh and hung up.

She let out a sigh of relief. Brandon Jones scared her to death. How could she fall for such a sick bastard? She fell hard, too, head over heels, before he turned into Satan. There was a time when he made her feel young and beautiful.

Girls night out, her best friend said, not taking no for an answer. Why hadn't she said no? She was too old to fall into peer pressure.

A night out turned into bar hopping and throwing back too many martinis. She didn't want to be there, and after a few she started to feel numb, just like she'd hoped. She saw him coming long before he made it to her table. He wanted her and she knew it. His eyes scanned the room but continued to come back to her. She'd never been one for dread locks, but she couldn't imagine him any other way. The whole vibe he had going on: dread locks, muscles, good looking, confident, and one fine body. She'd seen plenty of his type but found herself stealing glimpses of him.

"Hi," he said, his voice deep. "You are one beautiful lady," His eyes kept hers, not noticing her girlfriends gawking. "May

I," he asked. Her friend Lisa jumped up and still he didn't acknowledge her, he simply took her seat. Her heart beat a million miles an hour. In her line of work, she'd met the bottom of the barrel in creeps and thought she knew what to look for.

They talked, they laughed, and he invited her for coffee the next morning. He didn't ask to come over that night and he didn't ask her to join him. They went their separate ways. Dumbfounded, she couldn't believe how much of a gentleman he was. They met for coffee the next morning and it was spectacular.

This one is different, she told her dead mom. In a letter her mom wrote, she said, *If they don't treat you good, leave them.* And she'd always done just that. The years flew by and at forty-two she found herself alone, but she didn't care. She never needed a man to make her happy. She'd been disappointed too many times to worry about it.

At her office, she poked her head into her boss's sanctuary, what he called his little office space. "Coffee?" she asked.

"Yes, please. We still on for ten?" he asked. Her boss had a small potbelly but insisted on wearing a collared shirt much too tight with his dress pants tucked below his protruding stomach. He rested his hand on it often like a pregnant woman. He said his wife was too good of a cook and he couldn't say no to anything she put in front of him.

"I'm going to be a little late. I have a meeting with Josh and the Perkins family at nine. We might run a little past ten.

"Oh, right, the Perkins. No problem, fill me in when you're done."

"Got it," she said.

She hurried out of his office and made her way to the small room that doubled as their break room and supply room. Filling her own cup, she took a sip making sure it was fresh.

Satisfied, she filled a cup for her boss and added a little cream.

His door was closed when she returned, and she could hear his muffled voice. Tapping the door before opening it, she poked her head in. He motioned for her to come in and continued his phone conversation. She set his coffee on his desk not sure rather to wait or come back because she needed to talk to him about leaving early, she stood there looking around the office she already knew by heart.

He hung up, "Perfect timing. You need to be in court this afternoon. I know it's last minute, but Sylvia just called and said she can't make it. Her mother was just taken into the emergency room."

"Not again," she replied. Sylvia always had emergencies. Her mother, her uncle, her son—you name it. She had no empathy for the woman.

"I know, poor dear."

Every part of Max screamed inside, but on the outside, she wore a straight face and replied, "I'll be there. I already went through the case files, but I'll go through them again to make sure I haven't missed anything." She had to be there, being the supervisor. She had nothing to argue about. She closed his door and everything she'd been holding back hit her at once. Feeling weak-kneed and as if she might hyperventilate, she rushed to her own office and shut the door.

How was she going to tell Brandon she couldn't do as he asked? How would she convince him to wait? When it came to his business, he was an arduous and cruel man.

Pulling up the file labeled, Boyden, she clicked to open it.

The mother had been charged with a DUI . . . again—her fifth. Only this time she hit a pedestrian in the crosswalk and fled the scene all while her four-year-old was in the back seat of her car. He'd been placed in foster care previously while she served a two-year sentence. After cleaning herself up and working with the system, her son, Caleb, was able to go back home last month.

She rubbed her forehead. Her day had only begun and the she felt the early onset of a migraine. The job had been tough on her in the last year. You had to have a certain kind of strength to do what she did, and your heart simply had to be in it. The tough cases—seeing what kids went through—can mess with your mind. She'd had a hard childhood, but she wouldn't begin to compare it to what some of these kids endured.

She called Brandon. Best to get it over with.

"Miss me already?" he asked on the first ring.

"Today's not going to work. I have—"

He cut her off, "I don't care about your excuses. I've heard them daily for the past three weeks. It's always something and I think I've been more than patient with you, Maxine. Now get me what I want, or I'll get it myself," he huffed.

"Wait. If you'd just listen. I have to be in court," she hissed. "I don't have a choice. One of my case workers called off."

"Fine. I'll do it," he said.

"No," she said too loud. "I will . . . tomorrow. She's sleeping at a friend's tonight; I'll do it in the morning."

"I want a two-for then," he said.

"You're sick. I already said I'd do it."

"You owe me. Come over after work. I have a job for you."

She didn't say anything.

"Maxine? My beautiful Maxine? I'd hate to think you hung up on me."

"What do you want."

"I want you—naked. All night long." He hung up the phone.

There was a knock on her door followed by Josh letting

himself in. *Every freaking time!* Just because he knocked first, doesn't give him the right to barge in without being invited.

"You okay?" Josh asked, sitting on her desk acting like a damn cat. He actually looked concerned.

"I'm fine."

"The family's here. I set them up in the conference room." Josh was her newest hire who did everything by the book.

"I have chairs for a reason. Why don't you use one?"

He jumped off her desk and made himself comfortable. "Oh, right." Like she'd never reminded him before.

He had a degree in criminal justice, unlike hers in psychology. She could see him as her boss in a few years. Aside of him acting like a barnyard animal, they were a good team and she found it hard to hate him.

Why didn't she ever fall for someone like Josh?

She thought of all the men of her past and lumped them into the same category—tall, dark, and handsome—which until now, she hadn't realized her love life was based on such a cliché. No wonder she was still single.

Josh may not be tall, dark, or handsome, but he was smart, compassionate, attentive, kind, dependable, and honest. Everything a woman wants in a partner. He was like the fifth in line to the throne with no chance of being king, but more noble than the king himself. Unlike the tall, dark, and handsome asshole who treated her like a piece of meat.

She needed to be rescued with no one to rescue her.

Foster care shaped Max into the strong independent person she used to be. Consumed by the impostor staring back at her, she longed for the strong version of herself. She leaned in for a closer look. *Disgusting*, she whispered, thinking of the night prior and what she'd had to do. *You're weak, and ugly, and a dirty whore! I despise you!* She grabbed the first thing her fingers touched and slammed it into the mirror. Glass exploded cutting her hand. Dropping the small stainless-steel canister, she fixated on the biggest shard, unfazed by the clanking across the floor.

How easy it would be to end this, she thought.

The shard reminded her of geometry class. Always an A and B student, she had received her first C. Shapes and angles weren't her thing, but she knew the shape of the stupid shard she couldn't get her eyes off. A scalene triangle—each side had three different lengths and the angles had three different measurements. Why did she remember? Did she know subconsciously her life would come to this? She held the shard to her wrist, shaking. Blood dripped from the hand holding her weapon, her grip tight. It reminded her of life.

His words echoed— *Bring her to me. If you don't, everyone you work with and love will pay.* She dropped the glass, knowing he would do it. Her living, or not, wouldn't change their destiny.

In her bathroom she found the remaining gauze from her wrist injury three months prior. Her first of many injuries caused by the man she thought she loved. When Max finished tending to her hand, the doorbell rang sending a shiver through her body. She quickly cleaned her blood-stained sink and hurried to the door. It could only be one person and he didn't like to be kept waiting. Her heart hammered as she peeked through the hole.

Here we go, she thought as she straightened her shirt, took a deep breath and let it out slowly in an attempt to calm her nerves. She opened the door and the sight of him standing before her caused her stomach to do a weird flip sending what can only be her coffee back up. She ran to the bathroom without a word. She felt his presence, watching, laughing. The thought made her heave more as she hung onto the toilet.

"I figured you wouldn't be ready, so I decided to come early. I know you all too well baby and we wouldn't want you to break your promise."

She continued to heave trying to drown him out.

When she finished, he added, "Oh, I brought you something to eat." And she heaved again. "It's on the counter when you're done being dramatic." His tone told her he was losing his patience.

She cleaned herself up and found him eating an egg croissant in her kitchen. The smell made her nauseous.

"Sit," Brandon said. "Yours is there," He pointed at another egg croissant across from him. She didn't move quick enough for his liking, so he took out his gun and set it next to his half-eaten croissant.

She glanced at the lady who had come with him. She'd been standing in her living room looking around, keeping quiet. "What's the plan?" She looked at the clock on her stove. "She's a teenager. When weekends roll around, she sleeps till noon." She'd known her for six months and knew she never slept in.

"Call her," he demanded. "Find out when she'll be home."

Her heart beat faster. "I can't, it'll be on record."

"Then we go and wait. I have the time."

Part of her wanted to go for his gun on the table, but she'd never be fast enough, and he'd shoot her. And if he shot her, he wouldn't kill her. Brandon didn't kill his assets.

"Someone will ID our car," she said. "We can't be seen hanging around."

"You have little faith in me, my love."

They'd never link this back to him. He was careful, with everything he did. He stood behind her and kissed her neck. She shivered as his lips touched her skin. "My darling Maxine,"

He pointed the gun at her temple, "you should use the brains in that beautiful head of yours more often." He turned her to face him, the gun still pointed at her head. "You're lucky your body is so fine," he added, grabbing her ass and sticking his tongue down her throat. She bit down knowing she'd pay for it later. He grabbed a handful of her hair and pulled, hard, glaring into her soul. After a few seconds he laughed. "You're a naughty girl, aren't you? You know I like you naughty, but we have business to do." He turned and gestured toward the lady watching.

"Meet your ticket out of being a suspect," he said. As the woman came in closer, Max thought she could have been her clone. If he had her, why did he need Max? He smiled, "Teresa is your alibi, baby."

She pleaded, "We don't have to do this. You can pick anyone. You have plenty of girls already. Why—"

He held his gun under her chin, running it along her jawline, landing it in her mouth. He licked his lip. "Damn baby, you're hot. And you're mine. All mine. Which means you do as I say. Besides," he said, dropping his hand and gun to his side, "I'm doing this for you."

"I never asked you to."

"You didn't have to." His nostrils flared. "Fuck! How many ways do I have to show you how much I love you? Have you forgotten what your father did to you? This is for you. Now stop arguing and appreciate the fucking gesture!" He swung the gun around as he spoke.

Desperate, she dropped to her knees. "Please, Brandon," she cried, grabbing his shirt and meeting his eyes. "Please don't do this. I beg of you. I *don't* want this. My father's dead. My mother's dead. I don't want retribution. I forgave him a long time ago and my mother wouldn't have wanted this. I don't want this."

For a moment, she saw the Brandon she fell in love with, his eyes, his mouth, his face. He knelt to her level and said, "I'll do it." The moment gone. "But you're coming with me. I don't trust you."

Deflated, she dropped her head. This was all a game to him. She could never change his mind. Once he had a target in sight, they were his.

He said to Teresa, "Get her ready. You have ten minutes."

Teresa pulled Max to her feet and led her to the bedroom. Max sat slumped over on her bed. She'd never seen Teresa before. How long had she belonged to Brandon? The whole time she'd begged Brandon, this lady watched in silence, no remorse, no feeling. It'd do Max no good to reach out and beg this lady, she lost herself years ago. Somewhere Max was headed.

Teresa removed the black wig from her head and placed it on Max, revealing her natural blonde hair. Max thought she looked like her clone before, now she was her identical twin. She proceeded to apply makeup on Max, she guessed sloppily. Finishing up with fake eyelashes and lipstick, she directed Max to take her clothes off. She didn't argue. They swapped clothes in silence.

When done, Teresa said, "Don't fight it, Hon. Brandon and I go way back. I knew him as Derek back then. I don't even know his real name. Once you're in, you never leave." She straightened Max's hair and added, "There. Now I'm you and you're me." She smiled.

If she went to the police, what's the worst that could happen? Teresa took Max's hand in hers and said, "Whatever you're thinking, don't do it." Max pulled her hand away. "I had a sister . . ." she paused. "Anyway, it doesn't matter now. Stop fighting Brandon. You think you have it bad now?—Believe me when I say, you don't. You haven't lost everything, yet."

"If he takes Isabel, I won't have anything to live for."

"You think you're better than the rest of us? You're not, and the sooner you get *that* baloney out of your head, the better. So stop arguing, stop begging, and just do."

"Help me get out," she pleaded. "I have to save her. There's still time . . . please. You don't have to do this."

She laughed. "That's laughable." She shook her head. "You don't get it. He'll find you. He always does. I've paid more dues in ways you can never imagine. I'm not going down for you."

Every part of her bruised and scarred body screamed for her not to give up hope. If she lost hope, she'd die. "Please, one woman to another, I'm pleading for mercy."

"We're done here." She opened the door and walked out taking any hope Max had left.

Brandon entered and looked her up and down. "You look good baby. Now let's go."

"I thought . . ."

"Oh, I almost forgot to ask you, how's your brother? Last I heard he didn't get along with some inmates. I'd hate for him to die because his sister *thought*. So stop thinking and know I'm taking care of everything." Brandon always thought two plays ahead.

She was in deep and didn't see any way out. She had nothing, yet he always found a way to make her follow orders.

She glanced at the gun sticking out of his pants.

THIRTY-FIVE

PRESENT DAY

JOINING THE MILITARY WAS THE EASIEST decision he'd ever made. Coming from a military family, he never felt as if he had a choice. It was an expectation. So when Frankie turned eighteen, he enlisted, and found it suited him. Even when he married Raven, his career worked; that is until she gave him Helena. He made a promise then to find another career where he could be with them every day.

He'd been too late. Raven and Helena died in a house fire, when he should have been there to protect them. It ripped him wide open. For a tough guy who could lift a car off someone if need be and make split-second decisions, he wasn't fast enough to save his family.

Not knowing anything else, he became a Green Beret. It came easy, too easy. Sometimes he let himself believe that it was his calling, why he was put on this earth and his wife and daughter were a small part of greater things to come.

It wasn't until he met a man years later who'd told him the story of his youngest daughter, who'd been missing for over a year. The police were convinced she'd run away, and she didn't want to be found. Frankie practically jumped at the chance to rescue her and bring her home. He did and the enormous shell he'd built started to crack. The enriching experience gave him a purpose—to save children, because he couldn't save his own.

He'd being doing just that for the past twenty-three years and every child he saved, he remembered Helena.

He watched Skinny Black and all the Johns file out of the house, the same scumbags he'd dealt with most of his life. They were a reminder to him—there will always be more of them. He didn't have to like it, but he knew he was helping by reducing the shithead count in the world, one by one.

Ugly Lady Gaga, anyone's daughter, stepped out, her face hardened knowing what was to come. He could tell by her face this isn't the first time she'd been caught prostituting. What she needed was intervention, not a jail cell. As much as he wished he could help her, he'd done his part. Isabel was a different story.

He picked up the phone and dialed Corneal. "She's not here."

"We're doing everything we can to find her. This bust was a win."

"The asshole I told you about last night is here. Can you get to him?" Skinny Black lied about not working with minors. He should count himself lucky Frankie didn't barge in there himself.

"I'll find a way. What do you think he knows?"

"The weasel lied straight to my face. He knows more than he let on. We may have removed him from the streets for now, but he's working for someone."

"The man with dreads?"

"Bingo." Max popped in his head. "Any information on Max?"

"None. We found her car parked at the ice arena and her phone has been disconnected. It's like she vanished."

If there's one thing Frankie learned, no one vanishes without a trace. They just had to look hard enough, where no one else thinks to look. "I half expected to find her in this shithole."

Mabel gave him a look telling him she'd thought the same. Her phone buzzed as he hung up his own.

What now? he thought.

She pulled it out and stared at the number across her screen. He leaned over, unknown number. Letting out a puff of air, she hit answer. The phone to her ear, her eyes grew.

"Max?"

THIRTY-SIX

ISABEL'S BLUE EYES FOCUSED ON THE BLACK curtain in front of her. The lie, the sense of hope. Her bed cover, still bat-shit green. A six-drawer light brown dresser stood against the wall. One drawer for each girl, but instead they shared everything down to underwear. Jackie told her if nothing fit, too bad because they wouldn't get anything else. They could request items, but it was never guaranteed they'd get it and when they did, it belonged to them all.

The room, the beds, the bedding, dresser, clothes, food, and private bathroom, were all a mirage meant to give the girls hope. Even the drugs, ones she thought she'd never take, were given to ease the pain, make her forget momentarily, make her not care what happened to her body—then taken away at a whim. Mr. B and his crew did this to prove they were in control, they owned you and your life was theirs to do with what they chose.

They were prisoners, sex slaves, nothing more. Mr. B, the puppet master and the girls, his puppets.

Jackie sat next to her. "Want me to do your makeup?" she asked.

Isabel nodded, and turned to face her. She opened a small black bag stuffed with makeup. Isabel never wore makeup. She'd asked her aunt once and she told her not until she was in high school.

"How old did you say you were?" asked Jackie.

She hadn't. Two weeks ago she'd been free to act like an ungrateful brat. She'd turned thirteen, hitting a milestone she'd thought would never come. She had a best friend, a boyfriend, an aunt, a dog . . . even a dad. She'd been mad at him for so long, but there was one thing she knew for certain, she wasn't taken from her home when she lived with her dad.

Sensing her unhappiness, Jackie said, "It's okay. You don't have to say. Hell, make up a birthday. You can be as old as you want." She dipped the brush in green and said, "Close your eyes." She did, seeing her dad. The soft brush swept across her lid. Jackie placed a hand on Isabel's shoulder to hold herself steady. Her warm hand—small, not giant and hard like the men from the night before—felt good against Isabel's skin.

"I shouldn't be here," she whispered, tears forming in her newly painted eyes.

"I'm sorry, Barbie, but none of us should." Jackie sighed and proceeded to apply blush across her pale cheeks. She made facial expressions as she worked, seemingly enjoying what she was doing.

"How . . . how old are you?" Isabel wondered, aloud.

Jackie paused. "Hasn't anyone ever told you it's impolite to ask a woman's age?" she asked, with one eyebrow lifted.

"I'm sorry."

She turned to see if anyone was listening. Satisfied, she whispered, "Sixteen, but don't tell the others. They think I'm nineteen." She continued working on Isabel, then added, "There. Now you don't look like a baby."

"I've never worn makeup before," she admitted.

"No, shit. Listen, in this work, the younger you look, the more trouble comes your way."

"But I don't—"

"Just trust me. The Johns—"

"The who?"

"The men who pay to have sex with us."

She cringed. "Oh."

"They like two types of girls. They like them young and innocent or young and experienced. Either way, they'll treat you like trash, but sometimes they can be rougher with the young ones. It's like breaking a horse. It makes them feel better about themselves."

She shut her eyes to remove the images, but the night before flooded in. *Don't cry, don't cry,* she scolded herself.

The door opened and one of the men entered with bottled water. "I come with the goods," he said.

Jackie grabbed hold of Isabel's wrist and she winced. "Oh shoot. Sorry. C'mon, let's get in line. Isabel followed her behind the other four girls already in line.

He handed each girl a small pill in their hand and then a water. They happily popped the pill in their mouths and drank it down, returning to what they'd been doing. Isabel followed Jackie's lead and when it was Jackie's turn, she nudged Isabel in front of her. The man looked at Isabel. "None for tonight, baby, you broke the golden rule."

"That's bullshit Tony, just give it to her."

"Nope. Bosses orders."

Jackie put her hand out and he placed one small tablet in her hand. She put it in her mouth and took a drink. He smiled and left the room. When the door closed Jackie took the pill out of her mouth. "Here, take it."

"But—"

"Just take it. You need it more than I do."

"What is it?" She thought of the pill she was given earlier which helped lessen the pain she had, but this one looked different.

"Angel dust. It's how they control us. They get you addicted so you'll do anything for them just to get more."

"Then I don't want it," Isabel shrieked. Did they get one the night before and she missed it somehow?

"Barbie, right now you have a choice. Tomorrow, they'll force you to take it and most likely beat you first for denying it. Believe me, you want this opposed to the needle."

"I don't want it," she held firm. She thought of Sam giving her a joint and how she trusted him and smoked it. She liked how it made her feel, but she couldn't bring herself to accept this one by these people who cared less about her well-being.

Jackie popped it in her mouth and swallowed. "Your loss. I was trying to help. It'll make you feel . . . less. Anyway, let's find you something to wear." She had on her clothes from the day before, holding on to some piece of her old self. She followed Jackie to her bed where she pulled out a suitcase hidden under her bed. She shuffled through clothes, satisfied with her selection and handed it to Isabel. "This is perfect! Put it on."

Nothing had been perfect since she left her aunt's house. She missed her room, the purple thick comforter on her bed, the purple and white curtains, the lights she had hung around her room. She missed her dad. She took a deep breath, held it, and forced the tears back.

With the bathroom finally free, she went inside to change, not wanting the rest of the girls to see her naked. It never bothered her before dressing in front of Abby, but she didn't think she could ever willingly allow anyone to see her naked again. She didn't like the girls staring back at her bruised and naked body, judging her for something she had no control over. She'd showered earlier in the day, now feeling like she needed to scrub every inch of her body, inside and out. Thinking of what she'd have to do that night made her sick to her stomach.

A single tear escaped, and she wiped it away.

Don't think.

I'm not Isabel, I'm Barbie.

She put her chin up, her eyes cold as steel.

THIRTY-SEVEN

MAX WORE BLACK JEANS, A WHITE T-SHIRT, AND black low heels. Her hair was pulled up into a mess on top of her head and she walked slow with her hands out to the side. The more Mabel thought of how stupid Max was, the angrier she got. Max may not have killed anyone, but she sure as hell is just as malicious as her brother.

What kind of man had Wilbur been to spawn such evil children?

"I'm sorry," was all Max could manage.

"Where's Isabel?" Mabel asked. She didn't care to hear how sorry Max was.

"I don't have her, but I know who does."

"Keep talking."

"Brandon Jones took her, but I don't know where."

Once inside, Frankie led Max to the living room where Doc and her grandpa waited. Max was in Mabel's world now, sticking out like a sore thumb. She sat obediently with her eyes somber, like she had something to grieve for.

Frankie sat and Mabel remained standing.

"Thank you for listening to what I have to say."

"*Don't* thank me," Mabel spat.

"I . . . I half expected to be greeted by police."

"What the hell were you thinking?" Mabel asked.

"I haven't been able to think clearly in months."

"Fuck you and your problems. I don't give a flying monkey if you drop dead right now. All I care about is Isabel."

Max dropped her head and said nothing. Doc and Grandpa both sat forward, taking it all in. Frankie put his hand on Mabel's arm and she pulled it away.

"What have you done?" Mabel accused.

"I never wanted any of this."

"I don't want your sob story, Max. Who has Isabel?"

"I met Brandon six months ago."

"He has dreads, doesn't he?"

She nodded. Frankie had been on to something.

"He had his eyes on Isabel the moment he saw her picture on my end table." Her voice trailed off.

"So you slept with him. Yay for you."

"It's not what you think," she argued. "He's the head of a trafficking ring. I didn't know anything for a month. Only after I'd fallen for him, when he knew he had me."

Mabel bit down on her lip. Her gun was still in her holster. All she had to do was pull the trigger and shoot Max between the eyes. But she knew she'd never do it unless it was her last resort. And she needed Max to lead her to Isabel.

"I was there, when he took her," she continued. "He made me. I put him off as long as I could."

"You could have gone to the police."

"You don't know Brandon. He would have killed me and taken her anyway and killed Susan just to prove he could."

"You could have come to me."

"Because you would have believed me?"

Mabel didn't respond. She would have investigated the accusations and been able to keep Isabel safe regardless.

"Did you help him take her?"

"No. He made me go, I think mainly to get into her house. The last time Isabel was with me I made a copy of her key."

"You dumb bitch! You did help him," she yelled, ready to rip her head off. Frankie stopped her and shook his head.

Tears ran down Max's face realizing she played more of a role in Isabel's disappearance than she was willing to let herself believe. Mabel didn't feel a shred of sympathy for her. What she wanted was to tell her off, tell her she was an accessory and she'd go to prison like her twisted brother. Instead, she held her tongue.

"And then what?" Frankie asked. "You waited in the house for her to come home."

Max nodded.

As the sun disappeared and daylight faded, Mabel thought of what the night had in store for Isabel. She was running out of time. If she didn't find her soon, she feared she'd lose her forever.

"She never saw me. When we left, Isabel was alive, but knocked out."

"Where did he take her?" Frankie asked.

"I don't know for sure."

"You were with him!" Mabel accused.

"I was, yes. But when he stopped at the corner of Colorado and Walnut, I got out and ran."

If Max could see the inside of Mabel's thoughts, she'd see an avalanche waiting to happen. Her mind fracturing, unstable from all the shit the Dumel spawn have dumped on her for years. If she didn't find Isabel tonight, she would certainly blow. She needed a hard, treacherous workout to let out all the pent up energy over the last couple of days. She should have joined Frankie on his workout that morning.

"Mabel, I am so, so sorry," she said breaking the silence. "I love Isabel."

Her hand palmed the butt of her holstered gun. Max's eyes dropped to Mabel's hand holding her gun.

"Go ahead and do it. I don't deserve to live."

Not yet. She didn't have the information she needed.

THIRTY-EIGHT

MAX NEVER EXPECTED MABEL TO WELCOME her with open arms, to sympathize with her, much less listen to her story. She admired Mabel in so many ways and she wanted to tell her so, but she'd never get the opportunity. If they both didn't have an attachment to Jimmy, to Wilbur, to Isabel, she could see them being friends. God knows she could use a friend like Mabel.

From what she knew, Mabel, too, had a rough life losing her family and all. They're similar in so many ways. Both their losses stemming from Wilbur, even if he wasn't the one to pull the trigger, he'd had a hand it, raising a demented kid who eventually took Mabel's family. Now, here Max was, the cause of taking another important person in Mabel's life.

Being in a room with three strong men, Max realized Mabel was surrounded by love and support. Something Max never knew.

Her mouth dry, she began to speak, her voice weaker than she would have liked. "Brandon has two houses in Denver, one in Grand Junction, one in Greeley, and one in Colorado Springs. But he works with other dealers who swap out the girls like used cars. If she isn't in Colorado, she could be anywhere."

Frankie, the man who tucked her in the night before, stared into her soul. His arms flexed, but not to impress her. He was ready to fight. He looked at his phone and sent a text to someone. She could only imagine the police.

"These houses will have to be hit simultaneously. That means we have to take a back seat on this." He looked directly at Max, "The police will come to take you in."

The words sent her heart beating like a freight train. She knew it would come to this, it was always inevitable. But not yet. She had unfinished business.

"Wait," she said. "He's been calling all day. He's so confident in his ability to manipulate me, he knows I'd never go to the police."

"How could he be calling you, when you left your phone in the car?" Mabel asked.

"The burner phone he gave me." Mabel threw her a look, telling her to drop dead. "I'll call him . . . tell him I was scared. He'll want me to go to him." When she left earlier that morning, she had planned to never see Brandon again. To run away and start over. She'd plan her backstory—with a family, a loving father, and a mother who was very much alive.

Mabel audibly let out a breath. "No. I don't trust you or Dreads."

"I don't blame you. Any of you. But please, give me a chance to make this right."

"You deserve nothing more than a dark cell in the middle of hell."

She'd get nowhere with Mabel. She turned her attention to Frankie, "Follow me, bug me, I don't care."

"Let's say we go along with this plan," John said.

"What?" Mabel shrieked. "Grandpa, you have to be joking right now."

"Hold on now, Mabes. There's no doubt we need to involve the police, but who would you rather trust with Isabel's life?"

"Not her!" she pointed at Max.

"Just hear me out." He fell silent, all eyes on Mabel. She nodded, rolling her eyes as she did. "I adore Isabel, but I don't have the connection the two of you do," He pointed at Mabel and Max, "which gives me the ability to think clearer than either of you."

Mabel made a face, disgusted at the thought of her grandpa lumping her and Max into one.

"You say he won't suspect you're working with the police?"

"He knows I would never do that." Max bowed her head. After a moment she looked up to Mabel, "I'm an accessory, he made sure of it."

Frankie stood, interrupting John's thoughts, and said, "Mabel. John. I'd like a minute with you before we decide on how to proceed."

Max watched the three exit the living room and disappear down a hall. She turned to the only other man in the room with her. She'd never met him before but heard about him from Isabel. Isabel had said when she grew up, she wanted to be a doctor like Doctor Melvin. He hadn't said a word since she came into his house.

"You thirsty?" he asked, one eyebrow up, scrutinizing her.

She wanted to ask earlier for water, her mouth dry and all, but feared asking. The taste in her mouth made her think of a public restroom—grime, urine, feces, dead skin—like she'd licked it. She could see Brandon making her do such a thing. "Yes, please."

He looked toward the kitchen, then back to her, then the front door. Thinking better of it, he said, "Come join me."

She did as he requested, taking the stool nearest the

refrigerator. The water felt cool and smooth down her throat. With her eyes closed, she swore she would get even, with or without their help.

There are nearly twenty million children living without a father present in their home. Max was one. She grew up never knowing her father. In her mind, all men were bad. It started when one killed her mom. She never saw his face, but could never forget his voice.

The man she never met. He'd come over, uninvited, every couple of months. His voice felt rough, like sandpaper, and forever mad and deafening.

Her mom would say, *Mouse (she called her Mouse), it's time to play our game. You go hide and whatever you do, don't come out. Can you do that?*

Yes, yes, she could. She didn't like the man with the rough voice, he scared her.

Her mom would open the door, next to the oven, and Max would climb in pushing the pots aside.

Now you have to be quiet as a mouse.

She'd scoot back making herself as small as possible and cover her ears.

Good girl. And don't come out until I come get you. Her mom kissed Max on the hand and shut the door taking all the light with her.

Her mom said the man with the rough voice came to visit because he was sick. Not like the cough and sore throat Max got every year, but sick because he drank too much poison and when he was sick, he was very dangerous. If she kept quiet as a mouse, her mom would take her to get a sundae. They were best with extra hot fudge.

One night, she curled up extra tight, screwed her eyes shut, and listened to her mom's footsteps cross the floor. The bolt turned and the door creaked open. Her mom's words were faint, but Max heard her say, *She's not here.*

He made so much noise, Max thought the house was falling apart.

"Will, NO!" her mom screamed, followed by a whack and a thud. "Please, don't do this."

Whack! Whack! Thud.

Footsteps and the door shutting.

When it was suddenly quiet, she waited and waited, for a long time, for her mom to tell her to come out. Afraid to speak or make any noise, Max stayed put for what seemed like forever. She fell asleep and when she woke, she found she'd peed. Something she did in her bed sometimes. Her mom would be mad.

She never came, like she promised.

What she didn't know at the time was that her mom lay dead just outside the cabinet door.

THIRTY-NINE

SUSAN WOULD SAY THE COLOR BLACK IS perceived as an indicator of prestige, power, and intelligence. Mabel agreed and disagreed. She wouldn't exactly call a thief or murderer prestigious or intelligent, and power is a perception. For her, it made her feel invincible.

Show time.

She stepped out, her long black boot hitting the pavement. The cool breeze rushed in, enveloping her face and giving her energy. Her black trench coat hid a black miniskirt and tight lace crop top. It served two purposes—prestige and power. The power being the small arsenal she'd tucked inside. And she felt like a hooker, exactly what she was going for.

Butterflies flapped like crazy in her chest incriminating her frightened mind. She'd gotten used to the feeling, relying on the dose of epinephrine to shoot through her bloodstream.

She walked past four houses, her eyes on the small house on the corner—3750 N Cascade, the same address Roberto gave them was exactly where Dreads told Max to meet him. There was no guarantee Isabel would be there, but it was a start.

The streetlight was out, and she wondered how often the

city replaced it only for it to conveniently die out again. On the outside, the house looked empty, no light flickering from within. Two more homes to go.

"Well, what do we have here?" asked the man blocking her from entering. He kept his chin high but looked down at Mabel. She had a hard time taking him seriously because his thin goatee and beard reminded her of a Pac-Man ghost and his bushy eyebrows were permanently raised in surprise.

"Hello, there," she said in a breathy voice. "Are you Brandon?"

She'd been wrong about his eyebrows because now they furrowed. "Who sent you?"

"My agency, the Promise Land." Max confided Brandon hired escorts to turn them into his own prostitutes, promising them more money than they could make with any agency.

"He didn't say anything about this." He looked over her to the left and right. Satisfied she came alone, he pulled her in. "Wait here," he said, closing the door behind her.

The small living room looked normal. If an officer or someone came to the door and were only allowed in the first room, they wouldn't be the wiser. The room was uncomfortably quiet, and she wondered if Max had set her up.

A man, not Pac-Man, came through the same door Pac-Man had disappeared behind. This one looked like he swallowed Pac-Man. Think Jabba the Hutt kind of fat. "What do you want with Brandon?" he growled, dribble leaking from his mouth.

Grossed out and before she could answer, a half-naked girl flew through the door on the right, wild and bug eyed. His head whipped around at the noise. "What the hell are you doing?" he roared. Not waiting for her to answer, he swung his right hand across his chest and whipped it back across her face. The impact hurled the girl backwards and she landed on the ground with a hand covering her red swelling cheek. Tears poured out her black eyes and she screamed. "Get your ass back in there!" he yelled, kicking her in the stomach.

Mabel bit down, withholding the urge to pull out her gun and use it on him. Another man— how many freaking men worked here?—rolled in after her. He picked her up like a rag dog and retreated, closing the door behind him.

Jabba turned back to face Mabel, daring her to challenge him. Giving away nothing, she said, "Do you treat all your girls this way?"

"Only the ones who don't behave. Are you someone who needs to be taught a lesson?" He looked her up and down, undressing her with his eyes.

"I'm here for Brandon. If he isn't here—"

"Follow me," he said.

She could only hope he'd take her where she'd find the girl. Instead he went left. Left led to a run-down kitchen consisting of all the essentials—sink, refrigerator, counter, cupboards, table and four chairs. Continuing through the kitchen he took her through another door. This one he had to unlock with a key. When he opened the door, he flicked the light switch and a single bulb illuminated the narrow space. Before heading down, he turned and locked the door again. A lock on the inside and outside?

The steps creaked as they descended.

She thought of the Geico commercial about making predictably poor decisions and how she should be running the other way. Too late now, the door was locked, and he heaved his way down the creaky stairs to what she could only presume was the basement. What waited for her, she'd find out soon enough.

He unlocked and locked the bottom door, like he had the one on the top of the stairs. On the other side she stared into

Max's eyes, then into a man with dreads who could only be Brandon. He sat behind a desk. There were two doors on either side of him, and two hallways on either side of her. With no idea who or what was behind the doors, she relaxed a little because she'd much rather see a desk than a chain hanging from the ceiling with a cement floor soaked in blood.

"Who in the hell is this?" asked Brandon from behind the desk, pushing Max away, who sat on the desk to his right. She'd caught the last words he'd said when they first came through the door, *This is going to cost you.* Max jumped off the desk and stood submissively next to Brandon.

"She says she's from the Promise Land."

"What's your name?"

"Star." Frankie had given her the name.

"I asked for Kitty."

"She has the stomach flu."

"And Monique didn't think of calling to tell me this?"

"I volunteered and she said you'd be pleased."

Brandon sauntered over making a full circle around her. When he made it back around, he said, "Show me what's underneath."

She smiled and removed her coat, draping it over her arm.

"Mmm, mmm, mmm. You are fine, and brunette!" He turned to Max and said, "Baby, go get started without us. We'll be right there." Max nodded in agreement. This had all been part of the plan and Brandon played his part to the T, just as Max said he would. It wasn't over yet, and Max could still screw her over, but she was here with the man who took Isabel.

"We? Am I the lucky one to join you two?"

He laughed out loud. "Shit! I like you."

She smiled and watched Max open the door to what looked

like a bedroom, looking back with fear in her eyes. What was she afraid of?

"Except, you're late," he added. "And I don't like to wait."

"I know. I'll make it up to you."

"Bet your ass you will." He grabbed her ass and squeezed, to show her he was in control and he'd do anything he liked to her.

She glanced around the room, noting Jabba retreated and a man with an afro guarded the door.

Max said every Friday, Saturday, and Sunday, Monique sent one girl for Brandon to do with what he wanted. In return, he allowed Monique to continue her high paying escort business. The men who came to Brandon for girls were the bottom of the barrel in warped minds. Monique had rich men with a whole lot of money. She even went to the extent of running background checks on them to protect the women who worked for her. Women, not minors. And if one of her girls got the tiniest scratch on them, she'd cut her ties with the client—all, except for Brandon.

"Joe, you're in charge," he said to Afro. He looked at his watch and added, "They have ten more minutes with the girls, and not a minute over or they pay double. The man nodded in agreement, unlocked the door behind him and from what she could hear, locked it behind him.

Brandon wrapped his arm around Mabel's waist and led her into the room where Max waited. Brandon frowned at Max, who stood by the bed, fully clothed. "Why aren't you undressed?" he asked.

"I thought we'd play a game with the new girl." Not knowing what Max was up to, she slid her hand under her coat, resting it on her gun.

"You're in no position to make decisions—"

"But—" In two steps, Brandon lunged at Max and punched her in stomach. She dropped to her knees from the blow, holding her stomach.

He stepped back, into Mabel's gun. "Put your hands up— slowly," she demanded, knowing full well, he wouldn't.

Like she expected, he reached for his own gun, but she got to it first. Every asshole like Brandon carried their gun in the small of their back. She whacked him on the side of the head with his own gun. Down came the rock, first hitting the bed, bouncing off and landing on the floor. He was out cold.

"Oh my god!" Max said, eyes wide. "You killed him."

"Not yet. We don't have much time. She pulled two zip ties out of her trench coat and tied his hands and feet. "Let's go."

She held the knob, turning it slowly, and peeked out into the room with the desk. No one in sight, just like she'd hoped. "Is there anyone else down here?" she asked Max.

She shook her head. "No. All the girls are upstairs."

"Including Isabel?"

"I . . . I don't know."

"Does this door lock?"

"Yes, Brandon—"

Mabel shut the door and searched Brandon for the key. Finding it in his front pocket, she took it along with his wallet and locked the door behind her. She handed Max her trench coat, "Put this on. You'll find another gun and more zip ties in the inside pockets." She hesitated, "Stay close." Max did as she said. Mabel turned and crept up the stairs, ready to fire. As they neared the top, she heard two men on the other side, talking. "I've got these two. Watch my back," she whispered. She knew Frankie would come barging in at the first sound of gun fire.

She threw the door open and the two men pulled their

weapons, but before they could get a shot off, she fired two, hitting both in the chest. She glanced back to a tap on the back door where Frankie stared in. "Let him in," she told Max, keeping the gun pointed at the two injured men rolling around on the floor. "And then tie them up."

She nodded to Frankie to say, Let's go. He raised his gun and fired a shot causing Mabel to jump. She hadn't expected it. Jabba, lay on the floor blocking the entrance to the front room. With no time to move him, she stepped over the large body as Frankie kept his gun pointing at the man's head. He'd already hit him in the chest, blood soaking his black shirt.

In the front room shouting could be heard coming through the door on the left. She opened the door and men were running towards her, half naked with their clothes in their arms. Frankie holstered his gun and took down the first two men with his bare hands. With no room to move, Mabel stopped a man, both hands on his shoulders, and brought her knee up, hard. He fell to the ground, calling her every bad word she'd ever heard. Two men came out with their hands up and they tied them up, leaving them in the hall.

"I haven't seen the one who opened the door to me. He's white, six foot, 190 – 200 lbs, tattoos on his neck and both arms, looks like Pac-Man," she said.

"He's outside, tied up." Frankie smiled.

Frankie took the rooms on the right, she went left. Girls were squatting in the corner, drugged and afraid. One room left. She opened the door and found a girl, naked and tied up. Not Isabel.

"She's not here!" Mabel shouted, all blood draining out of her. Frantic, she ran through the hall into the front room, and shots rang out.

Isabel!

FORTY

THEY'D LEFT HER ALONE IN THE KITCHEN. MAX couldn't believe her luck. There were three men in the kitchen, all tied up and hopefully dead. She knew each one, too intimately. They deserved everything they got.

What did that say about her?

She came back for one thing and one thing only.

Brandon.

She never had much to begin with, outside of money. But before Brandon, she had a heart. A damaged one, but one that beat like any other healthy heart. *Does a broken heart beat differently?*

She'd made two mistakes with Brandon. The first, trusting him. Her mom told her to never trust a man and she had listened, until him. She'd told herself he was different. It turned out, he was. Just not the different she had in mind.

Second mistake was allowing him into her heart, her mind, her soul. She'd never confided in a single person. People knew she'd grown up in foster care, that her mom had died and she'd never known her dad. But they only knew fragments of the truth. She showed them what they wanted to see. A broken girl who had turned her life around and made it.

Sometimes she believed the half-truths she told people. She forgot every bad thing she went through growing up in foster care. She allowed herself to feel good when a foster parent ended up adopting a child, good for the kid and the parents. She celebrated when a child was placed in the care of a relative or back with the parent who once beat them. She told herself . . . No, she forced herself, to believe it was in the best interests of the child.

Since she'd met Wilbur, she realized it was not always best to be put back with the parent or relative. What if Wilbur would have had custody of her after he killed her mom. What then?

Brandon came into her life when she'd needed him the most. After Wilbur died. It had taken only three weeks for her to confide in him. That was all he needed. Her deepest, darkest, secret.

After she tied up the men in the kitchen, she shoved her hand into Joe's pocket searching for the key. He was a lefty, so she found it deep in his left pocket.

The men were predictable, and she'd spent plenty of time in this dump to know where each would be. Brandon, she knew, would be hidden away in the basement acting like a businessman when he was nothing more than a twisted man who took advantage of weak women and girls.

The door at the top of the stairs was already unlocked. No one else had come from that direction since her and Mabel. She hurried down the stairs knowing the bottom door would also be unlocked.

In the open room, she wondered why, if Mabel didn't trust her, she left her with her trench coat and weapons. Did she know what Max had planned? One of the many things Isabel had told her about Mabel, was she had a good heart.

She doubted anyone ever said those words about her.

Max had zero sympathy for Wilbur when he died. None. She remembered how it had felt when she learned he'd died within the hour after her visit. The only regret she had was not being there to see the light go out in his eyes, see his chest motionless, his face freeze, his cold heart stop beating.

No one could ever blame his death on her, but she'd known exactly what her visit would do to him. She'd known he had a weak heart. When she went to the nursing home that day, she had hoped he would die.

No one knows, but after Isabel and Susan left the nursing home, she told Wilbur what she knew. She told him everything down to her mom hiding her in the cupboard to keep her safe. Except, she told one lie. She told him she saw him. She told him she saw him kill her mom in front of his daughter and she planned to tell Isabel everything.

The next time she saw Isabel, Wilbur was being buried six feet underground. She thought she would feel relief, but instead her heart broke in two. She'd taken a family member from Isabel sooner than expected. He didn't deserve it, but Isabel loved Wilbur. She looked up to him, she confided in him, and he held her, hugged her and placed soft kisses on her head. A man, capable of murder, incapable of being a father, had family who'd loved him.

And Max had no one.

Until Isabel. She had a niece and a brother. A badly broken brother, but still family. She wanted nothing more than to be Isabel's aunt. To be the person she now confided in, spend quality time with at the zoo, the museum, the beach, anything. She had a niece.

She'd been around hundreds of kids in the worst type of

situations, and even though she felt compassion, she never felt . . . intimacy. Her bloodline led to this beautiful little girl with her whole life ahead of her. Max vowed then to do anything to be in Isabel's life.

She walked across the room, eyes on the desk, half expecting Brandon to be seated behind it in his black worn leather chair. She moved the key from her left to her right and stuck it in the deadbolt, to the door on the left. It clicked. She dropped it in Mabel's coat pocket and slid her arms through the sleeves. The coat came to her knees as opposed to just past them like it should. Max had six inches on Mabel. Other than that, it fit well.

Entering the room, her eyes fell to Brandon, splayed out on the floor. No longer a victim, the room felt different. Now the bed looked even dirtier and it told all her dirty stories.

Brandon lay on the floor, lifeless. Was he dead?

She approached cautiously, knowing to never take Brandon for granted. She held the gun from Mabel's coat and pointed it at the heap on the floor.

"Get up," she demanded.

He didn't move, but she knew he wasn't dead. His chest rose ever so slightly. She kicked him in the groin, jumping back afraid he'd grab her leg.

"Fuck!" He yelped, with fire in his eyes.

"I knew you weren't dead."

"You're going to wish I was after I get done with you."

"I said, get up!" She would not play his games.

He stood. His hands were still tied with the zip ties Mabel had put on earlier. "Give me that," he pointed his bound hands at the gun in her hand. "You're going to hurt yourself."

Don't listen to him.

"Come on baby. I'm sorry. Things will be different. I promise."

He's lying.

He looked at the door. "You need to trust me. I'm not going to hurt you."

Liar.

The gun wobbled from her trembling hands. Her eyes burned, her body felt hot and sweaty. She hated him. He'd done this to her. "Don't," she managed.

He reached out his hands. "Give it to me." His eyes were gentle liars. She could see it. He inched forward and she squeezed the trigger.

"I hate you," she said, firing again. "You can't hurt me anymore." She fired again. "And you will not take the only family I have." She fired again. Tears streaming down her cheeks. She screamed at the top of her lungs and emptied the gun into every part of his body. Every part he ever used to touch her.

FORTY-ONE

FAINT SHOTS CAME FROM ELSEWHERE IN THE house along with a piercing cry.

Without a second thought, Mabel had bolted passed Frankie, through the front room and into the kitchen. Men were tied up, shouting. Max was nowhere in sight. At the top of the stairs, she threw the door open, gun drawn, pointing at the door at the bottom of the stairs. Frankie touched her shoulder, letting her know he had her six. She could hear nothing more than the men shouting above her.

What if Max let Brandon out and he killed her?

She came to a halt before opening the door at the bottom of the stairs. Brandon could be standing on the other side waiting for her. She aimed low and Frankie aimed high.

"You ready?" she asked, and threw the door open to the empty room with crying coming from the left where she'd left Brandon.

She went low and left, Frankie went high and right. The same strategy they used every time, ready to take out whoever stood in their way.

After clearing the halls to their right and left, they

both hurried to the open door. All that could be heard was whimpering.

Inside, Max sat on the bed, wiping tears from her face. She turned as they entered and stared straight ahead. "He can't hurt me anymore," she said. She didn't show signs of pain.

Mabel's eyes fell upon the heap on the floor. The man with dreads, lifeless; blood draining out of his body from all the places he'd been shot.

"God," Mabel whispered. She did to Brandon what Mabel had only dreamed of doing to Jimmy.

"Max," she said. Her name came out harsh, not soft as intended. Isabel was still missing, and she couldn't help but fear she may be too late. "Where's Isabel?"

The spell she'd been under broke and she looked at Mabel confused, fear taking over. "Oh god. What have I done? I . . . I thought she'd be upstairs, with the rest."

"She's not. Where else would she be?"

Max's eyes fell to the corpse, oozing blood everywhere. "He . . ." she paused, and fell to her knees over him, beating his dead body with her fists. "What did you do to her?" she cried.

Is this what she had planned all along? Her only intention to kill Brandon.

Frustrated and angry, Mabel stormed out of the room. On her way out she saw the key sticking out of the keyhole in the door. She wiggled it free and handed it to Frankie. She still had the one she'd taken from Brandon's pocket earlier.

This is what happens sometimes, she told herself. At times the intel you received and bet someone else's life on didn't always pan out. It came down to trusting her gut. When would she learn to not second guess herself?

The first door to the right, led to a bathroom. No Isabel. The next door led to a bedroom with six beds and one dresser. No

Isabel. Her heart sank thinking Isabel stayed in these conditions. She ran to the other hall. As she passed the open room, Frankie was tying Max to the chair.

First door, bathroom, no Isabel. Second door, a bedroom, much like the first—six beds and one dresser—no Isabel.

"Mabel!" yelled Frankie. "I found her."

Adrenaline shot through her. She ran out of the second bedroom, into the open room, and her eyes met Max's who then dropped her head with her hands laid out in front of her.

"In here," he shouted. The other small room, to the right of the desk. Why hadn't she checked that one first?

As she turned the corner, Frankie was giving Isabel CPR.

"I'll call 911," she croaked.

"Already did. They're on their way."

Mabel knelt next to Isabel's legs and held her hand. Her two fingers naturally feeling for a pulse as Frankie continued to do CPR. There was none. They were too late.

"Don't stop," she begged.

He didn't, his giant hands making her look so small. She was completely naked, her body bruised badly from head to toe. Blood puddled from between her legs.

Her throat tightened, and she found it hard to breath. *Please Isabel*, she thought. *You can do it sweetie. Just breathe.*

Isabel moved.

"Stop!" Mabel shouted to Frankie. "Isabel, Isabel," she soothed, nudging her leg gently. She didn't want to hurt her any more than she already had been.

Her eyes opened. Her big beautiful blue eyes. Mabel looked past the smeared eyeliner and mascara. She pushed Frankie away and inched herself till she was next to Isabel's head. She looked drugged. The marks on her arm confirmed it. They'd drugged her.

"Hi, sweetie," she said.

Isabel tried to speak, but nothing came out.

"You don't have to speak. Save your strength."

Noise came from above as the police raided the house. She didn't want to take her eyes off Isabel, afraid she'd slip away if she did. Frankie's strong hand squeezed her shoulder, telling her he'd take care of everything.

In her time working with Frankie, she'd seen a whole lot of sickness in the world. To think that three years prior she thought the worst thing in life was growing up without a mom and dad. Girls like Isabel had to go the rest of their lives reliving everything they'd gone through while being held captive. The slightest touch sending them spiraling down into an abyss where they had to learn to fight their way out, learn to love again, and learn to forget.

Isabel's eyes were closed. Instinct told her to slap her, to wake her, but she couldn't. She couldn't bring herself to hurt her anymore. She put her hand gently on her shoulder. "You're safe now," she assured her.

Isabel's eyes flickered, trying to focus on Mabel.

FORTY-TWO

TO THINK, ONLY THREE SHORT DAYS AGO MABEL had visited Jimmy Dumel in prison. Now, she waited for his half-sister, Max Gallo, to walk through the door. She'd been right about her, yet in some way she felt guilty, as if her poor thoughts made Max the person she turned out to be.

The heavy door opened, creaking as it did. In walked two guards, with Max in the middle. Despite Mabel's dislike for her, she had always identified her as beautiful, poised, and resilient. The beauty she once saw had vanished. But even though she had been a victim herself, she held her head high as she walked over to where Mabel waited.

She stared at Mabel as the guard attached her chained hands to the table. She'd have a lot of answering to do for her actions, but she owed Mabel nothing. In truth, Mabel wasn't sure Max would accept her visit, but here she was, eye to eye.

"Why are you here?" asked Max when the guards left them.

"I could ask you the same thing," Mabel replied.

Momentarily Max looked confused, then it hit her. "You think you know me, but you don't."

Mabel never claimed to know her, she only had a gut feeling

about her and sadly it was worse than she had imagined. She didn't reply because she hadn't come to defend herself. It was Max who needed to do the talking.

Max looked away for the first time, glancing at the table next to theirs. Another prisoner sat with whom she presumed to be her mother. Satisfied they were not listening to their conversation, she said, "My lawyer told me to keep my mouth shut, but . . ." she bit her top lip and her chin quivered. "Listen, I just want you to know that I never meant to hurt Isabel."

Mabel sat silent.

"*She* was the best thing that has ever happened to me."

Max had no reason to lie, but why did she feel the need to say it out loud, it wouldn't help. Mabel felt no sorrow for the lady who sat shackled before her.

"You need to know, so someday you can tell her the truth. She *needs* to know the truth!" She twisted in her chair. "Can you tell her? Please." Her eyes were pleading now, her face suddenly pained.

Mabel stared at her for a few seconds, then said, "I promise you nothing."

"Fine. I . . . I see . . . and I don't blame you. But you need to hear me out."

She didn't need to do anything, but she wanted to. Something inside her told her to stay.

"This whole mess, my life, it started when my mom met Wilbur, fell in love, and ended up pregnant."

She already knew Wilbur was her father.

Wait? Is she saying this is some type of twisted payback!?

Suddenly defensive, Mabel glanced at the guard who was looking the other way. She wanted to reach across the table, it couldn't have been more than three feet, and slam Max's head into the metal. "I sure hope you're not saying what I think you are," she said between gritted teeth.

"Wilbur murdered my mom when I was four."

Her heart sputtered. Out of all the things she expected her to say, this was not one of them. "I thought you said she died of cancer."

"I lied. I had to."

"You lied to get close to Isabel and make her pay for something she had nothing to do with!" Her blood boiled and her eyes were on fire. Mabel sprang to her feet. Catching herself, she looked to the guard and sat back down.

Max shook her head, "It's not like that. I promise you."

"Then why don't you tell me. Why did you come into Isabel's life after all these years?" She leaned back in her chair to keep herself from tearing this woman's head off.

"My mother left me a letter. It was true when I said I didn't know Wilbur was my father. The letter contained a picture of him with no name. It wasn't until Jimmy . . . well that's when I saw the picture and found Wilbur."

"You met a man you knew killed your mother—" she stopped, shocked with what she suddenly realized. "You killed Wilbur."

"No! I didn't!"

"He died the day you met him, Max. You mean to tell me the man who killed your mother coincidentally died the day you met him?"

She shook her head in denial. "You have it all wrong. True, I went there to do . . . I don't know what. But I could never have killed him. I'm not a murderer."

Did she forget about Brandon? She'd put thirteen bullets in him. "Spare me the pathetic act. Your father and brother killed. It's in your blood."

"After I learned about him, I wanted nothing more than

to make him pay. The only thing I wanted more was him already dead. When I finally found him, I did go there with bad thoughts, but the man was already on his death bed and he was very surprised to see me as you can imagine. I guess if you want to say I killed him because he was so shocked to see his own daughter after all this time, especially knowing he killed my mother . . . if that gave him a heart attack, then I say he deserved it."

She's right. All this time Mabel thought of Wilbur as someone who loved Isabel and wanted nothing more than to make her happy. She thought he'd been dealt a bad hand with Jimmy. Now it made sense why he covered for his son for so long. Jimmy was just like his father.

"Let's back up. How did your mom know Wilbur killed her? It's not like she wrote the letter after she died. And if she suspected he would, why didn't she go to the police."

Max sighed. "I don't know. I was too little to remember any of it. I had dreams, but I'd always put them out of my mind thinking they were nothing more than nightmares. I was there, Mabel."

"When Wilbur killed your mom?"

Max nodded. Mabel wanted to hate her, but the look on her face was nothing more than sorrow and pain. "Here, read this later and then you'll understand." She pulled a letter out of her jacket and handed it to Mabel.

"What's this?" she asked holding it out.

"The letter from my mom. I was hiding when he did it. My mom hid me under the counter."

"If you didn't plan to ruin Isabel's life, then why did you?"

She sat up, composing herself. "Brandon. I met him a month after meeting Isabel. I fell head over heels for him, just like my mom did for Wilbur. She warned me in her letter, about men, and I didn't listen."

This was all confusing, but she listened, allowing Max to continue.

"I'd never told anyone about how my mom really died, but I told Brandon. We'd even talked about marriage. God, how stupid could I be. Don't you get it?"

No, she didn't.

"He was grooming me this whole time and I didn't see it."

Oh shit!

"He knew I worked with kids and his plan had always been to get me to bring the kids to him."

"I'm sorry this happened to you Max," and she was, "but you were free to walk around. You could have gone to the police at any time and you chose not to." She knew the accusations were unfair. Max had always been under his thumb, from the first day she met him.

"He threatened not only me, but he threatened to take Isabel if I didn't do as he asked."

Mabel snarked, "But he took her anyway."

"Yes, he did. I told him not to. I begged him not to. I'd done everything he asked of me and he did it anyway because Brandon gets what Brandon wants."

"Not anymore," Mabel mumbled, knowing full well he already got what he'd wanted. He'd done his damage.

"Please tell her. I never meant to hurt her." She shook her head and yelled out, "Guard."

Mabel walked back to her car with Isabel heavy on her mind. How would she explain this to her without adding to her pain? She couldn't and she hated Max for asking her.

Life can be unfair. Who decides who suffers?

Are you imprinted the moment you're conceived? She'd hate to think her family's destiny had been written before they even entered the world. Mabel's mom and dad were good people, and her little brother was never given the chance to make mistakes. As far as she knew, her grandparents on both sides were good people, too. So why did tragedy take her family?

Then there's Isabel.

Had she always been destined for sorrow? Her mom's death, her dad a serial killer, and now she learned her grandfather wasn't the man she'd thought he was. He'd fooled Mabel as well.

FORTY-THREE

THE CRISP MORNING AIR FELT GOOD AS MABEL walked across Susan's lawn. The grass had started to grow and needed tending and the flower beds waited patiently to be reborn. Bella pulled on the leash, begging her to move faster. You would never have known the dog had been stabbed, if not for her bandage wrapped around her body.

Just as her finger was about to press the doorbell, she stopped and looked out to the street once packed with emergency vehicles, media, and onlookers. A week had passed since Isabel had been taken and just yesterday, she had been released from the hospital.

Susan's street was lined with trees, and for the first time, Mable noticed the leaves starting to bud. It reminded her of the passing seasons and how all living organisms adjusted to the change. Then she wondered how Isabel would adjust to the most recent traumatic events.

Susan planned on putting the house up for sale. Knowing her house would sell quickly, she would wait till she found another place to live first. Somewhere across town. Mabel would probably do the same in her shoes, the once beautiful home now tainted by filth. The neighborhood had been one of the safest in Colorado Springs, but maybe nowhere was really safe.

Mabel wondered what it would have been like if her own grandpa hadn't moved her across three states at the young age of eleven. It took some getting used to, but of course, he had been right. She'd made new friends, and eventually found the love of her life. She'd like to think the same would happen for Isabel. She would move on, make new friends, and find a man who would love her, just as much as Lucas loved Mabel.

Mabel and Isabel and Max. Three completely different people with three very different tragedies. Who is to say one is worse than the other?

All she is certain of is she would give anything to have her family back. But nothing she does will ever bring them back.

How will Isabel get through this?

Whatever path she takes, Mabel will be by her side.

With a sigh of relief, she let out her breath and looked down at Bella who sat dutifully next to her, panting extra hard full of excitement.

According to Susan, Isabel still hasn't said a word.

The door opened and Susan's face lit up. "Mabel, I'm so happy to see you." Her arms outstretched and pulling her into an embrace. "I hope you haven't had breakfast. We were just getting ready to eat."

"Oh, I . . ."

"Nonsense," she replied, without letting her finish. "I already set an extra plate." She looked down at Bella. "You are going to make someone's day." She patted the black dog on the head and led Mabel into the kitchen where Isabel sat, her face in a trance.

Mabel's heart sank.

Will she ever come back from this?

"Isabel," Susan said, "look who's here."

Bella had been pulling, trying eagerly to get to Isabel. Mabel removed the leash and Bella bounded forward, jumping up with her front paws landing them on Isabel's lap, licking her face vigorously and whining as she did.

Isabel pushed her away and Bella laid next to her feet, letting out a sigh.

Stunned, Susan apologized. "I'm so sorry, sweetheart. I just thought . . . she's just happy to see you is all."

Isabel didn't reply.

Susan looked to Mabel for a lifeline.

"Hi, Isabel," she said in a soft, but normal tone. She leaned over, about to kiss her on the cheek, but Isabel turned away. She took the empty chair next to her and sat. Isabel needed time. And all the love and support she could get. Mabel could understand that.

They ate in silence.

Mabel would never fully know what Isabel went through. Her first day of counseling was scheduled for tomorrow. She could hope, in time, it would help heal her pain.

She'd practiced what she'd say to Isabel. She had to tell her the truth about Max, but maybe another time.

FORTY-FOUR

ISABEL SAT IN SILENCE ON THEIR DRIVE TO SEE a counselor name Karla Meyer. Every nerve in her body on end. She wore a long-sleeve sweater and jeans. When she looked in the mirror, she didn't recognize herself; the bruises were fading but still a reminder of the week prior.

The long mirror she once had in her room was now tucked away in the basement. As for the one she shattered in her bathroom, Susan replaced it the very next day for no reason other than to torment her. It's not like she used it, she had her own master bathroom and they still had a half bath near the kitchen. Isabel put a towel over it, but Susan removed that too.

She hated looking at herself.

Susan pulled into a spot marked *Visitor Parking*, and turned her car off. "Ready?" she asked.

No, she was not. She didn't even want to be here.

"I know you're nervous. We'll only stay as long as you're comfortable with. How about we come up with a safe word."

Safe word? Did she hear her right? *Safe from what?*

How about *pineapple*? The man who stole her virginity likes pineapples and if she hurt at any time while he penetrated her, she could say *pineapple*.

To that, she says, *Go to hell!* No one knows anything about her. Just like no cares she'd rather be dead than alive. Everyone expected her to go on like nothing happened, but she can't, no matter how hard she tried.

Every time she closed her eyes, she saw the men who took away her will to live. Their eyes, eager; their mouths, open and hungry; their bodies, grotesque, smelling of cheap cologne mixed with body sweat and sometimes piss and alcohol. But worst of all, their semen.

Where was her real safe word when she really needed it? *Help* didn't work. She wanted to be grateful when Mabel came to her rescue, but she felt nothing. If anything, she felt mad it had taken her so long. For god's sake, she saved kids for a living, but when it came right down to it, she couldn't save Isabel quick enough.

"How about, 'vile'," she suggested, speaking for the first time in the last eight days.

Susan's brows furrowed as she turned the word over in her head. "Okay, vial it is." She offered a small smile, not knowing for sure if Isabel meant vial, as in a small glass container, or vile, as in bad, disgusting, of little worth—exactly like Isabel felt.

Mabel had once told her that fear and anger made her dad into what he is today, and Isabel would be better off when she learned to forgive. She wondered if Mabel still expected her to forgive.

Inside the office, Karla greeted her. Her dark brown hair was pulled back in a loose ponytail and her bangs covered her eyebrows. She looked young, but according to Susan, Karla had been a licensed professional counselor since 1990 and specialized in trauma, specifically child sexual abuse.

Karla spoke in a soft voice. In any other circumstance, Isabel may have liked her. She told Isabel that what happened to her was not her fault. Part of her wanted to believe it.

"Traumatic experiences can leave us feeling confused, sad, doubtful, and even worthless. It can shake the very core of our being and make us wonder how we can go on. Together, we will work toward healing."

She didn't say you, she said us . . . It was almost like she had experienced everything Isabel had. She wanted to ask her but didn't know if she could trust her quite yet. Aunt Susan had said if she didn't like Karla, she'd take her to someone else.

Time was up before she realized it and Isabel agreed to see her again in a few days. Karla had given her a lot to think about, but all she wanted to do was not think.

Since Mabel had rescued her, Isabel couldn't stop thinking what she'd heard on the news—that there were nearly one hundred girls kidnapped for sex trafficking in 2017 in Colorado alone. She thought maybe if she would have been more careful, she wouldn't have become a statistic. She would have never fallen for Sam. Or would she? She knew now that Sam hadn't really cared for her. If not for everything else that had happened to her, knowing this would have hurt more. He had been sent to groom her. He was paid to get close to her . . . to watch her.

How dumb she'd been. Everyone keeps telling her it wasn't her fault. But how could it not be?

FORTY-FIVE

SIX MONTHS LATER

PART OF HER HEALING PROCESS WAS LEARNING to forgive. At the top of her list, her dad.

Hate would be too strong of a word for a man who raised her for eleven years, a man who made her laugh, a man who once healed her wounds, a man who loved her as if she were part of him.

Loathe is more fitting, for every disgusting decision he ever made which got her to where she is today. But today, they would talk and she would ask him why. Why did he take her mom away from her? Why did he kill Mabel's family? Why did he have to leave her when she needed him most? She would ask him—no beg him—to change his ways. She figured if he could do it, then maybe every other bad person out there could do the same. Maybe, just maybe, there was goodness in every person, because she hated to think she was destined to follow in his footsteps.

Counseling was helping her believe, helping her to see the flickering light in the dark world she had been exposed to.

Karla had been a gift she never expected, and Isabel wanted to believe she, too, could be the gift someone needed at the worst time in their life. She even thought maybe she could be a counselor one day.

Abby was also a gift. She'd taken the blame for the joint Isabel had left at her house. And when she found out Sam worked for Mr. B., Abby never left her side. They'd both been so wrong about Sam. It made them both question who they could trust. Abby had wanted to come with her today, but Susan didn't think it would be a good idea.

"Call me the moment you get back," Abby said. "I'll bring the junk food and the movie," she added.

It was just after 1:00 p.m. and the sun shined bright overhead. The place her dad lived was nicer than anticipated. She assumed the walls would be dark and falling apart, not an earthy brown with the mountains as a backdrop.

As they walked up to the front doors, she didn't know what to feel anymore. The whole process seemed bizarre: checking in, the guards, door slamming shut, people who seemed to know what to do, unlike her. She wanted to turn back, but the need to see her dad was too strong.

She sat on a bench with Susan next to her. The time had finally come and her stomach ached. She didn't think she could go through with it. She wiggled in her seat, unable to stay still. Susan put her hand over Isabel's and squeezed. "You going to be okay?"

Isabel nodded. Then she saw him. He looked so different. Bigger, and bald. Her throat tightened.

"Isabel Rose Dumel," he said, his smile lighting up his eyes.

She jumped up, excitement overtaking her, and ran to him wrapping her arms around his waist. He dropped his chained hands over her and hugged her back. She had done exactly what she was told not to do. Don't touch the inmate. At that moment, she didn't care.

"Oh, how I've missed you," he said as the guard pulled him away. He gave Isabel a stern look, but she couldn't stop smiling.

"I missed you, too, Daddy."

Acknowledgments

I N 2017, THE LEADER OF A SEX TRAFFICKING RING who victimized adults and children was found guilty on thirty counts, including kidnapping, sexual exploitation of a child, child prostitution and human trafficking of a minor. The Colorado man was sentenced to 472 years in prison.

When I read this news story, I thought, "I live in Colorado!" Then, "And I have two girls of my own." The girls victimized are daughters, nieces, grandchildren. What ifs started running through my head. As a parent, I try my best to be honest when it comes to talking about 'what ifs' with my children. We don't want to scare our kids, but they need to know. How else can they watch for warning signs?

The news of a sex trafficking ring, in my home state, inspired *In Plain Sight*. It motivated me to go deeper and what I found was scarier than I had imagined. It was a difficult story to write, especially from the victim's view. I humbly hope I have not offended anyone. That was not my intention. This book is meant to bring light to this horrific crime. The more we talk about difficult topics, the more we educate ourselves and others, we start to come together and find ways to keep one another safe.

First and foremost, I'd like to thank the multiple agencies who work hard every day on prevention and intervention, who are committed to end modern-day slavery, and who train and provide resources. Their endless devotion is extraordinary.

To my husband, my greatest support, thank you for continually being there for me and believing in me. Thank you to my children, who laugh along with me. You three are my light. I am grateful for my mom and dad, sister and brothers, for their endless encouragement.

To my beta readers, for their willingness to read my book it its rawest form and offer feedback, I thank: Heidi McCarthy—The Librarian, Pat Smith—The Veterinarian, and Marisa Holbrook—my daughter who isn't afraid to tell me when I don't make any sense.

To my editor, Kimberly Peticolas, who continually makes my work better, thank you. And a special thanks to those who helped along the way, Detective Dale Hammel for taking time out of his busy schedule to meet with me. To Gwen McClure, who helped give me insight into a very difficult subject, thank you.

About the Author

LAURIE HOLBROOK GREW UP IN A SMALL TOWN in southern Colorado, where she spent an excessive amount of her time playing make believe and watching movies. Her debut novel, *Still Out There*, was inspired by her love of thriller movies and the average everyday kickass heroine. After spending twenty plus years in the retail industry working in various managerial positions, she decided to pursue her lifelong dream of storytelling. She now lives and writes in the northern suburbs of Denver with her husband, children, and dogs. Find out more about Laurie by visiting www.laurieholbrook.com.

Author photo by Amy K Wright.

Enjoyed the Book?

If you enjoyed this book, please consider leaving a review on Amazon or Goodreads.

Want to know more about Laurie Holbrook or her next book? Make sure to visit www.laurieholbrook.com and sign up for her newsletter.